A Show
of Strength

And Other Stories

Also by Wendy Wright

Freerunners — Poems of Love and Italy

Sand Dancer and other poems

Gooseberries, Urchin Books

Fingertips, Urchin Books an interactive (V.A.K.) learning programme for the acquisition of reading and writing skills for early years and special needs children.

Wendy's poems have been included in several anthologies including 'War without Weapons', an anthology of remembrance of the first World War compiled by Gordon and Jocelyn Simms in 2014.

Praise for 'Sand Dancer'

"Wendy Wright draws the reader into image after image so that one not only hears, but also watches as she dances through her thoughts; thoughts that produce constant originality in word/sound combinations.

Her use of onomatopoeia and metaphor startles as each poem reveals Wendy's wonderful way with words.

The eponymous poem 'Sand Dancer' epitomises the dynamics of dance, its timeless quality, rhythms and contrasts; elements that thread the whole volume. Throughout, there is a sense of history that rewinds or fast-forwards to the present and whether in the description of people or places, there is a certain sadness often set aside unveiling the poet's determination to remain a survivor. 'I shall not go down alone' (Keeping Company).

Her style holds the element of surprise often delivered with a punch... 'icy patches and ruts are hidden / under the deadening flattery of snow / lies marriage (White Wedding) or 'when the words run out / in the lees of the will' (Finding You).

Wendy's work whether poetry or prose is always a delight to read as it jerks you from an earthy level towards a very different, higher, even erotic plain, but in this particular volume her 'pantheistic weave' includes the 'billowing outrage' of those who speak out against war and the 'belligerent silence' (Vimy) of those who lose their lives.

However she is forever optimistic and survives in a 'landscape of space, distance / and pure air tingling with discovery' (What Love Is)."

Brenda Walker Phd., award winning multi-talented creative artist in all fields including the creation of Forest Books Publishing, specialising in literature in translation.

"'Sand Dancer and other poems' is Wendy's first collection of poems. It is dedicated to Ivor Meggido, who was a dancer, teacher, choreographer. Well known for his work on both sides of the Atlantic.

One feels the book is also dedicated to the art of dance, especially on the opening sequence of Sand Dancer, the lines, written on the death of Merce Cunningham weave the theme with energy and panache – sound echoing sense, giving the dramatic flavour of the book its sinuous movement and immediacy, words shadowing the dance.

'I am only this dance / I am only this dust / even my thoughts / turn cartwheels then / stamp their feet to castanets.'

Wright is a talented artist as well as a poet and she has provided most of the widely varied artwork enhancing the book.

There are also helpful notes which outline her colourful personal history which has taken her from Walthamstow to boarding school to theatre, teaching and travel. Cosmopolitan to her dancing toes, she now lives in South West France.

These are poems of great feeling and insight, as in her elegy for her father who was killed in 1942 (N. C. O.) and the many other poems reflecting on art and life."

Katherine Gallagher, poet, in the magazine 'Second Light'

"Music, movement dance and spirituality – all close to my heart. The range of your poetry creating moods of poignancy and of delight as well as a fascinating choice of subjects drawn from both life and art makes for a very rewarding collection of poetry to which I shall return from time to time."

Kathy Howes, teacher and artist

"The poems beg to be spoken aloud and make me want to take to the stage again. I loved them all for different reasons.

The atmosphere in 'Tango de Noche' sultry, sexy, so very Tango.

The rhythm of the Pavanne in 'Faures Pavanne' and how it conjured up a picture of renaissance

aristocracy carrying on as usual despite the turmoil of the world when the music was written.

Your tribute to the men lost at Vimy really stirred my heart – as did the poem to your father, 'N.C.O.', who was killed in 1942.

So many poems about places I have never visited made me want to know more – Amalfi Coast, Bangkok, Naples, Corfu, etc.

I enjoyed the humour of 'Seventeen' as well as the excitement of getting ready for a night out.

The pathos and sacrifice of 'Ballet Girls of Degas' being eyed up and preyed upon by old men 'Top hatted and be-spatted' – your love of dance leaps off the pages, the poems draw you into your world.

The first verse of 'Fugitive' – I felt I was being tossed around by the high wind. – 'Dawn' – Corfu with its unfolding of a new day; the tingling lines of 'Altered state' 'I can smell the lemons and the melons of your skin'.

Art, music dance and life all come together in your poems.

I have ordered copies of your book for the bookstore and I am going to sell the heck out of it!!!"

Linda Bryant – bookseller, Barnes and Noble bookshop in, New York, U.S.A.

A Show
of Strength

And Other Stories

Wendy Wright

Perigord Press, part of GunBoss Books,
3rd Floor, 207 Regent Street,
London, W1B 3HH, England
www.perigordpress.com

ISBN: 978-0-9929653-9-6

Cover idea by Wendy Wright
Book design: Dean Fetzer, www.gunboss.com

*For all the friends I've met in writing groups
and scribblers everywhere.*

Table of Contents

INTRODUCTION

I inherited my love of literature from my mother along with a love of music, theatre, ballet, and painting – all the arts. That 'Christening gift' has sustained and nourished me all my life. Once later in her life I came across a book full of notes, jottings and ideas. I asked my Mum if she had ever thought of writing a story or a novel?

She said, 'No, I found I had nothing to write about.'

Of course, this was not true, her life had been brim-full of incidents and experiences, but I knew what she meant. She felt that she could never write a 'significant' novel and so somehow it wasn't worth writing anything.

I, on the other hand was an inveterate scribbler – poetry, stories, novels began to pile up on top of the wardrobe or under the bed over many years. I was a minnow in writing terms, but I enjoyed the numerous writing courses I went on and the writers groups I belonged to and of course other writers!

These stories span 60 years – from my teens to the present day. Those written in the sixties, seventies and eighties are almost from a different person – no definitely from a different person. Also, they are stories of a lost world – places that have changed beyond belief but were like Paradise when we first saw them in the fifties.

The earliest one is me being an irritating teenager on a touring holiday in Scotland with my Mum and stepfather –

'Foreign Travel'. Then, as I got older, got married, had children and travelled more, life opened up considerably, the stories become more introspective, thoughtful and laced with a little angst.

Some are autobiographical – 'A Show of Strength' is exactly what happened in Malta in the run up to the military and attached personnel being airlifted out in 1972. My husband was a teacher in a naval school and we had to leave when the troops were pulled out. I cried all the way to the airport.

Other stories begin with some true incident and then become fictionalised. I had that 'capacity for wonder' for letting my imagination run away with me. I also plundered other people's lives, of course, and some conversations in the stories are almost verbatim – never trust a writer!

The opening of 'The Sacrifice' is all true – the carpet shop meeting, the Bulgarian Professor and what he said. At the same time on the beach where we were staying in Sile in Anatolia on the Caspian Sea, we met an engineer who was building a dam for the Turkish authorities. How could I resist? So many stories begin with a real person or situation that metamorphoses into fiction.

I also have a very soft spot for children. I always enjoyed their company, their unexpectedness and how they make you laugh and lift you up wonderfully when you feel the troubles of the world weighing you down. Children creep into many of my stories – 'SMS' is one. I taught in East London for nearly thirty years and not only did it sharpen my story telling skills it also gave me eternal sympathy for the poor unsuspecting 'supply teacher' who often has no idea what they are walking into. I had a lot of fun with 'Talking to Tomatoes'!

It has been hard to choose which stories to put in the collection as I have hundreds, but I have tried to make them as varied as I could including some of my 'fluffy' stories that I hope you find amusing.

They are the writings of a scribbler – who will continue to scribble until...

W.W. 2021

A NOTE ON MALTA

Malta - Msida church and creek late sixties.

Our first few weeks living in Malta were a shock. We arrived in high summer in 1970 and from the air the island looked like a charred dirt patch. It was not as we imagined a Mediterranean island to be. It had escaped our notice that Malta is only sixty miles from the coast of Libya. It felt more as if we had landed in North Africa.

I wrote in letters home that it was like stepping out of *Brave New World* into an unknown landscape. Everything was an assault on the senses – colours, sounds, heat, the people, insects, diseases (the slightest graze could turn septic over night), and the colourful dramatic Catholicism. It took us a while to adapt to a completely different life, but slowly I began to be drawn into the place; its phenomenal history, its streets and buildings and of course the stunning blue of the sea and sky. I realised you either love it or you hate it.

Our first flat was in one of the roads that led down to the Msida seafront. We moved quite soon to another flat along the coast road (pictured) on the TaxBiex sea front. Several yachts were moored opposite our balcony and we slept to the sound of spinnakers tinkling under the stars and had breakfast watching our neighbours lowering their shopping baskets on ropes to the greengrocer on the street. His horse and cart slowly making its way along the road with the Karozzins sedately clip clopping along in the careful traffic.

So much has changed since those quieter, calmer times of 1970.

GREETINGS FROM MALTA G.C.

A Show of Strength

Malta, 1972

There were tanks in Testaferata Street, just a few, widely spaced on the long road that led to the sea. Outside the shuttered shops they stood, awkward and inappropriate, casting short jagged shadows under the high bright sun.

Anne turned a corner and passed the old man who always sat on a sagging velvet armchair on the pavement reading his newspaper. He was sitting there as usual, his coffee cup lying empty beside him on a baize-topped card table. A patch of yellow dust had settled in the wet coffee in the saucer, leaving it like an age encrusted relic.

Opposite him, in a small roadway, was another tank, half hidden by the blank sandy buildings set in wedge shapes littering the edges of the town. Fragments of building rubble, heaped into piles always remained long after the builders had left, like a series of untended graves of those who had died unexpectedly. She had often thought the new blocks of flats looked older than the old balconied houses. They appeared gaunt and derelict their plain dark doorways offering no hint of their occupants.

They grew up in a week and decayed in another, saturated by sun, soon to resemble the ancient temples of TarXien or Hagar Gim, reminders of the island's earliest beginnings.

A soldier in army greens and a red beret lolled over the turret, the sleeves of his shirt rolled up as high as they would go, his sunburned arms raw and painful in which he cradled his rifle.

Anne remembered how just the other day one of the big trucks from the base had stopped and picked them up. They had stood on the back, high up, looking over the roof of the cab. Friendly and smiling, the sergeant had jumped down and lifted her and the boys in to the back. Holding excitedly onto the rail, they had felt like Monty after a desert campaign entering Cairo or Jerusalem at the head of victorious troops.

This day was different, the quiver of nervousness in her would not be still. Now she was on the ground, not high above the crowd, sweeping past the population their heads turned to watch the impressive convoy of big trucks powering its way through their narrow streets.

Standing beside the tanks on the ground they appeared huge and intimidating. She stopped and stared at the big gun protruding from the turret, the end covered with a metal cap. What did they fire? She struggled to recall. Was it shells? What were shells? What did they look like? She looked at the green tank and the soldier. He didn't smile or whistle as they often did. He shifted his rifle to a more comfortable position and frowned slightly in the late morning heat. The street was empty now. All she could see were the Java sparrows in their dozen cages swinging on the wrought iron grille of the motor accessory shop.

She knew there had been rioting down at the docks. Some political demonstration had been staged to coincide with the closing of the shipyard. A tension had been tightening and relaxing for several weeks. It would wind up to a pitch and then suddenly let go. A strange pendulum had swung back and forth, bringing rumours and counter rumours. This rocking movement had lulled her into a forgetfulness that anything serious was taking place.

Only once before had she encountered the force of the mood of the islanders. In the grimy narrow alleyways of Cospicua, in Senglea, where her fair hair and skin shone out amid the darkness. She was a token English woman, a focus for hostile attention. She hadn't noticed it at first, wrapt in her own thoughts she had wandered around, curious and interested in what the English community referred to as the 'Arab Quarter'. A tourist

with tanned legs, thin summer dress, light sandals. But she was not a tourist and they knew that.

Tourists did not penetrate so deeply into the urban hinterland where so many floors of square-bayed Moorish windows almost touched each other across the street. It was as though the city had been built in one piece and then carefully sliced. In places there was barely room for a man's shoulders to pass through without turning. She could not see the people, but she knew they were there: a slop of mules, a tapping of the rattan, a hint of displacement inside the dense rooms.

She had strayed across some unmarked border into a territory where she was not welcome. She felt conspicuously healthy and pristine. Her clothes were simple enough, but they recognised it as the disdain of those who have plenty and choose to look plain. A person who has achieved the luxury of not needing to parade what they possess. It wasn't merely having money that distinguished her from them, for she was obviously not rich, it was that well cared for and tended appearance. Wherever she came from, somewhere within her society her needs could be satisfied, whether it was for a glass of water to quench her thirst, or a quiet hour to walk their broken dirty streets for her amusement. There was no reason for her to be there. No 'picturesque' shops for her to visit, no one she had some to see.

It was a mistake. Anne decided to go home.

There was a small square, stepped and overlooking the harbour. She sat on an iron seat under the tired lemon trees to wait for the bus and watch the heavy women in their dull black dresses and thick black head squares going to church, one of so many twin-towered churches on the island, royal, expensive and historic. A building nourished and revered by the people who lived in its embrace.

A young man passed her, heading towards the steps that led down to the waterfront. He had that frail and flimsy frame that she had noticed before in many of the young men. His hips and his ribcage were as narrow as a child's. The old trousers he wore, pulled in tightly at the waist, accentuated the sparseness of his body; the excess material bunching awkwardly around him. The too wide bottoms snapped at his bare ankles.

When he saw her he turned his head, pushing his hands deeply into his pockets as he walked and stared more openly than usual, carefully assessing everything about her. With his teeth and tongue he made a rhythmic ticking sound. His mouth opened a little and, surprisingly, he grinned. Then he spat. A large gob of spit landed a near her feet. He did not stop to watch her discomfiture. He slapped his upper arm with his opposite hand and rocked a clenched fist up into the air in the familiar local gesture of contempt. 'Ayah!' The hard sound was forced out from between his teeth and leapt up into the empty illusion of the sky, its triumphant blue reflected in the deep scallop of the harbour creek. Opposite, the intricate crenellations of flat roofs, domes, spires and carved towers confiding with crags and rocks rivening the hillside down to the water's edge, remained impassive and unmoved by the young man's cry.

Only a group of children playing nearby in the gravel of the square looked up and shouted in reply. Squatting on their haunches and flicking chips of stone, they echoed its call and mimicked his expression. 'Ayah! Ayah! Ayah!' They chanted until its novelty had been exhausted.

She had been too self-conscious to move away quickly, preferring to appear not to have noticed the young man, but her eyes were compelled to look at the gob of phlegm mingled with dust on the ground. Clusters of flies were settling on its filth, she was repelled and sickened by it. She took a handkerchief out of her small bag and put it to her mouth. As she did so she was aware of a flurry of little stones rattling down on the ground around her.

The children laughed as she almost involuntarily looked towards them. One of the boys stood up, made bold by the delight of his friends and aimed a sharp pebble in her direction. It caught the side of her ankle. She winced and put her hand down to where the stone had hit her, there was a small nick in the skin.

Alarm forced her to her feet, she wanted to go, go somewhere, but where? If she went down the steps to the harbour that would be much worse. She could hear the grinding of dock machinery and harsh shouts and grunts as men unloaded rusty freighters in the heart of the port. Then there was only the dark water in front of her. She had to wait for the bus.

Where could she go? She was alone, perhaps the church – surely she could wait safely in the church? But the children were between her and the church, she would have to pass them. She decided to walk up to the top of the square, back on to the road and down the far side that was in the deepest shade. It was the widest possible route around the children to the church steps.

As she reached the road there were several women with baskets grouped together, talking and gesticulating to each other. They stopped as she approached and just watched her pass by. She felt foolish, her eyes hard and dry as pumice and her mouth pulled back tightly over her teeth. This time she stared at them.

One of the older women in a shapeless floral dress broke away from the group and touched her arm. 'The children…'

She squeezed one shoulder against the side of her neck, the corners of her mouth turned down and she offered her open palms to Anne. The sentence she had started drifted away from her, not so much from a lack of English, as the substance of her meaning which she found painful to express. She turned and spoke loudly to the children waving a hand at them.

'Did you see the church?' An eager pride filled her small bright brown eyes, she hardly gave Anne time to reply before catching hold of her arm.

'Come, come, you must see the church. Our St Joseph's.'

Still holding her arm firmly she led her back down the clumsy terracing of the small dusty square. Their heads brushed the dry leaves of the lemon trees that crackled from months without rain, as they dipped their heads to pass beneath.

For the first time Anne noticed the railings above the wall overlooking the harbour, their fine tips pointing straight to heaven like spears arranged for battle.

This island has defended itself many times against the invader, she thought to herself. When there is nowhere to go you make a stand.

The children, sensing an occasion, had run on ahead, their wide eyelids rolling up and down like shutters beneath low foreheads burdened by thick hair. They stood winding their arms around the iron rails nearest to the open door of the church. They put their feet up on the wall and curved their bodies into bows as they hung by their fingers from the railings with serious expressions, their faces creased, eyes squinting upwards into the dark mouth of the church.

The woman climbed the stone steps one at a time, puffing slightly between each step. She took a handkerchief from her bag and dabbed at her forehead and above her top lip. The furious heat had gone out of the day, but the wall stored its intensity, Anne felt its sudden flare on her bare arms.

Inside it was not as cool as she had expected, the heat from the sun had permeated forever the heavy atmosphere of the church.

Incense mingled with lit candles and old stone dust hung in the air clogging every corner and crevice of the high vaulted building.

Tiredness settled upon Anne in slow waves, a weakness made her put out her hand to steady herself. The woman took her reaction to be entirely expected, she was naturally overcome by such splendour and magnificence. There were only a few rows of wooden chairs pressed close together in the main body of the nave, she led Anne to one of them and they both sat down.

Intermittent candles flared, poking their fingers into the spongy gloom. Those in an act of oblation knelt before mute statues petrified in attitudes of fervent benediction; above and below Baroque gilded decoration dominated the worshipers. Everyone seemed too small, too close to the floor, as though they had been drawn to the wrong scale for the lofty lines of the building that ran away from them in every direction.

At the high altar, in the chancel at the far edge, a young priest busied himself, smoothing and folding napkins and reverently wiping the heavy golden chalice, his head and shoulders moving up and down in the repeating pattern of his eternal prayers. His thumb described a tiny cross on his forehead, lips and breast. He performed his small religious duties swiftly and quietly, only the sighing swish of his cassock signalling his presence.

Anne watched and listened. It was like being inside a drum, all sounds were outside penetrating inwards, but their resonance was so refined and selected that each one reached the mind separately giving time for recognition and reflection. The soft burr of murmured thoughts and prayers rose upwards in redolent mystery. The outstretched hands of the statues and figures in the frescoes, with their beckoning curled fingers, were an invitation to come closer, to sit with the disciples, to touch the hem of the Madonna.

Briefly she was made to think of all the corruption and suffering of this world and felt it all to be redeemable.

'Here it is peace,' the woman said gently.

'Yes,' *the peace that passes all understanding*, Anne thought of tracts in gilt lettering. Directly above her was a depiction of the crucified Christ, its heart exposed, stuck with darts, livid with red and gold paint and pasted with glass rubies. All around them were vast paintings of the Stations of the Cross, cruel and violent. Christ being scourged, Christ being stoned, Christ being reviled and spat upon, Christ dragging the cross, Christ being nailed and crucified before throngs of people and overseen by Roman soldiers in their metal helmets and sharp pilums.

'Yes, it is peaceful here.' Anne looked around her thoughtfully 'And yet at the same time it isn't. This is a very strange place.'

'Strange?' The woman looked at her in disbelief, thinking she must have misunderstood the English woman.

'It is not strange, it is wonderful. This is the house of God,' she said with simple conviction and she dropped a few coins into the offertory box nailed to the side of her chair.

Anne hurried across the piece of waste ground that led to the Ta' Xbiex seafront. Somewhere above her, in the bright blue sky that spread itself like a great umbrella over the island, muffled sounds of hooting and shouting insinuated themselves into the drowsy morning already settling for its midday snooze.

Engines rattled over craters in the road, horns played strident jingles over and over again.

Directly in front of her was another tank slewed across the full width of the street, blocking the entrance to the little road, smelling of a mixture of oil and dirt. Several soldiers were grouped around it in the canopy of deep shade provided by high buildings on each side. One leaned against the tank stretching his long legs and banging his boots on the broken surface of the road. In their heavy boots and bulky flak jackets they looked to be bigger than they were – wider and taller, they filled the narrow space between the buildings without doing anything. They smoked and talked, stubbing out their cigarette ends with the round ends of their ammunition boots.

The young men wiped their hot faces with the backs of their hands. Lifting their berets, they rubbed hard at the livid sweaty red stripe around their temples, where the leather strip on their hats pinched their skin. Circles of dark sweat showed under the arms of their khaki field shirts and they pushed the rolled up sleeves even higher up their arms.

Gradually the swollen heat in their faces subsided as they breathed in a little sigh of a breeze that floated up from the creek, a bright blue patch at the end of the dark street. Although Anne couldn't hear the words she recognised the sounds and gestures of some kind of respite as they pulled their shirt collars away from their bodies to relieve the intense heat.

Too preoccupied with their discomfort, none of them noticed Anne until she was directly above them, then one glanced up the hill, and the others followed his interested gaze. They screwed up their eyes to appreciate the view of Anne approaching from the sunlight. In her thin sundress and long fair hair hanging past her shoulders, she was used to the friendly attentions of the servicemen.

But today was a different day, the whole mood of the place was different, the atmosphere was strained and tense. She came towards them more cautiously, more seriously than usual.

A service base is a young community with the majority of its men and women under thirty. At twenty-nine Anne was one of the older wives. Sometimes she felt positively ancient, a dowager among debutantes. Many of the wives were still dazed by being transported from one country to another, one kind of life to another, but for Anne, who was a Londoner and had lived and worked all of her life in a big city, it was the smallness, the closeness of everything that fascinated her.

Nothing reached you merely second hand, via newspapers or television. No longer was she sealed in, in an office, or a classroom, a bus or a tube train. Everything touched you immediately. It was a joke that the locals saw themselves as the metropolitan centre of the world and yet in some strange way she felt herself to be living more at the centre of something here than she had ever felt in London. Quiet suburban gardens of England receded even further in her thoughts as she reached the long barrel of the gun.

The tank straddled the road – it was going to be difficult for her to pass.

Crack! Crack! Crack! Crack!

Suddenly a violent repeating noise like machine gun fire blurted out, fiercely beating out a ragged taunting kind of anarchy into the warm sweet sky, its dogged mutinous rattle accompanied by furious honking of horns and fists and stones pummelling against the metal panels of buses and cars. Echoing and reverberating, the body of hostile noise spread itself wider and wider, eddying further and further its fervent message.

This exploding of sirens, hooting and drums banging burst upon Anne, bringing her down as though she had been shot by the velocity of the sound. Losing her footing on the loose stones of the street she was pitched forward, her head veering towards the big gun.

Without pausing to call out or move the nearest soldier caught her with both hands. Like trapeze artists they locked their fingers around each other's forearms, an instant before her teeth rammed the side of the barrel.

'Jesus Christ!' Shocked and panicked she clung tightly to the soldier's arms, then she let her head drop, feeling the warmth of his skin against her forehead. He pulled her body close against him, for she seemed likely to fall again, patting her shoulder comfortingly.

'S'alright luv. It ain't the second coming, though they're making enough bleeding row.'

The other soldiers clustered round her sympathetically, grateful for the unexpected diversion.

'You would'na have tae throw yourself into *my* arms lassie,' the soft burr of Scots could be heard among the general teasing as they soothed her.

Anne's adult composure was quite destroyed, she felt embarrassed and at the same time amused at her predicament. She laughed nervously and apologised to her rescuer, who was still only a boy and, close to, was rather slight and small.

'It's a good thing I'm only light or I might have flattened you. I feel such a fool.' Anne cast around for her belongings. 'It's been such a funny day, seeing the tanks out on the street made me jumpy.'

'These ain't tanks Miss, these is armoured cars. Tanks is a lot bigger. There's none on a little island like this. You get them in Germany and places like that.'

The boy who had caught her spoke to her kindly, but knowledgeably, as though to a child who would find such matters difficult to comprehend.

'Alright lads, alright, shows over, let the lady through.' The Warrant officer took Anne's arm and led her through the interested throng of young soldiers who had retrieved her bag and various items that had scattered as she fell.

The officer was older than the soldiers and acquiring prematurely those whitish lines around the eyes that spoke of a long time spent in bright sunlight.

'Do you live round here Miss?'

'Yes, just at the bottom, on the seafront.'

'I'll walk down with you. Pandemonium seems to have broken out down there.' He turned to his small section and called over his shoulder. 'It's getting a bit lively down there lads. Don't forget what we're here for.'

'What is that?' inquired Anne.

'Oh it's nothing much. Green alert Miss. Officially it's to protect British installations and property. You know the sort of thing. Show the flag, bang the drum, the natives are revolting and all that.'

'But this island's independent...' Anne was mystified.

'Yes, but independence costs and Britain doesn't need this little rock any more. No one does. We're pulling out soon and taking our money with us. A show like this doesn't mean a thing to them. They're more afraid of poverty.'

They had reached the seafront. Petards were still being let off outside the church at Pieta at the end of the creek. The fireworks were falling into the water near the cheerfully decorated Dhgajsas and Luzzus. Lorries and buses and cars were lined up draped with political flags and bunting. Dozens of young men and girls were squeezed into each vehicle, leaning out of the window, shouting and chanting slogans and the name of their political heroes.

'They're used to this kind of thing here, you know.'

The N.C.O. steered Anne carefully through the steadily gathering crowd and stood with her by the rail overlooking the Marina. He pointed to the dark bastions pockmarked by shell and cannon, the fortifications of the city rising out of the jagged rocks in the sea.

A testament to the island's violent history.

'They took a hell of a pasting in the last war you know. Nearly all round here was flattened.'

'Was it?' Anne looked incredulous. 'You mean all this has been rebuilt since the war? It looks so old. It looks so...' Anne paused for the right word to describe exactly what she meant, '…historic,' she said at last.

'Perhaps it's because the island's so old. People have lived here for thousands of years you know.'

'Yes,' said Anne, 'it's odd, but you can sort of feel it all around you.'

'They'll manage somehow when we've gone. They always have.' The officer was alluding to the very well known history of the island. A history packed with Greeks, Phoenicians, Romans, Byzantines, Ottomans and Knights, of which the people were deeply proud.

Outsiders smiled patronisingly to hear them speak as though they lived in some vast Archipelago and yet in a way it was true. It was a geography of depth rather than breadth. This tiny nation had held out twice under siege and bombardment, nourished only by its prayers.

The demonstration was revving up impatiently, clamouring to move on, ready to show they would grasp the moment. They would stand or withstand whatever might be asked of them.

Klaxons were being sounded even more exuberantly. The officer put his arm across Anne's back to protect her from the eager crowd now pressing forward, anxious to follow the coughing throttle and vile smelling exhausts of the battered lorries. Those on board the open lorries were pulling the extended hands of others on the road eager to join the demonstration on its journey around the island.

Anne was thankful for the presence of the officer. They stood together for a while and watched the untidy procession pass along the Marina, both drawn deeply into their private thoughts.

A Karrozin clip-clopped sedately behind the last of the following vehicles, an antique beside the modern cars. That was how it always was, the very old interlocked with the most new and mysteriously, everything here became old more quickly than anywhere else. The past protruded and overtook the present, held the people, held their pride as fealty for their own time.

The Marina ended at the bridge, but the procession followed the road that wound around the cleft of the creek and rose steeply towards Castile. The lattice of little streets and houses closely fretted together held tight above those ramparts in crowning display, their golden domes a beacon shining out over the city and far across the harbour, the bay and the sea, piercing the heavens, an invocation for the blessing of God.

A Visitation

Shakespeare sat in his usual corner of *The Swan* tavern. He was almost pleased to smell the pungent odours of the town again. He welcomed the hustle and bustle of the unruly population, their sounds, their street cries – even the usual violence in some quarters of the city. He was still bemused by his recent adventure – not undertaken by himself, but brought upon him by others. Whether he could speak of this to his companions, he was dubious.

He was hungry for real food and tucked into his ham and leek pie washed down with good ale. Once he had eaten he felt rather better. He had not realised how hungry he was. He fell to ruminating on how this had happened to him.

Those persons in the 25th century had fully explained it to him – that it was a mistake and they were truly sorry – they had had no intention of 'time travelling' him to the future.

Somehow in the transference of matter of some kind, his hologram must have been introduced accidentally. Shakespeare had no idea what they were talking about – the only thing that made sense was that these persons were collating a World Library of many things including literature and his name had become mixed into the process. Apparently all knowledge itself was at risk in their time.

So much they had spoken of – in a language he did not understand and had to be communicated by a strange beam of light – meant nothing to him. He was interested of course, but as a child might be when given a new box of tricks.

One thing he did impress on them was to be careful as many people from bygone ages were violent and dangerous. They had smiled at him gently. Evidently they did not consider conjuring up Attila the Hun or Titus Andronicus, or Tamburlaine to be a threat.

'Well I have warned you...' he muttered. They seemed to consider people from ages nearer to their own century far more dangerous.

Shakespeare found this troubling. Surely the human race would become more civilised and educated with knowledge and experience. They indicated that this was not the case.

It had happened one afternoon when the rehearsals at the Globe were not going too well – so many arguments and mounting money problems.

It was one of the history plays they were preparing and Shakespeare had struggled to ensure that all the royal forebears were presented in a good light and all of those out of favour were seen to be villainous. The Queen was coming to the first performance so a lot was at stake.

Babbage was being difficult and the rain had kept audiences away from the theatre for many days. Will felt he had the whole world on his shoulders. He pulled his warm winter cloak over his padded doublet and wrapped it closely around him.

He'd barely set foot outside for a breath of fresh air when he found that with his next step he was no longer in London town.

His journey had been instantaneous. At first he thought he had died and was in the next world, having been struck by falling beams from the house being constructed nearby. But he was not injured at all. His surroundings were not even anything he could imagine from his wildest dreams.

'I am dead – I must be,' he said out loud.

A person answered him. 'We deeply apologise.' A curious voice that did not sound like any voice he had ever heard before spoke to him.

'If I am not dead, where am I? And who are you? Am I in a foreign land? Have I been captured to be ransomed? Have I been sent into exile? Are you the gods of Olympus sent to judge me? Forsooth what sorcery is this that I am here without anything of my own will to bring me here?'

'Shhhhh…' the crooning sound of the strange voice calmed him. 'None of those things have happened to you and you will be returned to your own time when you wish.'

'Ooh…' Shakespeare did not know what to say so he took time simply to breathe again and try to settle himself. For the first time he looked around. So many huge windows he had never seen the like, so much glass everywhere. A great domed ceiling brought the heavens themselves pattering down into this mysterious realm.

He put his hands out to touch the moving pictures in the windows.

'Please do not touch the screens, you may make changes we do not wish for.'

'Screens?' was all he said. 'They are glass windows of an extreme magnitude is true, but windows still.'

'No, they are not windows…They are like glass, yes, but not windows as you would understand and yet they do give you a view of the world. You can see what is happening anywhere and everywhere at the same time.'

Shakespeare shook his head in bewilderment. 'This is strange alchemy, I cannot but think it is but a spell you have me in – a trance.' He looked around. 'How very perplexing. Why would you want to do that? Can I see any of you? Or are you in the pictures on the windows?'

'You cannot see us, as we are different beings from yourself. We did not originate on the same planet as you. We did not come into being in the same way as earth people. Earth people were formed from earthquakes, fire and tempest. We were formed from light and air, waves and finest particles. We are from music and sound waves, we are harmony – while earth people grew slowly from destruction to creation. So many things we have learned in Earth's history were the result of destruction that became creation. In your own plays, the theme is always disorder moving by many events towards order. We can see it is what you yourself would wish for.'

'So you are creatures of the air.'

'You could describe us so.'

'But on the windows I can see earth beings, in different clothes – I would call them undergarments – rather dull and drab I observe, all very similar, but people nonetheless like to myself.'

'Yes of course, we are here to observe – we do not exist among earth people – only occasionally do we have contact with them, perhaps to revive a memory or encourage an original thought, we are interested in their evolution.'

'What is the earth like here and now?'

The voice stopped and the beam of light went out. Shakespeare was left alone in what seemed a hall of mirrors.

Terror swept over him. 'Please don't leave me – I know nothing of this place and cannot find my way.'

A different voice, higher and lighter replied. 'We are not leaving you. We are configuring a system that will enable you to go further out on to the planet to see for yourself how Earth is in this century.'

Without any movement of his own Shakespeare found himself in an arid desert-like place with heat such as he had never known in his life. He cried out as a fresh terror gripped him.

'Am I to be burned alive in this place?' He tore at his clothing ripping off his old fashioned high collar, his feet prancing like a mad man on the scalding sand. He heard distantly the high light voice of the person who had brought him here.

'Please, please take me back to the cool of the domed palace,' he pleaded.

And he was back in an instant, but in what he considered to be another chamber. The room was softer, even the air smelled perfumed.

A great chair – almost a throne was in the middle – he could not stop himself from falling on to the seat where he rested his head on the padded headrest. He took long gasps of air to revive himself.

'We were not aware that you were different from the beings on the planet. We can see you are unaccustomed to such heat.'

The frightening experience had put Shakespeare in a poor humour. 'I should have thought my apparel would have told you I am from a cooler clime.' He adjusted his collar and shook sand from his shoes irritably.

'You said I could return to my own time when I wish – I wish to return now. This place is not Earth.'

'It is Earth – it is the exact spot you where were standing when you came here.'

'Fiddle-faddle, you jest with me. London has splendid houses and churches and palaces and a castle, it is great city. I saw none of this.'

'That is because what you would call the 'clime' is vastly changed from the age in which you live. The people of the planet grew in huge numbers and inventions created a demand for a life that we cannot explain to you.

'This growth overtook the planet's ability to sustain life in the way humans had known it for thousands of years. People and animals and plants and rivers and seas changed – damaged beyond the ability of the planet to repair itself. Storms, tempests, forest fires, wars swept across the lands too often for the population's ability to properly control their world.

'In the early twentieth centuries travel changed until it became usual to visit other planets and once the resources of the Earth were exhausted many millions chose to live their lives on satellites and other planets many light years from Earth.'

'So who are the people who are in the windows? Are they not Earth people?'

'Oh yes, they are those who were left – who lived at the margins of your planet – in remote regions, who were not part of the tremendous change of a life controlled by machines. These people did not understand what was happening to them and now they are what we might call slaves or people kept on reservations to serve people they have never seen. Their bodies have adapted physically to the conditions into which they were born. They know no other existence and are unaware they have a remote ruler in another universe solely dedicated to the prosperity of his own people.

'We watch them and ensure they have food, water and shelter. We wish to help them in any way we can, but still they fight and quarrel among themselves and cannot agree on much.

'We have encouraged a return to planting and growing food in the earth. We harvested seeds and plants from an earlier eon, for they had lost a sense of purpose and necessity to think for themselves and solve problems that confronted them in order to survive. But they are not half-man and half-machine like those who left the planet, so we have a hope they can evolve into a higher human form. It is why we are gathering together as much knowledge of this world as we can. To build a braver new world. We hope that in time they will take advantage of what we have done. It may take millennia, but we have time.'

'And I am part of this experiment?'

'Exactly – you will go on to become a great writer and make a huge contribution to the sum of the new world's art and culture and knowledge. It is vital you continue to write and be read and your work watched in the playhouse, for many centuries.'

'I hope I can live up to your expectations – it is a responsibility to which I have given little thought.'

Shakespeare did not like to add that he was really only concerned about paying his rent and having enough money to feed his family. What happened to mankind in the future was more or less up to them. He would not be there. Now these creatures of the air had implanted an idea that he would indeed be part of the future. Forsooth, all men are part of the future. This was a lot to think about.

'I think I am ready to leave now, this place is the stuff of dreams – troubling and frightening dreams. I wish to return to rain, green grass and trees, my sylvan forest of Arden. I need to eat too, I cannot think on an empty stomach.'

Back at the Swan, Shakespeare requested pen and parchment (as he had done many times). *It was but a trance that came to me...nothing of it was real.*

But as evening drew close and banished the light from the inn and candles were lit, he wrote.

'Ariel' a creature of the air who hears all, sees all with
a clarity unknown to humans.

Pros...Prosper...then it came...Prospero...a ruler who cares nothing for his subjects whom he considers to be slaves. However, after some disturbing events, enlightenment assists him to acknowledge his own false nature and past misdeeds.'

Shakespeare felt the full flow of inspiration, writing in the dim light with all the speed he was able.

'This ruler learns regret of his decisions and slowly
comes to an understanding that the future for
everyone is more important than his own petty
desires...Such little lives are rounded by a sleep...'

Shakespeare closes his eyes to hear the music of the island.

'Yes, yes Ariel will sing, a creature of harmony.'

'This ruler conjures by his magic a Tempest and
causes a shipwreck to drive mariners and travellers on
to his Island...'

———∞∞∞———

Unfortunate
Accidental Deaths!

It all started as a favour for a friend, but maybe now is the time to tell the tale of a scheme that developed for helping people quietly with 'no names and no pack drill.'

Some years ago I had a friend who was in enormous difficulty because after many years of fairly complicated marriage she finally had to acknowledge that she had married a crook. A con man – a man who had not only worked his way through his own family's money, but had stolen from the law firm where he worked as an advocate. He had gambled on the stock market and lost and was now forging my friend's signature on various loans from banks and building societies. The situation was grim. She had been to the banks she had been to the law colleagues of her husband, she had been to the fraud squad – but nothing apparently could be done.

When she was very young and dazzled by her handsome new French husband, she had signed a document giving him power of attorney over her financial affairs and no one was prepared to concede that the document was forged, the original being long out of date – and that it was not her signature on the loan contracts.

The house had been remortgaged several times and now they owned nothing and the husband, Serge had condemned his family to penury. She still worked for a prestigious firm and Serge was

24

living off her – with the post bringing fresh demands for money to her door everyday.

She was at her wit's end and mentally broken. She was advised to divorce him, which she did as, being France, all the debts would be on the shoulders of her and the children when he died.

The children disinherited themselves to stop this happening. But my friend found that she was still getting endless demands for money from all kinds of bizarre sources. When he was disbarred from practising law Serge had done some legal work for the Mafia.

I watched my friend sink lower and lower and I feared for her life. So, after much deep thought and speculative conversations with unsuspecting friends I decided my friend's husband must die. It turned out to be relatively simple.

Every night in the hot summer he, Serge, watered the garden – he had always nurtured the illusion he was a peasant at heart!

It took a quick visit: a check on the loads of steps and shiny tiles, a little water in the appropriate place and, hey presto! he fell down the stairs one evening, hit his head and was out of my friend's hair for good.

My friend was away at the time visiting her mother in the U.K. and accidental death was declared. There were sighs of relief all round.

Many friends helped her to properly go through all his papers and prove to these various banks, companies and the police that my friend's signature on so many contracts was a forgery and she was able to start a new life.

* * * * *

I did not think of it again until another friend was telling a similar tale of a member of her family being in an equally tragic situation.

'How well do you know this man? His movements, his way of life, his habits?'

'Oh very well, he is my son-in-law and he lived with us for some time.'

And so we had a little chat. I gave her some advice and, hey presto! the deed was done. Accidental death – some faulty wiring in a PlayStation – something only he ever touched and was obsessional with, no one ever going near it. But he was a heavy drinker.

A few months later I had a letter from said friend who had recently 'lost' her son-in-law to tell me of another tragic case. Well, we were ladies of uncertain years with a taste for knitting, comfortable shoes and leading lights in the Women's Institute. We sang our hymns fervently in church every Sunday and took communion at Mass.

We never communicated by phone – mobile or otherwise, never used a computer. We met at self-improving courses on social diversity – made very good friends from the ethnic communities and did good works. We made sure there could be no trail to connect us with any of these tragic accidents. We sent flowers, the colours became important, the wording on Christmas/ Birthday cards, sometimes presents, a pattern on a sari and somehow a small but effective multicultural network developed across the country.

The golden rule was absolutely no violence. Nothing messy like stabbings and shootings. Fortunately the police were far too pre-occupied with stabbings, shootings and terrorism to pay much attention to small accidents in the home or at work.

Oh yes, work was always a favoured place for an 'accident'. Also, the bereaved family could often claim compensation for work related accidents, which was a bonus.

We investigated this line of inquiry for a long time as one of our small group was in the Insurance business. She had invaluable experience and expertise, not only because she knew the 'ins and outs' of her industry – but also the many different kinds of accidents, that we had not thought of, that led to compensation being paid. We began to ask our members if they would dig deep into their lives and share any other very special talents they might have to assist with our valuable work.

One of our ladies turned out to be a private detective, another had been a serving police commissioner. We had a retired research scientist who had specialised in little known untraceable toxins, which was very handy – food poisoning was as popular as falling off ladders with our members. Engendering strokes was also popular.

We had an ex railway engineer, also very handy, an expert in Chinese medicine and an African MP who spoke several African languages that proved to be astonishingly useful. The Asian community was very well represented and opened up a whole new dimension to our understanding of tragic family situations.

The list grew over time and experience and of course another golden rule was that no one was to be there at the time of these unfortunate incidents. Everyone had to be noticeably surrounded by other people at the time. Body doubles are very useful in areas of heavy CCTV and relatively simple to organise. Fortunately most women, once they reach a certain age, become invisible.

* * * * *

It all took a lot of research and preparation, which could be expensive. We managed to cover that by getting very good grants from the local authority and various charities for our work with the 'needy'. 'Save the Children' were especially generous and so appropriate, don't you think?

We were all glued to the 'Padsy Bear Telethon' every year – one of our members was a director who thought highly of our endeavour. It all worked so well and it meant we could use Ubers and taxis for speed and buy any necessary specialist equipment or pay for occasional overnight accommodation.

Our local churches held 'Bring and Buy' sales to raise money for our charity and several local Primary Schools put on displays of Art Work. I managed to get Grayson Perry to adjudicate a competition which bumped up the number of visitors through the door, and they kindly shared the money from the ticket sales.

We gave a splendid service and contributed to the health and welfare of countless families. But of course there comes a time when all good things have to come to an end.

We are still needed, of course, and from the way society is developing we can see the demand is growing. The time has come to share our experience and the 'silent' side of my life with you, in the fervent hope that one of you may like to carry on the good work where we have left off. I await your response with some eagerness.

There is a great need for this work to carry on and grow – pick up any newspaper and you will see how invaluable a contribution it is to the mental health of society.

Harry and Meghan have already expressed a wish to be involved in our 'Improving Mental Heath programme.' I hope that will tempt you into joining our small 'but perfectly formed' band of well wishers.

We like to think of ourselves as the fourth emergency service. When all else failed there we were waiting and ready to help.

ANOTHER TIME, ANOTHER PERSON

Ibiza, 1958

My chiropractor had suggested a massage would be beneficial and gestured for me to go upstairs.

I found the room. It was light and airy with a view across Chingford Plains where we lived. A very pleasant young woman greeted me, helped me into a gown and arranged me on the massage table. A new experience for me.

She chatted easily 'You alright love?' Rather like a hairdresser her pleasantries and inquiries soon settled on to the subject of holidays.

'Are you going away?' I asked her.

'Yes, I beetha.' Her soft kneading fingers, the warmth of the room and her almost whisper of a voice had relaxed me into a pleasant soporific drowsiness.

'Ibiza...I remember...' I could not see her face – it was as if I was talking to myself.

It was late September 1958: a tiny, tiny airport, a hut with a flag on top and stones painted white to mark the runway. A long boat journey from Palma Majorca – a slight swell of a deep purple sea, full of flying fish and on deck chickens, goats and sheep with local people in local dress. The unmistakeable grin of Terry

Thomas propping up a brass railed 19th century bar. It was our first meeting with the Mediterranean.

A boneshaker of a 1930's taxi took us (my friend May and myself) to a hotel a little further on from San Antonio.

It was not the crumbling potential catastrophe of today, it was a traditional white, white villa at the very heart of the bay, with a deeply arched arcade all around the building keeping the large rooms cool all day. They were high ceilinged and sparsely furnished.

We were a little disappointed our room was on the ground floor in an annexe, but we very soon understood it was a huge advantage for two teenagers, as we could come and go unnoticed. The annexe was even closer to the sea than the villa.

The next morning every expectation was fulfilled and more much more. The beach was deserted – no families, no kiosks – a tiny bay with craggy cliffs either side.

We were too young to concern ourselves with deck chairs and umbrellas, we had the eternal ravishing blue of the sea and the sky, the playful waves and the rocks to climb and explore. We basked like dolphins in the water. A small sailboat was heading down the bay towards us. Two lads – I suppose young men – waved to us to come closer.

'Would you like a trip around the island?'

'Of course we would. Do we have to pay?'

'No, no we take you for a sail.'

So it began on that first morning. We spent some time of every day with Juanito and Paco. We were entranced by them and they were entranced by us.

Ibiza was hardly known then as a tourist destination. Only film stars and the like stayed there. I imagine St. Tropez was similar – they were undeveloped fishing villages by the sea, still mainly the preserve of the rich and famous. We stumbled across Peter Finch and a luscious lady on one outing. Two teenagers on holiday alone was very unusual.

To us the island was a paradise island. It was hard to believe that anything could be so perfect. Only in films and dreams. The boys had to work I suppose – we never knew, we lived in the moment. A mixture of a little Spanish and a little English between us gave us just basic information. (I still have the phrase book and dictionary, a little sea stained.)

'You want go to a dance?'

Of course! We would have gone anywhere with them – there was an accepted and unquestioned trust between the four of us.

It was the local hop. The entire village turned out in their best clothes. Grans and Grand dads, babies, toddlers, mums and dads, uncle Tom Cobbley and all. A little local brass band Paso-dobled and Sardanaed us through the evening.

The boys could not dance unless they wore a jacket. It was in fact one jacket they passed around each other so they could dance with us. We were swirled and promenaded, initiated into the intricacies of the footwork by the older women and held in masterful embrace by the boys. A blur of joy, laughter and music over flowed into the night.

At night – and I mean night, night, as nothing started until 11 p.m. – the boys would take us back to the hotel on, probably borrowed bikes, and we would go swimming.

The glitter of the stars was only rivalled by the glittering spray from the phosphorescent light show of the sea, as we splashed, raced and dived. We made dazzling patterns against the black velvety sky. We had a certain decorous English protestant reserve and wore our bikinis and Paco had a certain Catholic reserve and kept his pants on, but Juanito threw off all his clothes and swam naked. Like something from a Greek myth on a frieze, he became a creature of the sea – with sparkling droplets of water dripping from his thick hair. He always refused a towel, preferring to pull his trousers up on to his wet body, bundling his shirt under his arm.

'Will dry, will dry,' he indicated the ride home with Paco on the bikes.

They were eager to show us their island, its history, its coves, bays and hillsides that even today modern tourists are unlikely to find. A bar where a well-known painter (I can't remember his name) who could not pay for his food painted on the walls for his supper. I remember swiftly drawn people and shapes and some cartoons filling every crevice of the bar.

I remember a restaurant carved out of the rock in Ciudad Ibiza – it was cool and we had to sit on cushions on the floor, but mostly we ate in small cafes by the harbour. May referred to those as 'mad hatters tea parties,' for, like the French country people, plates were not wasted on extras: crumbly bread was put straight on the table and we whiled away the evening with laughter, jokes flirting and being young.

There was no such thing as 'Happy Hour' it had not been invented and, as I recall, we drank very little alcohol. The boys might have had a beer, but it was a small bottle. It may have been expensive? Cost was the usual curb on drinking in my teens. We had a slight brush with a 'so, so' Flamenco group at a 'laid on' tourist event in a nightclub, but it was not for us and we were gone in minute.

We had been thoroughly spoiled by the mystery and magic and sheer exhilaration of youth and simply being together.

One day the boys took us to the spot where relatives had been shot in the Spanish Civil War and WW II – many families on the island were opposed to Franco and fascism. They showed us the bullet holes in the wall – kept as a memorial to all who had been killed.

Juanito played football and had especially organised places for us to watch him and his team. These places were tiny brick walls with numbered places to sit on – brutally uncomfortable they were too. We did our best with the football, but the greatest entertainment was the endless scuffles on the ground and the drama surrounding them with resonant indignant Spanish rising and falling, echoing musically in the sunset out at sea. Mercifully his team won – I can't remember who scored!

'You have nice time?' Juanito anxiously enquired.

'Yes, yes, it was wonderful!'

Everything was wonderful. One very special night we were given instructions on what to wear and how to behave.

'Very quiet, say nothing – don't move – this man very famous, my cousin, best in all of Spain.'

We wore our best dresses – even high shoes, not easy on bikes. We were taken to an old winery for a performance for the extended family and us two. We felt incredibly honoured – I have always absolutely adored classical Spanish guitar.

I was seriously in awe of the musician. It was as if we had been invited to listen to Chopin in his own music room. Juanito had known we were exactly the right English girls who would appreciate such an experience.

At the end I was fighting back tears because it was over and I would never again have such an opportunity to sit at the feet of a master. His playing was superb, he touched our souls; it stayed with me became part of my life. I felt I had lived Spain, not just the clapping and stamping of feet – there is so much pain in Spanish music, a lot of pain in Spanish history. At first I was embarrassed, but it was taken for granted that I would be overwhelmed by this man and his playing.

We had paired off of course and there were many more adventures. Paco wanted to marry May and when we returned the following year he cried on my shoulder when she said 'No'. It was sad, but we came from different worlds. I often wondered if she regretted saying 'No'.

* * * * *

And my beautiful Juanito? We had to spend a night in Palma on our way home to get the plane the next day. Juanito was playing in a match in Palma.

May nursed her tears in the hotel and Juanito took me to a rather sleazy downtown nightclub that the team seemed to know well. Almost as soon as we sat down, he whipped me up again.

'Out of here, out of here.' I felt like the Virgin Mary in a brothel.

We walked down to the harbour and sat by the sea. He turned and looked at me strangely, his face was lit by the harbour lights, but his eyes remained dark. He took my face in his hands.

'You are a very bad woman,' he said with that particular Spanish intensity.

I was astounded. 'Why am I bad? What have I done?'

'Because you are in me now – when I am with other woman it will not be you.'

Juanito went on to be a professional footballer and played for Barcelona. I am quite certain he had a lot of other ladies in his career, but I like to think that the tiny, tiny piece of him at twenty that I enjoyed, was the best and the most beautiful.

When I had finished rambling on and reminiscing I sat up and the young masseur had tears in her eyes.

'You are so lucky to have something so wonderful to remember – those boys treated you so well and were so good to you. It's not like that now: I-beetha is a trashy place and full of drunken English louts.'

'I sometimes think that in young people the capacity for wonder has been beaten out of them. I have never wanted to go back – it would have spoiled what we had.'

* * * * *

I still have a photo of Juanito and myself, a bit battered and dog-eared as it has travelled around with me for more than sixty years. No mobile phones, no iPads, no earphones, no computers, no booze…

We had the island and each other and that was enough.

BRIAN

Brian put his hands in his pockets and stared out of the window at the 18th century terrace with it's rampant lions and elegant stone steps leading down to the maze and the ornamental lake. It was the beginning of May, the cherry trees he had personally requested to be planted were in full blossom a delicate pink and white dusting of petals eddied and whorled around the smooth water of the lake in the late spring breeze.

'This room seems so big,' he muttered almost to himself.

'Well it was always so stuffed with stuff,' his sister said. 'Now it's empty.'

'Yes, I, or we, certainly liked our "stuff".' Brian continued to stare out of the window. 'Well, it was fun while it lasted,' he said bitterly.

He picked up a small over-night bag and with long strides he was soon out of the room, down the great staircase – across the imposing wood panelled hall, out the door, down the steps to the drive and into the car.

As his sister followed him she looked back at the huge double doors in banded oak and the substantial portico, probably added in Georgian times and murmured to herself, 'We'll all miss it – especially at Christmas!'

* * * * *

'I'm sorry to have to dump myself on you Sis.'

'That's okay Bri – we wouldn't have our lovely house if it wasn't for you!'

'Thank God, at least you and Steve and the kids are okay and they can't touch this house!'

'Steve will be home soon with Marc – let's enjoy dinner together.'

'I would have checked into a hotel, but...' he pulled out his trouser pockets and counted out the loose change on to the kitchen table. ' I don't think that £13 and 74 pence would have quite covered the bill!'

'Actually it's nice to have you here Bri.'

'Thanks Caro,' he said ruefully and patted her shoulder. 'I'll get a job a.s.a.p. and I'll take anything until what I really want turns up.' Brian emphasised the "anything". 'I'll shelf fill at Tesco's or be the pot man in the local pub.'

'I'm sure something will turn up.' Steve his brother-in-law was encouraging and kept his private assessment of the situation to himself.

A while later, Steve handed Brian a whisky and felt he could broach the undiscussed subject.

'What went wrong Brian?' Steve waited.

Brian took several deep breaths. 'In a word – Me!' He looked at Steve blankly. 'I just got it all wrong!'

'But you were doing so well...' Steve probed further, wanting the details.

'Yeah I was and it all started from there. I was just so damn good at my job in the City – they used to say money stuck to me like glue. I had a flair for making lots and lots of money. So I got promoted and promoted. I was doing so many deals and they all just flowed and flowed like a dream.' Brian wafted his hand through the air.

'After a while, I thought why don't I start my own business and make all that dosh for myself? By then I knew just about everyone who was anyone and major companies and powerful men queued up for my services to place their millions in advantageous places. I was so pumped up that I didn't really grasp who these people or companies were. I was on the crest of a wave.

'It went on for years, then it crept up very slowly – you know the "you scratch my back and I'll scratch yours" situation. I got sucked in so deep. I was young and flying – literally all over the world.

'I was just making money and not asking too many questions and then of course Melissa – the gorgeous Melissa, my Morgan le Fay – no tycoon is complete without one.

'Gradually, it finally sank in: shit! I could get into serious trouble, even face jail. Melissa's affections waned in direct relationship to my diminishing bank balance. Over the years the F.S.A. brought in tighter and tighter restrictions and checks and balances. I could no longer fly by the seat of my pants!

'Then of course –the divorce – she wanted her pound of flesh of everything she had done nothing to acquire or achieve. Thank God she couldn't sign the decree nisi quickly enough and Hey presto! she was out of my life and enjoying yet another vast and vulgar wedding, filling column inches in the tabloids!

So here I am with thirteen pounds and fifty pence in my pocket sleeping in your spare room.'

'So you didn't manage to salvage anything?'

'Well, I thought my little nest egg in the Seychelles was safe but some bastard hacked into my computer and cleaned me out.

I knew some pretty lousy people so I was in no position to go to the police and have them take a magnifying glass to my affairs. So that was that. Thirteen pounds and fifty pence – and Melissa happily ensconced on a Caribbean cruise with one of my ex-clients, filthy rich of course.'

Caro put her head around the door. 'Obe rang and asked after you, he's phoned before.'

Brian's mouth opened in astonishment and he grinned for the first time in months. 'Obewele Okana!'

'The very one.'

'How did he know I was here?'

'He has a small nursery near here – just go down the High Street and it's the first turning past the church.'

'Obewele Okana…Blow me that's a blast from the past.'

'You were thick as thieves when you were kids – he was always in the house along with your endless band practice!' Caro put her hands together in religious piety. 'We must have had the patience of saints!'

'We practised in the shed…' Brian protested.

'But still the whole street could hear you!'

'He was a bloody good musician!'

'You weren't so bad yourself.'

After some thought Brian agreed. 'No, I wasn't. I'll drop in and say "hello" one day.'

As Brian pushed the trolley around Tesco, trying to be as helpful as he could to the family, he remembered himself and Obe at school – the local Comp.

What great mates we were, he thought. *Music bound us together.*

Obe was a great Jazz and Swing fan and played just about any brass instrument you could name. An unusual and enterprising music teacher had formed a school Swing Band and the two boys had been the leading lights of any performance.

Brian spent ages browsing through the Situations Vacant section of the Financial Times, the local paper and pouring over the computer. A few days turned into a week and a week turned into a fortnight. Rejections and impossible demands depressed him. His CV looked wildly overdone and, of course, slightly dubious. He became anxious.

One evening Obe phoned and Brian was happy to have a distraction and eagerly agreed to go round for a meal with the family. Obe said he needed to speak to him and Brian was puzzled. After so many years what could Obe need to talk to him about so urgently?

'Come in, come in!'

Obe and Brian 'Hi Fived' and punched each other on the shoulder several times until eventually Obe gave him a breath-squeezing bear hug. Obe's voice, warm as treacle pudding rumbled and tumbled over Brian and he felt back in some kind of haven.

He felt he had come home. Obe's wife Haree and son Kojo welcomed him with the same overwhelming affection.

'Why did we leave it so long?' They chorused over and over again.

'There's rather more of you, Obe than there used to be.' He teased his friend about his expanding waistline.

'There certainly is my man, my Haree's cookin' is…Ma, ma, ma…' Obe made ecstatic ticking noises as he waved his generous arms around the dining table. 'I have a jewel in my Haree.'

Haree beamed and her face shone with joy. 'Just eat up, be quiet Obe and let Brian speak,' she chided him affectionately.

'Well my story is a bit of a let down, so tell me about yourselves...How did you meet? We have a lot of years to catch up on.'

'Yes, yes, yes...lots and lots of years. I meet Haree when I was with the 'Kings of the Swingers' band: she was the jazz singer, beautiful...beautiful...We toured for many years. It was so successful, beyond our wildest dreams – we even had a spot on the Proms and TV quite often. We travelled all over the world! Played in fantastic places.'

'Don't remind me Obe...Remember Accapulco! What a time we had!' Haree agreed enthusiastically.

'We made lotta money, but we spent lotta money as well. We lived that life – plenty of booze, dope, late poker nights, lousy mornin's – you know what I mean man.'

Brian nodded knowingly. 'Yeah, I know – easy street. – I never told the family, but part of me losing the plot was too much coke. All those fancy dinner parties and always a dish of the stuff beside your plate! It took ages to kick the habit.'

'Me too Bro...Long time. But when Kojo was on the way we both knew we had to make big changes.' Obe's eyes opened wide as wardrobe doors. 'And we thank you from our hearts that you helped us so much.'

Brian looked blank, not understanding.

'You don't know how much you helped us. Haree do you want to tell him?'

'Yes Obe, I think so – better from me.'

'My Haree is a maths wizard and a genius!'

'Obe! Am I tellin' this story or are you?'

'Sorry, sorry – got carried away!'

'Well it was me Brian, who was the poker player – Obe preferred to be stoned. Sometimes I did well but, like you, sometimes some players were shits and they cheated us. I had to learn and fast.

'I was always very impressed when Obe boasted of his fantabulous friend. So I started following your career. I read the FT and the financial section of all the heavies. I could see a pattern. You do know that Melissa's father was bad news? Pushin' always pushin' you in the wrong way. Then I could see you were headin' for the skids.'

'Fortunately I got out in time and now have no debts and no one is chasing me.'

'Yes – it is very good – you are squeaky clean now. So…'

'There's more?'

'Oh yes!' Obe's eyes shone like car headlights.

'Oh yes, yes, there is more. I began to look at what you had done in the early days and began to see that I could do something too in a small way. You know music and maths go together…'

Obe was impatient and interrupted. 'She made loads and loads for us – is how we managed to buy the Nursery. Sorry Haree do carry on.'

'Thank you Obe…Well this is the hard bit to tell. You had money in the Seychelles.'

'Wow, you have been digging deep!'

'Yes, Kojo very good on the computer. Well, I was the thief who stole your money!'

'You??!!' Brian leaned so far back in his chair he nearly fell off.

'Careful man, you must not die now – you come to the good part.'

'I did it to keep it safe for you.'

Brian was thunderstruck. 'But how did you get my unbreakable password?'

'Brian, you two been friends a long time – we tried locker numbers, birthdays – the usual. Then Obe had a fantastic idea: it would be something no one would have a clue about...'

'Yeah...of course...'

'Only you and I knew about those few notes that were our signature tune!'

A light went on in Brian's head.

'Exactly. I just added the date when we played our last gig together and Open Sesame, it was easy! And with Kojo's computer genius we were home and dry.'

'Well not quite,' Haree was keen to finish her story. 'The hard part was where to put such a lot of money.'

Obe giggled. 'It's very well travelled, I can tell you, but it's safe.'

'Yes, having a Minister of the Willesden Church of the Tabernacle of Ebeneezer as a father was very helpful – I will explain later, it's complicated. We put the money in small amounts in several places. It attracts less attention when it appears in a new account.'

'Haree and Obe I don't know what to say – I'm gobsmacked! Where were you Haree when I needed you? Now it's all too late!'

'Maybe not: you and I together, living quietly in retirement running a Nursery. No pictures in the paper, no fuss.'

She and Obe grinned at Brian. 'A winning team! After all Brian, your name is "Brian Phoenix"!'

'And on that note, Mr Phoenix – we have a gig tonight at the Fox and Feathers. We'll stop off and pick up your horn on the way!'

CABBAGES AND KINGS

Beryl had worked for 'Cabarage and Kings' (affectionately known as 'Cabbages and Kings') for ten or twelve years.

No one was really sure how long she had been there. She was cheerful and smiled a lot. The staff exploited her good nature shamelessly, but in those years they had come to know very little about her. She did her job quietly and efficiently, wore chunky gold jewellery and gaily coloured scarves and was in charge of the biscuit club. She made sure every one paid their sub on the dot and had exactly the right kind of biscuits they wanted with their cup of tea.

She listened to everyone's trials and tribulations: lost dogs, lost wives/husbands, elderly parent – sick/demented – general problems with other halves and scooped up the occasional teenager on work experience crying in the loo over lost boyfriends/girlfriends.

She put up decorations in the offices at Christmas and strung the cards along the walls – put up paper chains and tinsel and baubles on the tree she had bought herself some years ago and which came out each year. This was much to the irritation of the trendier members of staff, who would have preferred something ecological or right on politically.

'Whatever that may be,' she said to the postman.

'They're lovely Beryl, ignore them.'

'At least I "do" something other than get totally totalled at the Party – is that the latest word for being plastered?' She giggled to the postman. 'There's so many, I can't keep up.'

He sniggered and cheekily asked for a kiss under the mistletoe. They pecked each other on the cheek and the postman went on his way feeling a lot more cheerful than when he had arrived with a heavy sack of post.

'Another Christmas,' Beryl said.

'I think that's stating the obvious,' her boss snapped.

'Oh come on grumpy boots,' Beryl was the only person who got away with telling him the truth. 'What's up Roland?' She was also the only person who got away with calling him by his first name!

'Oh don't ask,' he said and then proceeded to tell her. 'Melanie wants thigh-high patent leather boots and a whip – reading too much *Fifty Shades,* if you ask me. Tristram is harassing me for racing car lessons, wants to be Lewis Hamilton. And my beloved wants to go to Chamonix for three weeks!'

'Oh is that all? I am sure you can manage that Roland – you tell them you can't afford any of those things. And absolutely no putting thousands on your credit card – I sorted that out before, I don't want to do it again.' She looked at him over the top of her glasses.

'Oh all right Mary Poppins – but you tell them...'

'I will Roland in my own little way.'

'That sounds slightly sinister, Beryl.'

Beryl just smiled. 'You have a meeting with the board of directors at 10.30 a.m. I have put out all the reports and arranged the computer screens for the presentation. You have the agenda before you, all you have to do is click on the remote and refer to the notes in front of you. If anything goes wrong Stevie is on stand by and just like a High court Judge, you say, genially, "I think it is a good time for a recess".'

'Yes Beryl.' Roland said.

'Ah yes,' she continued, 'I have given them some folders with what I think is necessary for them to know. If you give them great dossiers of info they only throw it in the bin, so I've stuck to bullet points. They should listen and make notes if they have any queries! It's such a waste of paper, when it's all on the computer anyway!' Beryl aired her personal crusade about the waste of materials and time that was too commonplace in the company.

'Yes, dear,' Roland patronised her gently. Beryl was his secretary/PA/PR – she was a gem and Roland knew it. And often right in her finicky little way.

At 12.30 Roland returned from the meeting clutching sheaves of paper and looking a little preoccupied.

'Everything okay? No probs?'

'No, no everything was fine…Sure, yes fine…we'll talk after lunch.'

Beryl took her sandwiches to the rest room and munched thoughtfully. Did something she hadn't bargained for happen at that meeting?

She hoped Roland didn't have too good a "business lunch" at Gows – the best, the oldest, still Dickensian underground restaurant in the City, where all the top Johnny's met and drank far too much before returning to their desks.

A lot of tongues were loosened at those "lunches", a lot of things were bandied about that should have stayed in the office.

* * * * *

It was after 3.30 when Roland returned, a trifle red-faced.

'Umm…'

Whatever it was that he wanted or perhaps did not want to tell her had probably kept him standing at the bar a bit too long, thought Beryl. *Oh well, he'll tell me when he's ready.*

Before they had a chance to talk, a message came through that both of them were wanted in the Boardroom.

Beryl seemed unphased by this summons, but Roland was definitely jittery.

'I wanted to tell you myself,' he muttered.

'Yes, I know: they want to make me redundant.'

Roland was shocked.

'You know!'

They had reached the door of the Boardroom. They pushed it open and both sat down on the imposing carved ebony chairs around the huge table.

When all the board members who were on site were sitting down, Beryl got up and went to the top of the table.

'Gentlemen, this extraordinary meeting has been called because an emergency has arisen. Most of you probably have no idea who I am. Well, I was concerned about what was about to happen this morning so I had a word with my husband and asked him to call an extraordinary meeting.'

All the men around the table looked at each other and began to protest. 'Get this woman out of here – she's lost her marbles!'

'My name is Beryl Astramovicz, I use my maiden name as most people can't spell my married name.'

The people around the table fell silent. A tall white haired man who had been sitting quietly beside a table in the corner came and stood beside Beryl.

'My friends and colleagues, this lady is my wife of…He turned to her. 'How long have we been married?'

'Heavens, donkey's years.' Beryl replied.

'I think that has answered a lot of questions. Beryl would you like to carry on? I will leave you to it and see you downstairs later.'

Beryl drew herself up to her full five feet four inches and continued. 'As you know my husband and myself own the company. Well "the time has come, the Walrus said, to talk of many things: of shoes – and ships – and sealing wax" – of Cabbages and Kings. It has been run quite well for a long time, but in the last couple of years the bonuses and pay rises that you give yourselves have ballooned out of all proportion to the prevailing economic climate. Igor said I was not to interfere.

'I have enjoyed working here and we have left you to do as you please, but this recent round of increases for the fat bums in shiny suits concerned me. And then, when, on top of that, you planned to make several valued members of staff redundant just in front of Christmas! I could not let this happen – it was a monstrous thing to do! So here I am.

'There will be no redundancies at all, but there will be a significant restructuring in the New Year. There will be big changes and any pay rises and bonuses will in future be shared in a more equitable manner. It is a fallacy that you have to pay bosses hundreds of thousands of pounds or you won't attract the most capable people to the top jobs. I know this staff very well – better than any of you. There is talent and commitment and real ability under your noses that you are all too blinded by greed to see. I propose to foster that talent and ability. I am afraid the Walrus and the Carpenter were eating all the little oysters and I am not going to let them "eat every one".'

Beryl felt as if she had given a speech in Parliament. She moved to leave the room – then remembered something and came back.

'By the way gentlemen, the company apartments that are retained for emergencies will – once again – be for emergencies and not for fat bums to entertain their girlfriends and enjoy extra marital affairs on the companies' money. What you do in your private life is up to you, but from now on you will have to pay for it yourself. I have also left a basket for resignations if you feel so inclined.'

There was a palpable collective intake of breath from a silently stunned Boardroom. 'Good afternoon everyone and Merry Christmas.'

Closing the door behind her, very quietly, Beryl left them around the table, expressions of amazement and disbelief on their faces.

Beryl felt her smile growing as she walked away.

—∞∞∞—

CAUGHT IN THE LIGHT

It had been a long time since they had passed the last cluster of busy cafes and candle-lit churches. Uncertain of where they were going, driving in such darkness seemed perilous.

The heavy heat remained trapped in the streets of the town. Higher up in the countryside, cooler air whisked into the open windows of the car.

Following the beam of the headlights, they drove carefully along the narrow stone-walled roads. Previous experience had made them wary that the road might peter out into nothing. They continued in the silent hope they were going in the right direction.

In the moonless night the roadside was peopled by shadows of humpbacked prickly pear, their pink palms stretched out to catch the flecks of light that sprayed from the car's headlamps. Gradually they became accustomed to the empty silence. The timid scattering of stars grew bolder and impressed themselves more brightly upon the swathe of the deep purple sky.

They motored onwards, now climbing as the road threaded its way across the rocky landscape. As they reached the crest of a hill two rows of pearly light glowed with a slight lustre in the dip below.

'That must be it. Joan said she would put out lights to show the way.' Their unspoken anxiety now seemed foolish as the car came to a stop.

Several cars were already parked along the sandy ledge. On both sides of the path candles had been placed in glass jars. Their eyes shone in the spears of light that pointed directly up at them.

The villa glittered like a Christmas tree at the top of a slope, quite alone, dim folds of countryside rolling away from it on either side. Tinkling sounds of voices and laughter pattered down from the open doors and windows. Each note sharpened and defined in the dense bowl of land and sky.

The road ended at the slope that led up to the villa. Without speaking, they made their way up to the wide doorway, where the high wooden double doors were held back in an attitude of welcome.

Inside the house a throng of people stood in amiable groups. They immediately saw several familiar faces and raised their hands to them and smiled.

Joan detached herself from one group and came forward to greet them, her dark face alive and vivacious. 'You found us all right then?'

'Oh yes,' Tom replied casually. 'We just followed our noses. You couldn't really have missed it.'

'Well I don't know, it's a bit remote,' Sally said less confidently, but more honestly, than her husband. Tom rubbed his hands together, anxious to leave the uncomfortable topic.

'Come on, lead me to the booze. What kind of a party is it when the guests don't have a drink?' Tom's idea of jocular badinage always verged on downright rudeness, which often embarrassed his wife.

'Give Joan a chance dear, we've only just arrived.'

Tom pulled a face of instant repentance, but his black eyes sparkled wickedly as he assumed his customary role of likeable rogue.

'Of course the man needs a drink after such a long drive!' Joan led them further into the main hall where the party was being held.

The hall was very large and filled with guests. Along one wall at the back, a curving staircase led to the upper part of the house.

Joan asked them what they wanted to drink, passing on their request to the neatly dressed maids who were serving. As she did so a voice called to her from above. She looked up and answered in her own language, then turned to the couple and excused herself.

'I'll see you later, just ask for anything you want,' and she disappeared into one of the doors at the back of the stairwell. Tom and Sally took their drinks and turned to the company. Someone on the far side was waving and beckoning to them.

'Look there's Marjorie over there,' Sally said as she began to squeeze through the crowd as Tom followed.

'There you are! We wondered where you'd got to,' Marjorie carolled, once they were close enough to speak.

'Where on earth are we?' Sally spoke more freely now she was in familiar company. Her question was not a genuine inquiry, but an intimation to her friend of the curiousness of her surroundings.

'You're right out in the bundu now,' said Dave using an army term that was familiar to all of them. 'This is the other side of the island and the back of the villa overlooks the sea.'

'Didn't you realise that?' said Tom in mock horror shaking his head at Dave. 'You women!'

'Well you didn't seem all that certain on the way here,' countered his wife.

Dave, Tom and the other men in the group fell into a discussion of their precise geographical position and how many wrong turnings and dead ends they had encountered on their journey.

'There's some funny people here,' Marjorie lowered her voice and looked sideways over her shoulder.

Sally followed her glance. 'I haven't really looked yet, but I saw Madeleine on the way in.

'Not Madeleine!' Marjorie giggled and dug Sally in the ribs with her elbow, both of their drinks wobbling precariously, which made them giggle even more.

Ruth stood opposite them, her blonde hair swept back behind her ears into a wide black bow, she wore an expression of pleasant vacantness. 'I don't know many people here,' she said vaguely.

'That's what I mean – they're funny.'

Billows of laughter eddied around the room. One higher voice broke through the general babble of conversation concluding some story on a triumphant note.

'Well, I said to her if that's the best you can do Good Luck to you!'.

The company around him rocked on their heels in fresh gales of merriment.

Sally turned to focus her attention on the particular set of people.

'You see what I mean?' Marjorie looked slightly appalled. 'They're really enjoying themselves!'

The large hallway was lit by one central wrought iron chandelier holding only a few bulbs. It spread a dull flat light over the heads of the company, their eyes sunk into their sockets and all colour had drained from their faces. Their usually bright tanned skins faded into an eerie pallor. The women's dresses assumed a uniform greyness and the figures at the edge of the hall disappeared into mere smudges. Only the group directly beneath the chandelier, who were enjoying themselves so hugely could be clearly seen. They were all men. One of them had his hands raised, his fingers coiled in emphasis and several large rings shone boldly in the light.

Sally screwed her neck around painfully to get a better view through the crowd. The men were quite elderly she realised with some surprise and very colourfully dressed. Closest to her she could see a maroon velvet jacket and a tumble of white hair. As the man bowed his head to listen more attentively to his companion, a snippet of lace settled on his lapel. The man who was gesticulating so expressively was dressed in a pale green velvet suit with a large floppy silk bow tie in a brighter green. A maid with a tray of fresh drinks stood at his elbow and they opened the tight circle to let her in to serve them.

For the first time, Sally noticed their faces.

A trickle of pale yellow light infused them with a slight aura and she could see they were all quite garishly made up. Highly rouged cheeks and lips and mascaraed eyelashes set weirdly on their wrinkled faces, at the same time complimenting their gaily-coloured costumes. Others wore pink and blue satin shirts and heavy gold necklaces that gleamed, each golden sheen enhancing the others' radiance.

As their voices rose and fell, their hands fluttered and rested on the arms of their companions. Suddenly Joan was in the centre of the circle.

'Darling how good of you to invite us to your lovely party and such charming people.' A velvet arm was raised and a hand wafted above the heads in one graceful movement embracing the entire assembly.

Joan put her arm around him and kissed him affectionately on the cheek. 'It wouldn't be a party without you,' she said affectionately.

Sally allowed her glass to be refilled. 'I think they're old theatre friends of Madeleine,' she speculated.

'Well, I think they're ghastly,' Marjorie twisted her mouth into an expression of distaste.

As if to confirm Sally's conjecture, Madeleine swept down the curving staircase. A long chiffon scarf billowing behind her, she moved lightly on the balls of her feet. When she reached the floor she turned a small pirouette and her skirt swirled around her legs. The guests parted to allow her to join the charmed circle.

'My dear how lovely to see you!' Madeleine was greeted like a beloved daughter by the elegant men, extending their hands and patting her. 'You look wonderful!'

Madeleine laughed delightedly. She looked younger and more animated that Sally had ever seen her. Her personality sparkled and flowed unfettered by discouragement.

Sally turned away from the unfolding little scene. She suddenly felt rather tired and a little sad.

Dave had returned. 'They're just a bunch of old Queens,' he said and lit a cigarette. The men sniggered, the matter settled.

'You heard about old Gerry?'

Sally left the men to their usual talk of petrol and alcohol consumption.

It was getting warm in the crowded hallway.

Ruth was beginning to look buttery and was gurgling happily to an attentive young man. People were moving and spreading themselves into other rooms.

'Let's get some food,' Marjorie suggested.

Sally followed her as Marjorie found a pathway through the crowd. Slatted doors were being folded back into a room at the side of the main hall. It was large and more brightly lit than the main hall. A few upright chairs were set against white walls and people were sitting down balancing plates of food on their laps.

It was quieter and less oppressive than the hall. Slight strains of music stole into the room from a balcony at the far end. Sally felt her mood lift.

Marjorie took a breath of cooler air. 'It's better in here,' she said.

'Dear God!' Sally stopped suddenly. 'What on earth can Joan have been thinking of?'

In front of them was a large oval table that was the centrepiece of the room. It was piled with dishes and laid out for a banquet. An elaborately ornate deep silver bowl dominated the table overflowing with scarlet poinsettias, their slim pointed petals arching delicately on to the white lace tablecloth. Candles flamed in four-branched candelabra between the dishes of canapés, pates and trays of sliced roast meats. Multi-coloured salads topped with red, green, and yellow peppers shone in the golden light. Slices of orange, pale cucumber, curling lettuce and crescents of pink and amber watermelon were exquisitely arranged garnishes.

Here and there were glazed poultry and game with peacock feathers fanning out of the nut brown flesh and creamed potato piped and scalloped around salmon mousse and shellfish with the odd mock pearl left in the shells just to amuse, with rose petals scattered around the plates and at the corners of the table.

It was a painting of an earlier more opulent age come to gorgeous life. They walked around the table dazzled and horror-struck at the same time.

'It's a bit over the top,' Sally murmured.

Nearer the centre of the table were trifles and gateaux studded with gold and silver balls and grated sweets and jellied fruit of all kinds ruffled with cream.

Mountains of raspberries, apricots, loganberries, white peaches and pineapple rings lounged on a bed of crushed ice. A cornucopia of fruit tumbled out on to the table, spilling languidly in all directions.

'It looks like a picture. I don't want to touch it!'

The two women had been joined by other guests eager to know what was in the recently opened room.

'Heavenly spread! It looks out of this world.'

'They certainly know how to do things in this place!'

'Come on, dig in.'

Large serving spoons were rammed into the meticulously arranged dishes of food.

Plates and spoons rattled around the table as more and more people crowded in, elbow-to-elbow, leaning and stretching to pile food on their plates.

'We'd better get something before it all goes.' Marjorie looked rueful as she collected two plates.

In no time the dishes were ravaged. Tomatoes and anchovies were squashed in to the lace cloth, mayonnaise dripped into the trifle, the crisp colours sagged and ran into each other in a sloppy mess.

'Well it was there to be eaten after all,' Marjorie said consolingly to Sally as she popped a shiny black olive into her mouth.

'Yes, but all the same...' Sally didn't know what to say.

'Come on Marge, it's time you stopped feeding your face. How about a dance?'

A large man in a light coloured lounge suit stood behind her, beaming and glistening with sweat, his mouth half open, his hands spread and raised to his shoulders in a gesture of invitation.

'Oh hello John.'

'Excuse us,' he said to Sally and led Marjorie away.

Sally took her half-finished plate back to the table and wandered out on to the balcony. She was curious to see where the music was coming from.

A light wind lifted her hair and she could see the sea. The curved balcony was deep and wide with small painted stone tiles set in a geometric pattern. There was no one out there. She walked straight forward to the stone balustrade. Below her the cliffs fell away in a sheer drop to the quiet water. The arms of the land stretched around, encircling a rocky bay with the villa at its heart.

Now there was a moon: a clear, jewelled eye that stared down at her, its translucence feathering the tips of the waves. A shimmering breaded pavement to the stars rolled itself out toward Sally.

Sally posed a little, her head tilted back allowing her long fair hair to fall to her waist, her arms spread and extended as far as they could go along the stony ledge. She was allowing herself to be swallowed up by the night. The soft breeze caressed her face and arms – she was quite lost in the moment.

'Sally.' A young man was standing behind her. 'I was hoping I would see you here.'

Sally didn't turn round, but brought her arms in and put her hands together. His rather precise English held only a trace of an accent.

'Sally,' he repeated her name softly, placing the emphasis differently, it didn't sound like her name at all.

She put her head down, turned a little towards him and looked into his face. He moved closer, close enough for her to feel the tension inside him.

'Are you happy?' he asked.

Oh God, thought Sally, *it's awful – I want to laugh.*

He was trying so hard to be part of her reverie, she didn't want to hurt him.

At seventeen this would have been the perfect romantic idyll – a balcony and all that. But now...she assumed a world-weary expression.

'What is happy?'

Sally was aware of how she looked. She had dressed very carefully for the occasion, checking herself from every angle in a long mirror. She had chosen a simple long white silk dress, which was fitted to flatter her slim figure, with wisps of straps to show off her golden tan. She had let her hair fall naturally as it always did. She was satisfied with her appearance. This little charade was partly of her own contrivance, so why did she feel so ridiculous? Perhaps when you belittle the richer imagination of others you deride your own. It was an iconoclasm and it left her timid and bereft.

In the stillness of the night only the whispering waves were there to overhear them, it was like a brand new world.

The young man lifted his hand and ran his fingers over the strands of hair that strayed over her shoulder. 'When I came out here the moon was shining directly on to you...you looked made of silver.'

'It sounds like a cue for a song,' Sally said and immediately wished she hadn't, it sounded so trite.

Faintly in the distance she could hear the same cadence of delighted laughter as before. Madeleine was singing now, a song from one of her shows. Her light soprano voice echoed in the soft air.

'There,' he said gently, 'you asked for a song!'

He had moved round to lean back against the balustrade, so he could look at her more closely.

She looked into his serious eyes, which held something of the shining feast of the sea.

He took her fingers, stroking them gently with his thumb.

Wretchedness swept through her. The carefully constructed pattern of existence suddenly shifted. The recognisable order of real and unreal slipped out of place. She saw her life was only ever the scrapings and never the flesh. She felt exposed – caught out – playing a game.

Here in this place amongst such extravagant beauty, she didn't know how to live.

Unexpected tears formed behind her eyes, she swallowed and tried to blink them away, too afraid even to grieve for what she had lost.

THE WORD

Cyril sat in the darkened room with his hands folded. He had been instructed to imagine unspoken words.

He was at something of a crossroads in his sojourn at the seminary and had recently begun to search around for more than the rigorous, but ultimately unsatisfying, religious intellectual fare that he was served up daily.

Cyril clasped and unclasped his hands for no other reason than to experience the sensation of the warmth of his fingers moving against each other. It had been a fast day; he was hungry and could hear low rumbling complaints from his stomach.

The darkened room was an exercise to encourage his deepest thoughts and spiritual contemplation. He was quite enjoying the silence and the solitude, as unspoken words were what came to him when he was asleep.

The chair had no arms so there was no chance of him falling asleep, as if he did he would fall off and perhaps hurt himself. He was not as keen as were some others on self-inflicted injury – perceiving it to be the ultimate in false testimony diminishing the genuine suffering of others.

So he sat on the floor for a while. The stones proved to be too hard and cold so after a certain length of time he stood up and gave his situation some serious contemplation.

He decided to organise for himself a simple regime. He would sit on the chair for a while, then walk around for a while and finally sit on the floor for a while.

He was pleased with his little arrangement and felt he had achieved something and that the time would pass fairly equably and, because of this, his thoughts turned to systems, programmes and routines. Cyril found this an amazingly fruitful avenue to explore. His mind wandered across the idea of life's various forms of organisation.

Survival itself, he knew, had to have some pattern, some order and communities living together extended this need as did communities living with other communities. He thought of webs, nets, honeycombs and other self-regulating structures with some internal dynamic that held them together.

The room was not in a basement, but on the second floor so a scattering of light crept through the closed shutters. The random patterning of the floor, highlighting the surface of old stones attracted Cyril's attention. Dust particles shivered in the air and cobwebs swayed gracefully in the slight breeze his cassock created as he passed the corners of the room. He found himself concentrating on this – it assumed a curious importance.

The silence, the pinpricks of light, distant muffled sounds from the awakening afternoon of the town, the dull tread of his own footsteps on the cold floor created its own universe. He no longer felt like Cyril sitting in a darkened room, he felt he was at the centre of an organism with a will of its own, unrelated to his will.

He had previously decided he would become bored by his confinement, which he later realised he had brought upon himself, by being constantly over-talkative and irritatingly questioning.

Father John, who presided over their group meetings, was a Jesuit and had suggested this lengthy period of meditation for him in a neutral space. It had met with rather more enthusiastic support from his fellow brothers than was comfortable.

It was some kind of ruse to shut him up and make him think about something other than being contentious about every aspect of his religious training.

Cyril stopped in his latest lap of the room. A majestically large spider sat in his pathway. He was beginning to realise he was not alone and that almost without meaning to, he was in fact imagining unspoken words. He looked at the spider.

The spider looked at him. It was a daunting creature and normally Cyril would have shooed it as far away from himself as possible, but today he saw it as a companion, a fellow traveller, a creature with a perfect right to inhabit the darkened room – more right than Cyril, as Cyril had been taken to the room. The spider belonged there, had a prior claim, a superior position in the hierarchy of the darkened room.

Cyril put out his toe to the spider, not to harry or frighten it, but as a gesture of fellowship. The spider remained very still and Cyril was sure it was growing, getting larger by the second. He looked away. He was becoming preposterous: he, Cyril, was much larger than the spider, but for some unfathomable reason he no longer felt himself to be.

The pinpricks of light had begun to change position as the sun slipped down the sky outside. They had re-arranged themselves and were fanned out like the facets of a crystal recalibrated into a luminous prismatic carpet. Cyril thought of ripples on water, the perfection of soap bubbles and their iridescent colours. He felt the continuous act of creation all around him.

Cyril fancied he could see the galaxy as a map and the constellation of the stars spread out before him as he travelled across a universe that was at once both complex yet simple.

In St Peter's in Rome, when Cyril became Pope, the first Pope Cyril, he would often tell the young celebrants of his long afternoon in the darkened room, where he had learned more about life and his future than from a lifetime of books and learned texts, when he had to imagine unspoken words.

In the long galleries, behind the marble columns and in the small chapels of St Peter's, the cardinals would 'tut' and swish their scarlet robes, pulling their silken, sashes tighter around their waists in exasperation, as they muttered and hissed to each other.

'The man's a heathen – a pagan! How on earth did he ever get to be Pope?'

The old guard at the Vatican shrugged their shoulders sagely. 'Well all the others were so much worse. And anyway, to have a Pope who believes God is a spider is not as bad as you might think!'

COMING HOME

Her friends had a villa in St Angiello, quite near the Cocumella hotel that stood on the cliffs overlooking the Bay of Sorrento.

'You absolutely must come stay with us – you need Italy, it's food, it's sunshine and it's people to help you get well.'

Freya 'ummed...' for a while.

Sarah interrupted the 'umming'. 'You must come, you must,' her voice becoming more and more insistent.

'I would absolutely love to, but...'

'Pass me over to the "but". He's absolutely NOT invited. He will manage.'

Sarah restrained herself from saying 'he's got that monstrous ego to keep him company.' Instead she settled for, 'He's got plenty of "mates" to drink and chat with at that club he practically lives in. They seem to be able to switch off the "Me, Myself and I" 24-hour-radio-station that he's become.'

Freya laughed. She and Sarah had known each other since they were kids and that gave them a certain licence to express an opinion that other friends might keep to themselves.

'He might kick up...' Freya began.

'Pass me over to him.'

Freya complied.

'Stan.' Sarah always called him Stan when she knew perfectly well his name was Robert.

'Stan,' Freya could hear her friend.

'We have a well-known Art historian coming to our neck of the woods. I know Freya would absolutely love to join his group visiting and lecturing at the galleries around here. It would be good for her – just the pick-me-up she needs. That's settled then. We'll book her flights and check-in stuff and email them to her. We'll pick her up on the 14th at Naples airport. So glad you're happy about this. She wont need money – we're filthy rich – we'll pay for everything. Must rush…Byee, Byee.' And she was gone.

Robert stood in his Tesco woolly slippers and looked mildly shell-shocked. It had been a hurricane of language and it had taken away his power of speech.

'Well…Well…I suppose I have no say in the matter…And you're my wife!' His emphasis exposed an indignant wagging finger.

'Yes, exactly,' was all Freya said.

Robert made no further reference to Freya's impending departure except in a brief phone conversation to his sister.

'Oh she's off with her little mate – I dunno…one of them all-wimmen things.'

The sheer adventure of taking a cab to the airport, steering herself through the rough and tumble of the busy concourse, ordering herself a G&T on the plane, squeezing herself into the herding Italian crowd was exhilarating.

Freya stepped out of the airport into blinding sunlight.

Her friends swooped down on her and scooped her up like ice cream that would melt in an instant in the warm Italian afternoon.

Their spacious air-conditioned 4x4 crooned along the raggedy motorway – through the new tunnels – the longest in Europe they told her proudly, that cut the journey from Naples by at least 20 minutes.

Freya was quietly thrilled. 'Will we be able to go to the Cocumella?'

'Of course darling – that's where our Professor is staying.'

'There really is a professor of Art History? I thought you had made him up!'

'Oh he's real enough.'

'And he's staying at the Cocumella?' Freya's jaw was so firmly dropped she could hardly lift it. 'That's fantastically expensive!'

'Well he was in a rather naff hotel so – as he is working with Gigi – we suggested he might like to be our guest at the Cocumella.'

Sarah gave Freya a slight nudge. 'You do remember, don't you?'

'Of course I remember.' Freya said softly. 'How could I forget?'

I thought we might enjoy a few old times while you're here.'

'Is that wise?'

'We had great times when we were young.'

Freya's laughing rumbled deep inside herself. 'Didn't we just? I always thought that was why you married Paolo.'

'I think it was – I didn't want that time to end.'

Sarah almost pushed her friend on to the balcony of the room she was to have for as long as she wished.

'What do ya think?'

The compelling blue of the sea and sky all around her was hypnotic. Freya just stood and looked and looked. 'I'd almost forgotten,' she said to herself.

Freya slipped into the shower, the cool water restoring her to life. A heavy yoke had somehow been lifted from her shoulders. She breathed in for the first time in ages.

Nowhere to go, except…*Except what?* she thought?

Dinner had been laid out on the terrace overlooking the sea, a very slight breeze raised the edges of the napkins. The table was set out for several people.

Sarah and Luigi were nowhere to be seen.

Freya leaned over the stone balustrade. A tall man was walking through the garden towards the villa. She watched him stoop slightly to pass under the arches of bougainvillea. She watched him brush the escaping loose petals and leaves from his hair. There was something about him that was faintly familiar.

Freya turned and went inside speaking to herself sharply, 'Don't start that again!'

She caught sight of herself in the mirror satisfied the years had been kind to her. 'Like my mother,' she thought.

Sarah and Liugi came in with a visitor on each arm.

'They were wandering around the ruins…lost and forlorn.'

Drinks were handed out amid a general hubbub of hellos, ciaos and other greetings with much kissing on both cheeks.

'Remember it's Italy – two kisses on both cheeks!' Sarah and Freya laughed, putting their heads together conspiratorially.

The tall man had come in from the garden and was now leaning inwards towards the group.

Sarah whispered to Freya, 'You're here by special request.'

'Hello Frey.' The tall man was close to her and kissing her more than was necessary, putting his arms right around her, holding her tightly against him.

'Ben!' Freya could hardly answer him. She was almost off her feet. 'Ben…I wasn't expecting you…'

The warmth of his body filled her completely like stepping into a warm bath. Memories of their time together were in the feel of him, the smell of him, the sound of his voice.

'I thought I would never see you again.'

The dinner was a joy, laughter and chatter fluttered over the sea and hung in the starlit sky.

Freya and Ben sat together as if there had been no intervening years.

'Do you remember, do you remember?' they chattered on and on and the years when they had been students and worked together at the Cocumella hotel were relived over and over again.

The days and nights Freya and Ben were together spread out into the lifetime of a love that had been lost.

'I am not going to lose you again Frey.' Ben looked at her very seriously. 'Nothing worked out for me – it was always you.'

'It was the same for me, it made us both lousy partners for anyone else.'

Freya sat at the computer thinking about what she would need to pick up from the house and she started the email *Coming Home*.

But after a moment, she thought, *That is not true,* and wrote simply:

Returning at the end of the month.

DOGS AND CHILDREN

'Dogs and children upstage everyone,' Rita complained, 'and we've got the damned Infant Prodigy and blinking Fido in all our scenes,' she muttered to Joe who she was playing opposite.

The cast looked weary, it had been a long rehearsal and they prayed there would be no more notes – no more changes – no more crises over the new set and they could go home to their beds.

From the darkness of the auditorium the voice of the producer could be heard above the slight mumble of the tired cast.

'Delilah has had to go home, but we'll just run through the last act again.'

'Pity Fido wasn't taken home,' Joe hissed to Rita.

'Pity he wasn't put down in the first act,' she replied.

Fido's owner and trainer Felicity looked hurt. She stroked the dog's soft fur.

'You've got more talent in your left paw than the whole lot put together,' she whispered into the dog's ear.

Fido nodded – he knew this was true. He'd been on X Factor. He was on Facebook and had a following on Twitter. He was much photographed and was now on tour in a new show.

He brought the house down every night and by the end of the performance there wasn't a dry eye in the house when he sank down on his four legs and died tragically and heroically.

The show had been a huge hit, not since Lassie had there been such a canine star as Fido and he was not on film but performing live.

His real name was Monty and this unexpected talent for acting had been developed by Felicity since he was a puppy. She had been an only child and Monty had been thoroughly put through his paces by her games and the stories she'd taught him.

Felicity's house was filled with pictures of Monty: in bowties, sailor's hats, crowns and capes. Dressed up as princes and princesses, Kings and Queens. He could dance and sing – well sort of – enough to be a crowd-puller at local fetes and church halls.

Then he got his big break – an audition for the TV show.

Felicity had him practising every day: his funny walks, his high kicks, jumps, leaps and twists in mid-air, his smiles and his sad doleful faces.

Fido loved the attention – he was a star!

Some bright spark called Damien Dollor with cash register eyes had contacted Felicity to say he had written a show around the dog and another child that he felt sure would be a huge hit with the public and would she be interested?

Felicity was about fourteen and reluctant – she did not want Fido taken away from her. But her parents (who also heard the siren call of cash tills ringing) persuaded her to sign on the dotted line. She agreed as long as she was there to look after him. And so there they were backstage in this imposing theatre for the final London run, surrounded by actors and stage crew etc., most of whom hated dogs, but loved the work, the money and being able to add the smash hit *Dog's Army* to their CV.

It was a dramatic, romantic and sentimental little tale of heroism. It had been a bit of a stretch to include Delilah and her ringlets, but somehow a Shirley Temple fantasy number had been worked into the unlikely script to raise audience numbers.

Fido was not sure about Delilah, as she pinched him when no one was looking. No one knew, not even Felicity, who was only aware that something was not right.

Fido was a docile animal, but recently when Delilah came near him, he would bare his teeth and wag his tail at the same time.

'Don't know which end to believe with that dog,' the producer expressed concerns to Felicity as to whether he could trust Fido to finish the run without doing something they'd regret.

Felicity had a long talk with Fido and at the final rehearsal, before the 'dress', she watched Delilah closely and realised what was happening.

When questioned Delilah shook her golden ringlets and cried buckets.

'I hate that dog!' she wailed.

The producer threw his hands up in despair.

'Always knew it – never work with dogs and kids! One of them has got to go!'

Fido tossed his head and plonked himself very definitely on the nearest chair and crossed his paws.

'Well, I can tell you it's not going to be me – I'm a pro!' he said loudly and clearly in his best Felicity-trained accent.

'My God, it even speaks!!'

Rita and Joe stood open mouthed – the headlines in the press flashing before their eyes and the sound of stampeding audiences and soaring ticket sales filling their ears and their bank balances.

EMERGENCY EXIT

'Keep passing the empty windows,' Maggie called to Sam after their conversation.

Sam looked back at her a bit bemused.

Maggie knew he had no idea what she was referring to and it would have been too convoluted to explain, so Maggie continued on her way to lunch leaving Sam to think it was just the usual Maggie being her strange, slightly enigmatic self.

Maggie sat at her usual table in the canteen and studied the large wide windows that overlooked the car park. It was a warm day, so the windows were pushed wide enough open for anyone to sit on the sill.

It would be so easy, she thought, to just lean out and let gravity do the rest.

She ate her lunch alone. It was Monday and most of her colleagues were at a senior departmental meeting where, mercifully, her presence was not required.

She sat for a while after she had finished her jam roly-poly and custard drinking a glass of water. *I should not have had that*, she thought, *all those calories!* Never mind.

The canteen emptied of people slowly. It was so quiet, as if a phone was about to ring or a door open and someone say, 'Hello everybody.'

The shutters on the serving hatch had been rolled down and to Maggie that was a signal to leave the canteen and return to her office.

She took her time getting to the door, not anxious to begin another afternoon of form filling and student admissions.

It was very quiet in the corridor too. It was a strange almost supernatural silence for a Monday.

She peered at the doors along the corridor – they were all closed.

Maggie wondered if she had forgotten some major event and everyone but her was gathered in another part of the large campus or in another building. She began to walk more quickly, anxious to get back to her office and speak to her line manager.

She reached the stairs and the clip, clipping of her heels echoed on the stone steps. As she reached the bottom, she saw the classroom doors were open, but there was no one there.

Maggie began to run, then she caught sight of a man in a blue shirt hiding in a recess, 'Shh, Shh,' he gestured to her to be quiet. 'Take off your shoes,' he hissed.

'What's happened?' Maggie whispered.

'We have a hostage situation,' the man said. 'The building has been evacuated. I don't know how you were missed!'

'I didn't hear anything.' Maggie was trying hard not to breathe. 'I was in the canteen and as I came down here, I saw no one.'

'Well,' the man said, 'I am going to suggest that we go back to where you were and wait. It could be safer than wandering around here.

Maggie didn't fancy the idea but could see the logic of it.

'Is it terrorists?' Maggie asked.

'I don't think so, I think it's one of those crazy students with a grudge against humanity – you know the sort of thing.'

The man had something of a gleam of excitement in his eyes.

'Do you know if anyone has been shot or anything?'

'No,' said the man.

They crept back up to the canteen. As they passed the windows, Maggie caught a glimpse of armed police in the car park. They seemed to have taken up defensive positions.

The two of them looked out of the wide canteen windows. The man sat on the windowsill.

Maggie began to take more notice of her companion. Who was he and why was he not downstairs with the police? He seemed to be wearing a flak vest and was obviously armed. There was something about the expression on his face. A small ripple of nervousness ran through her.

Who was this man?

They both looked out of the open window.

Maggie was sure she heard a shout from the police below, she was sure it was.

'There he is – up there. That's him!'

At the inquest and major investigations later, she was to repeat her account of the incident many times.

'It was just a reflex action,' she moaned miserably. 'He was sitting on the window ledge and I knew he just needed to lean out and gravity would do the rest. So I gave him a nudge.'

Maggie sighed. 'It was just unfortunate I hadn't been to the meeting and hadn't been told it was just a training exercise.'

—⊗⊗⊗—

Every Picture Tells a Story

'Looks astonishingly like my old uncle Tom.'

Jessie, Albert and Stanley were standing in the hotel lobby waiting for the taxi to take them to the airport.

They all peered at the picture again. It was an enlarged photo of three fishermen carrying lobster pots in what they took to be Breton fishermen's clothes.

'Well really Stan, any old bloke in a black and white photo looks astonishingly like your old uncle Tom.'

'Was he a fisherman?' asked Jessie.

'Well no,' said Stan, 'but if you take away the French beret and the baggy trousers – he does look like him.'

'It's difficult to take clothes off in a photo,' Jessie muttered. 'What did your uncle Tom do?' Jessie continued.

'I don't know I never met him.'

'Well how do you know he looks like him?'

'I've seen photos.'

'So,' Bert wanted to clear up things. 'Actually he looks like a photo of your uncle Tom.'

'Suppose so…'

'Right' said Bert glad to have got that straightened out.

'He disappeared in the war.'

'Oh?' the flagging interest of the other two was revived.

'Was he in the forces?'

'No he was too young, but his Mum, my grandma's sister, and her husband lived on the south coast at that time. They moved away later. They had a motor boat and the story goes that they were part of the flotilla of small boats that brought back a lot of the soldiers that were stranded in Dunkirk.'

Jessie and Bert looked immediately respectful.

'I take it Tom's Dad took his boat across the channel?'

'Yes, so I believe.'

'Why do you always call him old Uncle Tom?'

'Oh that's because when they told me the story I was just a nipper. They always said – when they looked at old photographs – they would say "that's Tom, but he must be old now". So I always called him old uncle Tom.'

'When you say he disappeared...how did he disappear?' Bert's interest was piqued.

'Very sad.' Stan looked pensive. 'He went with his Dad to France to help bring back the troops. It was – if you'll pardon the pun – all hands to the pump. All able-bodied men and boys pitched in.'

'So Tom was just a lad really?' Jessie looked at the photo more closely...trying to see a lad in the faces of the grizzled and careworn French fishermen.

'What happened?'

'Well the little boats went back and forth across the channel as often as they could – especially at night. They turned out all of their lights – as the closer you got to the shore the more likely you were to come within the range of the German guns. It was an amazing thing for those blokes to do.'

'Yes' said Jessie, thinking of the wives and mothers worrying themselves sick on the quayside, probably filling flasks and making hundreds of spam sandwiches.

'Were they shelled?'

'Well yes…not completely shot up, but holed below the water line and slopping water badly – they just about limped back to port. They managed to get about twenty soldiers back. The tragedy was that it was only then they realised that Tom was not with them.

'It was such chaos – there were thousands of soldiers all hoping to be picked up and it was pitch dark – no one had noticed that Tom wasn't there.'

'How dreadful!' Jessie was quite distressed. 'Did they go back for him?'

'Well yes, when the boat was repaired. Everyone Tom's Dad knew asked the soldiers if they had seen a lad in a duffel coat and seaman's boots about sixteen or seventeen years old, but it was such mayhem – it was impossible and Tom was never found.

'How sad!' 'Was he taken prisoner?'

'After the war his Mum and Dad searched everywhere and went to every war department office they could think of, but no one knew anything about him.'

'That's tragic.' The three of them fell silent.

'I suppose he must have gone overboard and drowned – poor little fella.'

They all looked quite choked.

'I think they put up a plaque to him, along with others who lost their lives, in their little town,' Stan continued.

They all looked at the photo again – very solemnly.

The French taxi driver came into the lobby and called their names. The three of them piled into the taxi and the necessities of the present day, passports and check-in documents, brought them back to the present day.

Intrigued by Stan's story, when Bert got home he went on to the internet to see if he could mine any information with the resources available in the modern era: Ancestry.com, *Heir Hunters*, the military websites. It became a bit of an obsession.

It took him an age and proved quite fruitless. He learned nothing.

When he felt he had been down every avenue and, as a long shot, he phoned the hotel and asked about the photo. Did they know who the men in the photo were and was there any reason why that particular photo was on the wall of the hotel?

Bert could have kicked himself. He should have thought of it before.

Yes they did know – they were local fishermen and the picture was taken in the late fifties or early sixties.

'Could you tell me anything about these men?'

'Not really,' said the young receptionist, whose English was quite good. Then she had a thought. 'My Grandfather is here to give me a lift home – perhaps he knows something.'

After a pause and the sounds of footsteps a softly spoken Frenchman said, 'Hello?'

It turned out that the older man also spoke very good English. Yes he knew something of them, but it might not be helpful as the oldest of the men in the picture had been picked up as lad on a beach far away from here; he was badly injured and had no idea who he was or where he came from. He was very sick for a long time and they thought he would die. They realised that he had been washed ashore but could find no information about him to be able to contact his family.

Bert held his breath as the man continued.

'Some local people took him in and he has stayed here ever since. His grandson is our local Mayor.'

Bert was ecstatic!

A few weeks later the three of them were back on the plane returning to the small Normandy fishing port with video cameras, photos of Tom as a boy and a BBC reporter.

'You know if we'd been able to read French it was all written at the bottom of the picture...'

'Stan, how many times have you stayed in this hotel?'

Stan shrugged.

FETCH

The rain was coming down in bath-fuls. Scottie sat on the window ledge and watched it.

'No walkies today,' Roger said to his dog.

No, thought Scottie.

'Bloody weather,' Roger continued his conversation with his dog.

'You wouldn't like it anyway – you'd come in like a drowned rat, dirty and muddy and there would be BIG TROUBLE – you know what I mean. You'd jump on the sofa before we could stop you and well...' Roger's voice trailed away. It seemed unkind to say what precisely appalling things would happen to Scottie. '...you know what I mean.'

Scottie sank down on all fours with his nose pressed between his forepaws.

The sound of a key in the lock caught Roger's attention and he went to see which of his family had come back.

'Thought you were off for the day,' he said to his daughters.

'So did we,' Sarah spoke for both of them as she took off a soaking wet, rather skimpy but very expensive jacket.

'It was boring,' Jackie, her younger sister threw off her shoes and left them at the bottom of the stairs along with her very expensive handbag, scarf, half-open umbrella and sundry unidentifiable objects.

Roger remained forever mystified by the enormous amount of 'stuff' his daughters surrounded themselves with.

Scottie perked up and backed out of the living room.

Ooooh! he thought and rummaged around all the sundry objects left at the bottom of the stairs. The shoes became separated immediately: one to the kitchen, the other to the bedroom. The open bag tipped over as Scottie fell silently to a thorough chewing examination of its contents, diaries, purses, make-up bags, perfume, sweets, wallets all suffered the same fate as the shoes.

The girls had fallen into the fridge to recover from their abortive trip to the Mall. Once fortified by Diet Coke and a whole packet of Nachos they noticed Scottie lying quietly by his bed surrounded by their property – ready to take it into the garden as

soon as the opportunity presented itself.

'Ooh Noo! That bloody dog!' they wailed in unison.

'He's even got my bloody car keys,' moaned Sarah.

'I took weeks looking for my mobile phone last time and then had to go and buy another one!'

'That dog's a liability,' Jackie agreed with her sister.

'He's a kleptomaniac!' Sarah winged on.

Scottie did not know what kleptomaniac meant, so he wagged his tail and smiled triumphantly. So far his credit was good with the boy next door.

Scottie didn't know what bribery was either, but he did know that he would be taken out for a run in the park with a large ball if he continued to plunder the family's bags and drawers and cupboards.

The boy next door did not seem to mind what he brought him. When he had his 'mates' as he called them, round his house, they would share the things out.

The boy next door was ten and the girly things did not interest him, so sometimes he would give Barbie keyrings and such to the girls at school.

'You girls have got more money than sense,' Roger moaned at his daughters. 'You lose everything – you never know where anything is. It wasn't like this when your mother was here.'

'It wasn't like this before you bought the bloody dog!' The girls stared malevolently at him.

'That dog would be no problem if you were more careful!'

This was an argument that would rage for the rest of the evening.

Roger opened the back door. 'I suppose you'd better have a bit of a run in the garden,' he said to Scottie.

Scottie waited until Roger had turned before he scooted outside and under the fence.

The boy next door was in his room watching television.

'Hi Scot,' he greeted the dog warmly.

'Ready for another lesson? Sit!' he said firmly. The dog sat.

'Roll over!' The dog rolled over.

'Fetch the remote.' The dog fetched the remote.

'You're doing well boy,' he ruffled the dog's fur and romped with him on the floor.

'You're ready for the next level Scot.'

He took a lead from behind the bedroom door.

'Come on its stopped raining. Off to the park – Seedy's over there.'

Scottie trotted along the pavement obediently. At the crossroads they met Seedy with his little whippet.

'Damn good dogs – whippets,' Seedy said and they trotted along past the Town Hall.

As they approached the building, they saw two men running away. In their extreme haste they dropped something.

Scottie caught sight of a bulky white envelope lying on the stairwell leading to the basement.

The boy slipped off Scottie's lead.

'Fetch!' he commanded and Scottie tore over to the stairs, snatched up the envelope in his mouth and came tearing back, tail wagging.

'Good boy!' said the boys.

'Wow!' said Seedy in admiration, 'he's really coming on isn't he? He'll be robbing banks next!'

'All in good time my friend, all in good time,' said the boy next door as he examined the contents of the envelope.

FOREIGN TRAVEL

1955

I am a Londoner – never been serious about anything in my life. Much taken up with hair ribbons, hair spray, curls, frills, make-up, stiletto heels, rock and roll, Elvis Presley and looking like Grace Kelly.

Nature could have been kinder and dished out the requisite Marilyn Monroe figure necessary for any teenager in the nineteen fifties, but beggars can't be choosers and what are spare pairs of stockings for anyway – if not to fill your bra with those missing inches?

After all this is the 'look don't touch' era! I shall be perfectly ready to let it all hang out when the permissive sixties come along. But we're not there yet.

Here I am on a chilly, soggy, damp, uninspiring touring holiday of Scotland with my parents, both of them very serious about everything. We've 'Oohed' over Glencoe through storm and flood and 'Ahhed' at Aberdeen's severe religious grey. We've fingered Fingal's Cave and scouted round Fort William.

'Yes, yes, lovely…lovely…yawn, yawn.' I've counted the days. 'How soon? Oh Lord – How soon?' I've sung fervently in church. The pubs shut at nine o'clock and Mum and I get funny looks in them anyway – and we're tucked up in bed by nine thirty, safe and snug.

'Oh, how lovely. Oh how quaint! Heather tweed egg cosies – tartan underpants! I can't wait for the loom to loom!'

Desperation strikes. 'Yes, I will go pony trekking.'

'What do you have to press to make it start…NO! NO! I didn't mean that! What do you have to do to make it STOP!!'

A sore bum, a hot bath and bed again at nine o'clock. This is really living…Take me home country roads. Take me home, back to fog and fumes and traffic jams and long delays on the underground.

I have plunged into the depths of my soul and I have found a 'city girl,' right down to my painted toenails.

Now it is Kyle of Lochalsh. Highlands and pipers left far behind. Like Ariel, on 'yellow sands', I find the isle is 'full of noises'.

The daughter of the B & B – where my parents think we are staying, but I am convinced I'm serving some sort of sentence in an open prison – this lassie of few words, suggests, kindly, I thought at the time, that I go with her to something called a 'Kaylee'. The poster calls it a 'Cellidh' (Sellid?) – but I suppose it means the same thing.

I enquire suspiciously what it is.

'A dance', I am told.

I brighten – then wonder. 'What kind of dance?'

'Just a dance.'

Oh well it couldn't be too bad. I'd Paso Doble'd in Spain, and Cha-Cha'ed in Italy.

Hmm. It required a little thought. Yes, the green skin-tight number and the Italian black suede six inch heels, that no self-respecting City Girl could possibly be seen without and of course a chignon of indescribable complexity needing three tons of hairspray.

I tottered along beside this comely wench. This wholesome scrubbed – rosy-cheeked lassie and I looked at her pityingly.

I, after all, was a veteran of the 'Two Eyes', Soho's finest at the time, also the Marquis, Chris Barber and nameless Bond street Jazz clubs, where they smoked Gauloises and discussed Sartre and Cocteau!

I would grace them with my presence. I would decorate the walls gracefully – I might even dance with them.

The room was very large and very light. The people standing in tight groups were huge! And not just the boys!

For one brief second, my brave new worldliness wobbled. These people were different! They seemed to smile – a little – but, no, it wasn't entirely friendly.

I was being eyed up and down like a heifer at a cattle fair. I began to detect snorts and sniggers. My sophisticated feathers were ever so slightly ruffled.

I ignored them and turned to my companion, but I had been abandoned, she had joined the unwelcoming committee.

The music began – a curious mixture of wail and warble, pipe and drum. Absolutely no time was lost in polite eye-work and casual sauntering or...

'Would you like to dance with me?'

A hand like a shovel shot out and dragged me, like a chicken about to have its head cut off, onto the floor, where I was heaved and shoved and chucked from hand to hand.

I had been brought...such a dumb lamb...to this slaughter. The ghastly realisation dawned. I was the cabaret! This snooty southerner was to be brought to her knees...I panted and struggled...they weren't going to let me go. The girls were as strong as the men! The music got louder and faster and never seemed to stop.

Shoes went first: one, then the other, lobbed in a wild kick to the corner of the room. Hairpins flew in all directions as my long hair whacked me round the face – a very cross horse's tail.

I was vaguely beginning to make some sense of the pattern of the dance. Gasping with relief, concentrating frenziedly, I was beginning to pick it up, beginning to recognise some sequence, some repeating pattern. My bust went next…. I yanked it out of the top of my dress during a sort of 'do-si-do'. Strewn about the floor, those stockings lay like entrails that cast a Roman's fate. With that gesture my immediate destiny was sealed. I had taken up the challenge.

Now it is a man's life in the ballet and all that barre work had built for me thighs to grace a Rugby prop forward. In a brief moment they put me down I ripped my skirt to…well…those little bits of black lace around the edges of knicks. They had asked for this and they'd get it!

The honour of my tribe was at stake…Now I had bare feet and full freedom of movement…

'–and wi' you, wi' you and wi' you bonny lads…

I'll dance the buckles off your shoes,

Wi' you my bonny lads…'

They sensed me taking up the cudgels. Contempt very slowly turned to amused glee as I joined in with gusto and being smaller and lighter, when they threw me about, I went higher than the rest.

A great time was had by all – vast quantities of some nameless brew were consumed and the lassie from the B&B and I were chaired and serenaded home.

How were they to know? I was perfectly used to being thrown about, swung upside down and chucked over people's heads.

Rock and Roll hadn't quite hit Kyle of Lockalsh yet.

GAME ON

'Well 'spose it's "game over".'

Risby said nothing and looked at Tinder vacantly. 'Why, what ju mean?'

'Well there ain't much we can do.'

Risby still looked vacant. 'Why not?'

'Come on bruv he's split.'

'Yeah, but nuffin' was goin down.' Risby was doing his best to keep up.

'Then! Not now!' Tinder insisted.

'Come on bruv get wiv it!'

The young floppy haired drama teacher stopped them in mid impro.

'It's going really well boys, but we're going to need a few more words or no one will know what you're talking about.'

Risby looked vacant. 'Like what?'

'Well the audience will want to know what game?'

'Video innit?

'Does it have a name?'

'Yeah – 'corse!'

Tinder looked pityingly at his teacher.

'Well??' the teacher looked expectantly at the boys.

'The Revenge of the Ninja??' He cast around the room for inspiration. 'Cabinet makers?' He finished as his eye fell on a cupboard in the corner of the room. 'Or is that a bit long…maybe carpenters?'

The rest of the Saturday afternoon groups, at the Leyton Stagecoach drama school, were managing quite well with their various improvisations.

They were preparing for the inevitable Winter Show in January that was to be performed to parents and open to the public.

Stagecoach had affiliations to several other youth organisations and some youngsters were encouraged to join Stagecoach for reasons other than an interest in theatre.

There were some quite fearsomely talented children with their fearsomely ambitious parents – who were the lifeblood and backbone of any public performance.

The floppy haired drama teacher – whose name was Julian but preferred to be called Jools Jordan as he felt it had a ring to it as a stage name – was grateful for the paid work. After leaving Drama School he was keen to take any paid work between acting jobs.

He had something of a soft spot for Risby and Tinder as they had arrived in his group via Social Services. Julian had not delved into their history, but they were an odd little pair and he wanted to make sure they had their spot on the programme.

Due to the generosity of the caretaking staff Julian managed to give them extra time on their own. He half expected them to only appear intermittently, but every Saturday on the dot, he would find them waiting for the door to open.

During the class they hovered at the back and went to the toilet frequently. In the training exercises Julian would often call them to the front – but they remained stolidly in the back row. Unlike the other children they did not crave attention and appeared to want to remain anonymous.

They seemed to come to life when the rest of the class went home and they had Julian all to themselves.

'Well, what's it going to be? Ninja what?' Julian had a clip board ready to take notes and shape the impro into some kind of sketch for the show. He knew he would probably have to write it direct it and stage it for them.

The boys had been prowling around the various books on the shelves in the room.

'Choose something you know about,' Julian had advised.

Tinder handed Julian a piece of paper. He read 'The Revenge of the Ninja Apostles'.

He tried not to look too dumbstruck.

'I'm not too sure how this is going to work lads…I'll have to think about it – does it have a story line?'

The boys looked puzzled. 'You mean kind of what 'appens?'

'Well at Sunday School it's kind of Jesus dies – the Ninjas revenge 'im and he comes back, then he goes up to 'eaven.'

Julian felt it was unkind to dismiss the idea out of hand.

'Do you have any ideas how you will do it? Do you need a wooden frame as a TV?'

It was Tinder's turn to look puzzled.

'No. It's all effects innit, CGI's – right sounds…' Tinder was waving his hands about to indicate fairly frenzied movement. 'Lights and stuff.'

A glimmer of understanding struck Julian – he felt he knew what they were driving at.

'Ooh!! Yeah.. You mean black stage and some kind of back projection and a sound track?'

'What's 'at?'

'You need a screen.'

'Yeah we'll have a screen.'

'We can use the plain white cyc at the back of the stage.'

'But there's only two of you and there are twelve apostles?'

'Me and Risby's the Ninja's and we take your mates from the audience to be the apostles.'

Julian began to think about theatre in totally different way than he had ever done in his life. He became completely engrossed, in what he came to understand, was the vision of the two little boys.

Quite extraordinary was the verdict of the slightly shell shocked audience as the list of thank yous to the Technical team was read out.

'Performance Art', 'Pinteresque', 'Inonesco', 'Beckett' – Julian could hear the names being bandied about backstage as well wishers crowded around him.

'I liked the idea of with starting with "Game Over" as Jesus died and ending as he ascended into Heaven with the words "Game on", "Game on", "Game on" flashing on and off! So unusual darling.'

'I liked the bit with the Devil best!' Risby said to Tinder as they munched on the sausage rolls Julian's Mum had brought for them.

STRANGER THINGS

Penny recognised the handwriting even after all these years. Was it a joke or a coincidence from someone with similar handwriting? She looked very closely – it was unmistakable.

The writing was Maxine's.

Maxine was dead. Penny had gone to her funeral. She had sent flowers and spoken to the family who were – even to this day in shock at their daughter's death. So sudden and in such peculiar circumstances.

She looked at the postmark: the date was only a few days ago, but the postmark was too smudged to see where it was sent from.

Penny and Maxine had gone to school together, had shared so much of their teenage years and young married lives. Penny's mind ticked over how many years and put the letter in her pocket and decided not to show the letter to Ralph, who had spent the week tending to the needs of his beautiful classic Citroen DS.

'Don't jump to conclusions Penny,' she told herself. 'It may be something quite different from what you expect.'

It was a warm summer evening, Ralph stroked the shining chrome on his Citroen and waved a slight goodbye to Penny as he passed her sitting in the garden, before disappearing down the lane in small eddies of sandy dust.

Penny lived a few doors away from Ralph and when Maxine died, grief had brought them together for a kind of mutual support and assistance.

Ralph would have liked it to be more than that, but something had always held Penny back. Maybe it was those expensive cars? She didn't know. Something had made her keep him at arms length. They were friendly and he was unfailingly polite – almost too much so. Penny often wondered why he had taken up with Maxine as he never really seemed to like her.

The letter smouldered in her pocket until she saw Ralph drive away to spend the evening at the club, then she opened the envelope very carefully, rolling a pencil under the flap that was stuck down and it obligingly rolled back leaving an almost new looking envelope.

Penny took out one sheet of paper – it was not a letter. In Maxine's distinctive handwriting it said

Cornwallis Road…Aunty Ella

and there was a drawing of a rosette that horses are given at Gymkhanas and a little cartoon of their form teacher.

Maxine had been especially gifted at drawing cartoons and as a schoolgirl had often covered the black board with pictures of the school staff and various 6th formers who tickled her sense of humour.

Penny knew the reference immediately. Probably she was the only one who would know what it meant. Cornwallis Road had been demolished years ago and replaced by an estate of houses and a community centre. It was unlikely that Ralph would know either, as Maxine had always been anxious to obliterate her childhood and the years she had lived in a Warners one bedroom flat.

Penny remembered those years very well as she had lived a couple of streets away in a tiny 'two up, two down' with no inside toilet or bathroom and a filthy damaged sink with the only tap in the house wobbling from a wonky pipe in the wall. They were years neither of them had wanted to remember. The two girls had been friends from High School. They had always walked home together, taking the long route, ambling down the High Street, eating ice-lollies, or in winter a packet of chips, only getting a bus when the weather made it impossible to walk anywhere. Neither of them were particularly anxious to get home.

It was a dilemma for Penny – did she tell Ralph? It might be nothing. It could be a hoax and it seemed ridiculous to get all het up over what might be nothing.

Maxine had been very good looking as a girl and young woman. Penny had always taken it for granted that anywhere they went together it was always Maxine who would be asked to dance, or taken home from a party in a smart car. Penny thought nothing of it, after all if you look like the young Elizabeth Taylor it was inevitable. It was of course how she and Ralph got together.

Maxine had also been extremely successful in her business venture – something that happened almost by accident. In her travels, somewhere in the Far East with Ralph, in a local market she had been persuaded to buy a jar of the 'magic' face cream. She gave it a go, to be polite, and was astonished by the amazing things it did to her skin.

When she came back she took the cream to a chemist and asked him to analyse the cream to give her an idea of the ingredients. He in turn sent it to his chemistry Professor and who had access to a much more up to date and sophisticated lab.

Maxine had only wanted to be able to replicate the jar of cream that was by now nearly finished. She asked her chemist if it was possible for him to make up a jar for her. He said he would try – there was only one ingredient that was difficult to find. It was a moss that was only to be found on some remote hillside in Tibet.

Maxine accepted that it probably could not be replicated, when a few weeks later the chemist rang her and said he had been browsing through Chinese medicine on the internet for a friend and had come across the moss. Evidently it could be grown quite easily and was readily available in Chinese herbal medicine shops. So they decided to experiment with the formula.

To their utter astonishment it worked.

Maxine tested it for a year and nothing catastrophic happened to her and she looked blooming. She contacted Penny and asked if she was willing to be a guinea pig and test the cream.

'Of course I will and I'll ask some friends as well,' Penny replied.

Lots of friends used the cream and were delighted with the results. By now a small production line had been established – one that in a remarkably short space of time became a highly lucrative business.

Penny gave up her job at the Enfield Library, moved house and went to work for Maxine and had never looked back.

'Everything was coming up roses' for both of them.

Penny bought a house nearby to be close to her work as Marketing Manager for the 'Rambling Rose' beauty product company Maxine had developed. It was beginning to branch out into other products – like hand and body cream and also a range for people who had more serious skin problems – burns, acid attacks, surgery – which was proving to be hugely successful.

Penny became aware that Maxine and Ralph were now living rather separate lives.

'He has his toys to play with and his little playmates to keep him company.'

She sounds bitter, Penny thought, which was out of character for Maxine. But she could see that Ralph had no idea how to live his life with a successful wife and was becoming a playboy – perhaps feeling redundant.

He had ample opportunity to carve out any path he wished and when he joined the 'Companions of the Supreme Being' Maxine was almost pleased. Perplexed certainly, but pleased that Ralph had found a place where he felt he belonged and gave him some kind of purpose.

Penny viewed it as one of those rather shady cults, that attracted famous and illustrious people from all walks of life: politicians, pop stars, doctors even priests and on the face of it the adherents seemed to be happy and content.

Ralph persuaded Maxine to go to one of their meetings. She reported back to Penny that they seemed a harmless bunch who needed emotional support and a place to stay. 'A lot of them are bereaved, so I suppose it gives them somewhere to share their loss.'

So why was Ralph so taken up with them? Was he grieving? And for what? Penny kept her imaginings to herself. 'I suppose some are car enthusiasts,' she decided.

'They also seem to have a lot of money,' Maxine reported.

'Don't they always, these weird groups? It seems to go with the territory. People who have loads of money are often looking for something missing in their lives – and continue to pay out and pay out thinking these guru's will work a miracle.'

Penny was too busy with her own life to give the matter any more thought. She had lost her partner when they were still young and her daughter was growing into a challenging young woman who took all her attention.

As Penny looked at the piece of paper she thought about those years and decided to ring her daughter, now married and with a son of her own.

'Georgie, I have had the strangest letter – well not exactly a letter...' and she described what was written on the paper.

Georgie was silent for a while. 'You know Mum, I think you should follow this up – maybe even take it to the police. Don't say anything to the family, it will just upset them. How is the said Rafe?'

Penny could not see her raise her eyebrows ironically. Georgie pronounced his name in the upper class way with a slight edge to her voice – she had never liked him.

'Well he is much the same. He wants me to join the 'Companions...' She did not finish.

Her daughter almost bellowed down the phone 'No, no! Absolutely no! We'll be down at the weekend to see you. Don't do anything until I get there.'

Before she died Maxine had made Penny a full partner in the company.

Ralph only discovered this when the will was read after the funeral. He did his best to make light of it, but everyone could see he was surprised and disconcerted by the news. He and Maxine had never married so although he was entitled to a considerable sum of money he was not the immediate heir to her complete estate, which reverted to her parents and, in the event of their death, to Penny.

Maxine's parents were too devastated by the loss of their beautiful and incredibly talented daughter to be able to discuss the matter with anyone and then her father had an unexpected heart attack soon after Maxine's death.

Penny's daughter Georgie arrived in a fluster of arrangements, She couldn't stay long and was impatient to see the letter. She frowned as she studied the letter from all angles.

'I have no idea what the words and the cartoon refer to…'

'Well I'm not surprised, I think its meant to be cryptic. What it refers to is where she was born and lived as a girl – which was round the corner to me. Aunty Ella was who she saw as her saviour and where she went for holidays and half terms. All I remember is that Aunty Ella kept horses – I think somewhere in a village in Essex – and that Maxine had lots of shiny coloured rosettes around the mirror in her bedroom.

'The cartoon is of our form Teacher called Miss Park who was just a gem. She had her hair plaited then wound round her ears in what we called "ear phones" and she looked like Gertrude Stein. She was fearsomely clever and had been a Girton Girl in her youth, one of the first women to go to Oxford. She was a Classics scholar – quite wasted on us little "rock" fiends. I had no idea what she was talking about, but we loved her, as much as anything, because she was so eccentric! She cycled to school each day – that is why she is on a bike in the cartoon. I remember we clubbed together to buy new handle bars as hers were rusty and ready to fall off.'

Georgie could see that her mother was ready to relive all of those days so she stopped her. 'Mum when Maxine died was anyone called in to identify the body?'

'Well, no, they were all called to her bedside when she was dying and stayed until she died – her parents and Ralph.'

'That's pretty conclusive that she is definitely dead. I can't see that the police will be at all interested in this note. But it suggests that someone else got hold of an envelope that Max had written your address on and sent it to you.'

'But it is so long ago…and where has this envelope been hiding for so long?'

As a last resort Penny decided to ring Maxine's mother. She would have to be careful. She herself was unlikely to have had a letter as she had moved house after Maxine's father's death, but she might have her sister Ella's address or phone number. It was going to be tricky as they did not want to upset her unnecessarily.

Maxine's mother was delighted to hear from her and they exchanged pleasantries for a while when she suddenly said, 'Did you get Maxine's letter?'

'Yes, I did.' Penny hesitated not knowing quite what to say. 'Did you send it?'

'Yes dear. I was having a rummage around among some things for the charity shop when I found the letters addressed to you and Ella. My memory is dreadful these days, but the nurse at the Supreme Being clinic gave me Maxine's effects and the letters were among them.'

'Oh, so there is no mystery about her death?'

'No, I never thought there was.'

'I am so sorry.' Penny felt guilty. 'Only getting the letter made us think something was wrong.'

'Oh no, it was just another of Maxine's little notes she often wrote to remind herself of her premonitions.'

'Premonitions? I didn't know Maxine had premonitions!'

'Oh yes…Maxine was heavily into betting on the "gee, gees" as she used to call them.'

'I never knew that!' Penny was astounded and put the phone on to loudspeaker so that Georgie could hear too.

'Well how do you think she funded "Rambling Rose" when it first started? When she discovered the formula for the original cream she found that a particular ingredient had a very strange effect on her. She became quite clairvoyant!'

'Noooooo!!'

'Yeeeeeeess!! That's why Dad, and then me, have always had enough money to live on well and comfortably and Ralph as well of course. When she went into the Companions Clinic she left these two little notes for you and Ella so that you could benefit from her "special insight".'

'So what I read into the note was not what I thought?'

Penny and Georgie looked at each other, quite bemused.

'So what did it mean?'

'I read it quickly and it said Lord Cornwallis would be running at Kempton Park. Kempton being Maxine's surname. My married name of course. "Ella" referred to horses and the rosettes to winning. I have to apologise for not sending them at the time, but I was so upset I forgot. But I have had a message from her lately...'

'Pardon! Did you say you have had a message from her lately?!'

'Yes...'

Penny and Georgie just sat in silence, open mouthed.

'Are you still there dear?'

'Yes,' Penny said weakly. 'How did you get this message?'

'I was going on to say Ralph phones me when there is a message for me.'

'Where does he get the messages from?'

'The Companions of course! You do know they are a spiritualist organisation don't you?'

'No, I thought it was meditation, spiritual therapy and whatnot...'

'Well there's that too, but mainly people go to commune with the dead.'

'And...lost loved ones?' Penny encouraged Maxine's mum.

'Also other people who send messages...' Penny was beginning to cotton on. 'Like who is the winner of the 4.30 at Kempton Park?'

'Well, yes. And sometimes it can be news about the Stock Market or who will win the World Cup. You know helpful things like that...'

'I am getting the idea very well! I took no notice when Maxine said they were all incredibly wealthy, I just thought they were rich cranks!'

'Which of course they are! It's supposed to be a secret, but I think Maxine wants you to know now.'

Georgie grinned at her mother. 'That explains all those very shiny cars on Ralph's drive!'

'Well, I seriously think I may take up Ralph's offer of joining the Companions of the Supreme Being after all.'

'He did say he wanted to sponsor you. You can't just join you know, you have to be recommended...'

'I can see why!' Penny finished the conversation with pleasantries and promises that she would get in touch and tell Max's Mum how she got on and she put the phone down and turned to her now slightly puce-looking daughter.

'Well to mis-quote Shakespeare "stranger things – in heaven and earth Horatio than are dreamed of in our philosophy."'

Georgie rolled about on the cushions on the floor and laughed and laughed and laughed.

'Imagine if we had gone to the police! We would have blown the gaffe right enough!'

'Oh, I never thought of that!' Penny stopped waving her hands around.

'What about Ella? She doesn't live at the stables any more? Who got the other letter?'

Laughter turned suddenly to deep consternation…but that's another story.

HOLDING THE FORT

'Can someone help me – PLEASE!'

The member for Reading East sounded so pitiful that Mrs Atkins got up from her seat and went over to the photocopier. It was a machine of vast proportions and inexhaustible ability and complexity.

'What's the problem, Reading East?' The round, bald head of Reading East was shiny and sweating.

'I seem to have got the belt of my trousers caught up in the machine and I can't get it out,' he was spluttering and panic stricken.

Mrs Atkins pointed to the laminated notice on the wall that cogently outlined the machine's prodigious ability to detect in human beings anything related to a deviation from a calm and controlled state of mind.

It stated that anything to do with:

A hangover

bad feet

fiddling, sorry, 'juggling' your expenses

your position hanging by a thread

divorce pending

love at first sight

in a tremendous hurry

failed multi-tasking

rain

The list was endless and became more bizarre as it went on and concluded with:

murderous intent

'Which of these fills the bill, Reading?'

'I can't look, I'm trapped in the machine!' his bald head was wobbling like a blancmange as he tried once more to free himself. His trousers now being in imminent danger of following his belt.

Mrs Atkins squeezed herself into the tiny space between the man and the machine, passed her hand across a piece of plastic and Reading East was freed.

'Thank you, thank you Mrs Atkins! What would we do without you?'

She smiled and said, 'Which of the listed conditions do you think you were in when this happened?'

'Oh murderous,' said Reading East. 'It's been a hell of a week: two all-night sittings and the whips after us all the time, not to mention Jeremy.'

'Exactly, not to mention Jeremy – that's the best course of action,' said Mrs Atkins.

'What do you think about it all?' Reading East asked her.

Mrs Atkins had seen it all. She had presided over the A.V. room in its various incarnations 'since the flood' as the newer MP's would say.

'They come, they go,' Mrs Atkins said, 'and at the moment more seem to be going than coming.'

'But what do you think Mrs A? Do you think the party will split?'

'Well, it did before! People seem to forget that.'

'Umm,' said Reading East, 'and they all ended up in the Lib Dems and look what happened then!'

'Umm,' said Mrs Atkins.

'Bye Mrs A,' and Reading East waddled to the door clutching a wadge of papers in his hand. 'I'll look at the list next time,' he called as he disappeared down the corridor.

Mrs A went back to her desk and took out quite a large book that looked like a ledger and, finding the right page, she ticked the column headed 'murderous'.

The room began to fill up and became fairly crowded with researchers, secretaries, messengers, and reporters – the usual crowd who had no private office in the building.

All the computers were being used and the landline phones. Considering the number of people in the room there was a strange almost religious hush.

Mrs Atkins was occasionally needed to assist a junior or a less experienced MP – who always asked her opinion on the various issues.

The day wore on.

Winchester South came in. 'The PM is in fine form today Mrs A, he's really giving it to them!'

'Yes, he seemed fighting fit after his holiday, when he gave me a lift this morning.'

'He gave you a lift this morning?!' Mrs Winchester South's eyebrows shot up to her hairline. 'Does he do that often?'

'Now and then, if he sees me at the bus stop,' Mrs A said casually. 'He enjoys a chat.'

'Oh…Um…do you know him well?'

'Sort of, I suppose. I know his Mum.'

Winchester South digested this information. She decided to keep it to herself. She hurried to the chamber as she was late for Question Time.

She settled herself and her bundle of papers into her seat, in time to hear the PM begin a reply to the leader of the opposition.

'A very reliable source informs me…' he began.

Winchester South smiled to herself.

So now we know who's running the country.

IN A SMALL TOWN, SOUTH OF PARIS

Now perhaps it was over. His reflection stared back at her from the hotel mirror.

A reflection she had looked at so often, spoken to and it had answered her.

'The eyes,' she thought – eyes that creased into laughter so quickly. Eyes that had laughed at her day and night for too long. A brilliant smile, squeezing the breath out of her. Now she felt strangled by such beauty, it was draining energy from her, sapping her will. She had no idea of the real colour of his eyes, something from inside them had drawn her in and she had drifted closer and closer until she was caught in a disturbing power that ran between them, growing stronger all the time. The sweet softness of his face and body, the gentleness of him so near – his warmth penetrating her and a raw tenderness that spread to every nerve until she winced and the whole of her cried, every part screaming like a trapped animal.

Then there was the dream. One of those that wouldn't quite go away. It repeated itself. He was older, his hair quite grey, face waxen pale. Still slim and tall with long hands and feet, but now sick, with blood coming from his mouth. Leaning against her, stroking her back. The touch of his fingers – so real. though sick, though old, in the dream what she felt was love. Strong and powerful, her own love invaded the dream and his need. She wrung clothes out in a primitive sink of cold water and he leaned against her, looking so ill. The dream ended and she was left needing to care for him, desperate to lay him down and comfort him. So much pain and she wasn't there. Why would she dream a dream like that?

Ria held tightly to the few pages she had written. 'I am writing this for you,' she said to the mirror. It was time for him to go. She must move on. It had been a beautiful time, but now she must get back to her own life. To grow old in peace and not be caught out again.

Ria returned to her laptop...

Paris was stifling, the traffic on the Périphérique unendurable.

Bruno, sweating and bad tempered, changed gears aggressively. Screwing his neck around, his handsome face became distorted, made ugly by irritation and frustration. Following the green signs, he hurled his car off the major road on to the 'bis', the bypass.

No hurry, he thought.

Nothing to rush for.

On the less congested D roads the car gathered speed, the welcome breeze flowing around him from the open window and the sunroof. It cooled his temper as it cooled his body.

'What am I rushing for?' he asked himself.

'The children?' His mind wound on. 'They will be at Ecole de Vacance anyway. Not for Monique, who will ask for money and more money, as usual. She will say it is for the children and I won't believe her as usual and will point out that she is wearing the most expensive ensemble I have seen on any woman all year. She will become angry, and shout. "Do you expect the mother of your children to go around looking like a beggar?" And I will shout that Phillippe is enjoying all the benefit of these dazzling creations so perhaps he might pay for them now and again! She will scream at me "How do I know that he hasn't paid for them anyway?" and I will pounce, seize my chance. "Alors! So if he is giving you money why do you ask so much from me?"'

Bruno felt exhausted and depressed by this row with the unseen Monique and he was not yet clear of Paris.

Ria read what she had written aloud to herself.

'How will you be when you're forty? Still tall of course, unusual for a Frenchman. Still slim and lightly athletic as you are now. I think you'll still play tennis and ski or do some sport, until making money demands your entire attention, maybe squash?

'Anything that preserves that beautiful body you're so proud of and is worth the effort. The hair? I can't see you losing that thick dark mop. It's soft hair that goes quickly. Yours is coarse and springy and lasts well into old age. No, I think you'll still be attractive at forty, as now, at twenty-four. Perhaps more so. You should have more assurance, more sophistication.

'But what about you? Where have you reached?'

Ria put down the manuscript she was working on.

Pushing open the windows and the shutters, she looked down into a shady courtyard serving as a car park, decorated with antique farm machinery, now rusted and filled with trailing geraniums carelessly littering every step and corner. Opposite, red tiles of other rooftops linked and tessellated, neatly poised, formed the skyline. Beyond the roofs, small squares of careful fields fringed by tall poplars, completed her view from the window.

A smell of cooking pleased her.

'A beautiful country, like the cream of the milk,' she said.
'The French don't deserve it.'

Bruno turned on the radio, switching stations until he found one that suited his mood.

He was a man of unusually delicate sensibilities. This often made him cruel. Easily perturbed, easily thrown off balance, anything too harsh, too loud, too abrasive, distressed him. When he was young this sensitivity was almost too much to bear, so he suppressed it ruthlessly.

Solitude suited him, not being alone exactly – but keeping everyone at a safe distance – men and women. Because in any relationship there would be a moment when he would become unsure and suspicious and would withdraw for his own safety. He was extremely attractive to women and for a while everything would be fine, then he would do inexplicable things and be thought a bastard. Without knowing it he had acquired a reputation for being a man to avoid.

He was not a woman chaser. They should come to him, he felt and he allowed himself to be pursued and wooed. In this way he felt safe. To Bruno it was the natural order.

Then in his late twenties he had met Monique. Monique was everything he had always expected life would provide. Fairly tall. With a superb body, long legs, full, well-shaped breasts, slim as a whisker and a fine face with neat features.

At the time he was in partnership with a friend from University, operating a small airfreight company with useful contracts with the Arab states. Based in a rather flyblown, shit-filled little town just outside of Tripoli. 'Arsehole of the world,' he and Benoit called it. But it was to be endured for it was to lead to bigger things.

There were still a number of moderately wealthy Arab sheiks and dealers in various commodities who required certain private services of a small anonymous air company for cash to develop their businesses.

Ria stopped typing and considered this. She didn't know about either the Arab States or just how dangerous it was to smuggle guns, women, drugs or all three. Can you get away with that kind of thing for long?

No, I don't think he's going to be tough enough, she decided. *He's hardly streetwise now. He's drifted into it in a naïve way.*

Now the road was unrolling before Bruno as a smooth even black and white carpet. Driving was a pleasure when it was like this. The road to yourself, a private racing circuit, but he did not drive too fast. Too many scars, he had too many scars.

He had been loved, not often and not for long, but he had been loved. Though somehow it was never in the way he wanted. Often feeling there was an ingredient missing. But how did he know? Surely you can't miss what you have never known and yet, he did miss something. He had never truly loved Monique. He had desired her, who wouldn't? But when you are presented with perfection every single night even that palls after a while. He had found her tiresomely childish. Always wanting to be with him, hanging on his arm. Always wanting to know where he was and what he was doing. Sulking if he was late, or too tired to make a fuss of her or to make love to her. Wanting, wanting, always wanting something. Bruno felt he had given her the greatest thing he had to offer, namely himself. He had made her his wife. What more could he do?

Eventually her demands, her tears and the rows pushed her further and further away. At first he made some small effort to placate her but when the children were born, first Madeleine, then Antoine, he became completely frozen by the turmoil of the house. They all wanted, wanted. They all wanted something of him that he just didn't have to give.

In those years he had had to concentrate on the business. Among the many things Monique wanted was the financial and social position she was used to. A great deal of Monique's charm had been enhanced by the money that might come with her. Her father owned several well-known restaurants with enviable gastronomic reputations around the Cote d'Azure, where money was scattered without thought every season.

Pouring herself a drink, Ria decided he ought to have another woman by now. After all, he is French.

She glanced at the newspaper on the bedside table. Simone Lazare, TV presenter, smiled at her from the inside page. No, that's a bit obvious-glamorous. Monique was that kind of glamorous – a model – before she married Bruno.

No, I think Simone can be softer, more old-style French chic – more Juliette Binoche – not perfect, but effortlessly attractive. After all, even now he is not really keen on very modern young women. He doesn't like women who ask anything of him, so Simone can have some kind of connection with the business. Tax consultant accountant, something like that. It will have started as a business relationship that slowly became something much closer. He will be a little dependent on her and for the first time in his life make a definite first move towards a woman.

With Monique, who had made her interest in him plain for all to see, no effort was required from him. Everyone seemed determined they were perfect for each other and it all just happened as they planned it would.

Along the way, other women will have fallen into his lap and he will have casually knotted his tie, brushed his curly hair, put on his jacket and been gone with barely a 'Ciao' on his lips.

But Simone is different: she laughs at his jokes. He finds himself thinking about her a lot. In his mind he talks to her. Phones her for no reason, finds himself in her flat more and more often, cooking meals, sharing laundry effortlessly even joyfully, saving up funny stories about his work to amuse her. Mimicking his colleagues and customers for her entertainment.

'Tell me how is Bernard?' she asks him. Bruno mimes an immense pipe, with much huffing and puffing and incomprehensible conversation through dense clouds of smoke and Simone laughs and laughs.

'How do you work with this man?'

'With great difficulty,' Bruno replies. 'We say to him, "Look Bernard, don't talk, just send up smoke signals, it's easier to understand"...'

Simone wipes her eyes. 'You're so funny, Bruno.'

Bruno had forgotten he could be funny.

Now the light was slipping away, the landscape acquiring the sultriness of dusk. Bruno yawned a couple of times and took off his sunglasses.

No, he was not rushing anywhere. It was years since he'd passed this way, always using the autoroute, a mad dash to his destination. Cool forests and old towns were his companions this evening.

Bruno remembered the crisp freshness of the wind across a plain a long time ago. He remembered a woman who walked through a forest. A woman older than himself. It was fleeting, only half a memory. Dregs of daylight skimmed through the leaves. So dense, so pale did the scene appear to him he wondered if he had lost his way. His body told him he needed a stop.

The grey shadows of a very old town passed like dead soldiers. Across the bridge the road preened, sleek and smooth. For no reason he knew of, he felt lonely for the little town and its mouldering balconies.

At the traffic lights on the bridge, he glanced at a small hotel. The patron, short and squat, sat under one of his own umbrellas and watched the world pass by, rushing on to bigger, newer towns full of bright lights and colourful shops.

Bruno pulled the car into a wide sweeping arc in the road and turned back towards the little town. Something he needed was there, something he felt he had left behind. He parked at the back of the hotel in a courtyard that served as a car park, littered with trailing geraniums. He went in and inquired about a room. It was ludicrously cheap, so he took the best room they had, self-consciously doing them a favour.

Opening the shutters, he looked down on to the courtyard. He could see his car below, this pleased him.

Rapidly pulling off all his clothes, he stepped into the shower. Water poured down his body, slipping over his shoulders and his head. Putting his face up to the jet he drenched himself. He rubbed his hands over his chest and his belly and down his long thighs and around his small buttocks. He felt good.

He took several deep breaths, looking at his naked body in the mirror then looking at the bed. For a moment he wished he wasn't alone. But who did he want to share that bed with him? His mind flicked through women he had known, like fingers rifling through a filing cabinet. He remembered some very good moments, some very good sex, but he wasn't sure.

Simone perhaps, he felt so at ease with her in their lovemaking. With Monique, it had always been a little awkward and she talked about it, sometimes in public. Made sly little remarks about books and their covers. Bruno was sure she talked to her mother about his prowess as a lover. This made it even more difficult to approach her spontaneously. But the business had taken him away.

Frequent trips around the world made the distance between them even greater and the problem resolved itself. He found surprising comfort in the passing encounters in different hotels around the world and Monique found Phillipe. It was inevitable.

Bruno looked at the bed again, reminded of a particularly exciting Canadian girl he had spent time with. A whole world had opened up for him, he had reached sensual and erotic depths in himself that had never previously found expression. She had thought his somewhat slow response intriguing and a challenge.

'Wow, light the blue touch paper and retire immediately. Jeez! A slow fuse lover, but when it blows baby you're dynamite!' He'd lain back and stroked the few hairs he had on his chest, smiling his most beguiling Gallic smile.

'You're so gorgeous, just gorgeous!' she said and plunged back into him.

Being gorgeous was an act that Bruno had perfected over the years. He would never have admitted to her that perhaps she had something to do with it. Secretly he was thrilled with her and himself. Something long pent up had been released, now he felt like the whole man nature had intended him to be.

'A slow fuse.' He repeated her words to himself and smiled again. Quite the nicest thing anyone had ever said to him. He nursed those words.

One day he would take them home to Monique. He spoke to her unseen presence.

Ria heard a car draw up. She looked out of the window again.

Conjuring Bruno's image, she watched him get out of the car slowly in that infuriatingly languid manner, look around him, open the boot, take out a small bag, lock the boot, lock the car, throw a jacket over his shoulder and stroll across the courtyard.

She adjusted the image as it came closer, made him a little heavier and darker around the jawline. She kept the lithe youthful grace, but less delicate, less feminine. He still stood remarkably straight and upright for a tall man but was beginning to sink back into his hips.

A moustache? No, she decided no moustache and deleted it from the text.

Bruno came out of the shower and dressed himself carefully, wondering if there was a decent restaurant in the town.

Darkness had settled over the rooftops, over the trees, over spires and towers. Deep grey hills in the distance merged into a sky speckled with light and pushed to the edges of the world.

Dimly, Bruno perceived a strangeness about the town. It was not late, perhaps half seven, eight o'clock, but no one was about. Coloured lights drew him to a bar. Perhaps it was a restaurant too.

He looked in the window: two men sat at a table in silence with papers spread out in front of them. There was no menu and in spite of the lights it looked closed. Bruno walked over a long bridge, down to what he assumed was a main road, along a riverbank.

Passing a church he peered inside into blank darkness. Each house was firmly shuttered. The curling ironwork of the balconies and balustrades appeared flaking and naked. A few pots of geraniums that loitered on stone steps and pathways were thick stemmed and mature. Each narrow street led back to the river, dark and secret. Ducks huddled in weed patches, heads down for the night.

Bruno peered into the heavy secrecy of the water, mesmerised by thin strings of lights swaying on the surface. The ducks were silent. Bruno hated ducks.

Just a childish accident, but he had never forgotten. Squawking and the beat of heavy wings and Bruno caught up in the middle of it. Feet, wings and beaks swirling around him. He couldn't get out. He'd clawed the air, but the birds had beat their wings ever more furiously. Fear held them – birds and child trapped in a whirling mass. Covering his face, he had tried to run through them and tripped. A gash had split open on his forehead and he had watched his own blood puddle on the gravel of the bank and trickle into the muddy river water. Above him the squawking grew louder. He sobbed.

'They're laughing at me! They're laughing at me!'

The gash left a scar. It was the first scar. His overwhelming fear and his tears formed a scab, a crust that had hardened each time he ventured into some fresh challenge. The same adversary threw him back to land awkwardly and painfully.

So now he withdrew when he felt a warning – and it could be anything. Something trivial and unexpected, a glance, a tone of voice, the prospect of something he could no longer achieve.

At first, he had hurled himself against these distortions, but finally guilt had beaten him. There had been too many cars and motorbikes smashed and parts of him too. Too many courses embarked upon and abandoned. Finally, his father's death when he twenty-one. The last sure, secure footing to his life fell away and guilt had built the tight stone wall around him, so unnatural to the lively adventurous spirit he was born with. By the time he was twenty-four he had imprisoned himself.

His tears hung around him like storm flies and he hated them. Irritability, petulance assuaged them sometimes, but finally the most reliable defence was flight. Quite simply, he avoided anything that was likely to unleash those sleeping dogs. He became adept at recognising dangerous moments. Keeping everyone at bay so no one could ever, even delicately, touch a raw or tender spot. He only ever did exactly what he wanted. In this way he attempted to control everything. No longer could he be caught unawares.

He was walking down a long tree-lined road that led back to the hotel. Tall dark shapes loomed forever ahead. 'Dead soldiers', their ghosts criss-crossing the French countryside. He thought of Napoleon's troops as they marched the length and breadth of France – shabby, battle scarred and often hungry.

Ria reached for the bottle and poured herself another drink. Her third generous G and T, how excruciatingly English!

And I will spread my passion on paper like jam and cream and butter and chocolate until it makes me sick. There's nowhere else for it to go – only on paper – once blank pages, now gently steaming with unrequited love. No, that's not true…you loved me all right.

It was the impossibility – improbability – we didn't know what to do with it. This smouldering cinder landed in our laps and all we wanted was to get rid of it as soon as possible. You were embarrassed, I felt a fool – a kind of natural catastrophe!

Only when we were alone together were we quite happy with our feelings for each other. And I will cherish those moments, wrap them up, save them and take them out and look at them now and again.

What you couldn't forgive was that I cared about you. Sexuality goes on like eating and sleeping, it is the life of the affections that is so special. Your face, your body, everything about you excited me, I wanted you desperately – as you expected – but I cared for you. Your feelings, your dreams, your aspirations. I wanted your life to go well. I have learned to love unselfishly, but the strange part is that whilst it is good for me it's very bad for you. You need some demands made on you, or you will never grow up.

Ria made a note of her musings, not sure if they would fit in to the story.

Bruno shivered at his own thoughts, the trees had become monuments to the dead.

The little town, a cemetery filled with the graves of half-remembered bits of his own life. Intense silence unnerved him and he lengthened his stride, quickened his pace. The small hotel shone bright as a star in the empty blackness. He stepped gratefully back into its homely interior.

'Can I get a meal?' he enquired.

'Of course.'

The old man produced a plastic covered menu, rubbed it clean with his sleeve and handed it to Bruno.

'What would Monsieur like to eat? What is his pleasure?'

Bruno read the short list of meals on offer – they were Arabic. He looked at the old man more closely and realised he was Algerian.

'Just couscous,' he said quietly and sat down.

There was no point in running away or leaving the hotel at that very moment, it was not the old man's fault. How could he know that he and the town were prising open the coffins of his past? Every road had led him to this place. Every step, every action and now he was alone with nothing except his thoughts.

He put his fork into the slippery grains and remembered it wasn't the taste that had provoked Benoit to laugh at him – again, it was the texture.

'Didn't you realise? Didn't you know what you were getting into?'

His teeth had shown so white, like a beak against his black beard and dark skin.

He had thrown back his head and laughed and laughed for all the restaurant to hear. Before it overflowed Bruno had been out on the dusty street. The following month he had married Monique. Her father's money bought him out of the Air Freight business and into the food stuffs industry. His dream was over.

'What a fool, I was. If I could have just hung on, sorted things out. It need not have been such a mess – we could have made a go of it.' Bruno realised that on that evening he had lost something valuable. He had lost his independence, he had lost his pride and he had lost a friend. He suddenly felt his life as a series of doors closing and that too many people in his life now existed in unmarked graves – 'dead soldiers'…Who had said that to him? He couldn't remember.

Finally, in as sombre a mood as he had had in a long time, he left the lively Algerian family to their chatter and laughter in the small, cluttered dining room.

Once in his room he did not know what to do with himself. It was too early to go to bed. He opened his brief case; there were a few letters he'd picked up from the office. Most of them were the usual thing, but one looked different: it had a foreign stamp on it and it was hand-written. He left it to the last. Opening it carefully with his small paper knife, a letter and another envelope addressed to him fell out. Unfolding the letter, he did not recognise the handwriting or the name at the bottom.

> *My mother died recently and among her things I*
> *found this letter addressed to you. I have not opened*
> *it, but presume she wished you to have it, so I am*
> *sending it on.*

Bruno studied the words, they made no sense to him.

Why would the mother of a complete stranger be writing to him?

The envelope was addressed to his mother's home and she had re-directed it to his office. He opened the second letter.

It was the date he noticed first: it had been written seventeen years previously.

Bruno sat on the edge of the bed. It was extraordinary. The letter said she was coming to Paris and would he like to meet her? It gave the name of a small town just south of Paris.

But the letter had never been sent. He looked at her name and finally he remembered.

He remembered a family he had stayed with to improve his English. He remembered a pretty foreign woman – most of what she said he didn't understand. But he remembered how close he had grown to her in those months. A youthful infatuation of a young man for an older woman. He had told her things and talked about himself, talked about his father's death – he had even been able to laugh at himself when she teased him. He would put his face up close to hers and she would stroke his cheek.

'It's good for us sometimes to laugh at ourselves,' she'd whisper.

He wanted so much to put his arms around her and kiss her. This great tide of feeling that ebbed and flowed between them was tangible. Everyone around them could feel it – her family and, when they came to visit him, his family. He couldn't stand his sister's probing, his mother's enquiring glances.

So when she wrote to him – friendly letters – he never replied. He killed it in himself. He could not stand the thought that they may be laughing at him.

He remembered walking in a forest – it was her: she had called the trees 'dead soldiers'.

'They are a kind of monument to the past, like ghosts of dead soldiers. I can feel their presence, but then so many things become monuments to the past. Of course you haven't got a past you're too young.'

He had protested. His accidents with cars motor bikes and girls. 'Oh yes, your scars. Yes perhaps...But your past probably won't mean anything to you – won't fit together until you are in your forties. Then slowly it will begin to unravel. Those knots and twists and turns of experience will loosen and something recognisable may emerge.'

Bruno read the letter again. There was that same self-protective sensitivity so similar to his own. He had been happy with her, relaxed and more spontaneous than he had ever been, knowing his vulnerability was safe. Sitting on the floor by the fire, as close as he dared, he had wanted to talk to her to tell her things. He sought her out and wanted to be alone with her.

He felt it again that special kind of love they had shared. He could feel it across the years, it reached out to him from the letter she had kept with her all that time but he had killed it; and now by some strange fluke he was keeping the appointment she had never asked him for. Now he was ready to admit how much he had enjoyed her loving him – could even take some of that happiness on with him. She was dead now, but she had left him this tiny legacy – the letter – to remind him that his own feelings though deep, intense and often painful were to be experienced and not bludgeoned out of existence.

He suddenly realised she had felt his pain coherently, when she touched him and listened to him when he did not. All he knew was a blur, a discordant jangle of aching disappointment and anxiety. She had seen what he only dimly understood which was the burden of pressure to achieve, to 'be somebody', his father had placed on his shoulders. The traditional aims of the petit-bourgeois anywhere.

He thought of the long line of silent dark trees. His father had hurled himself into the struggle and was dead before he was fifty.

Bruno remembered why he had been happy in that house: he hadn't had to fight or prove himself in any way. It had been a stroll through a forest and in the garden he had watched the squirrels leaping from tree to tree. It was a completely different world. Out there in the wind and among the leaves there was nothing to be anxious about.

'This is my forest,' she used to say. It was a joke. They had shared a lot of jokes.

* * * * *

Ria took a letter out of her bag, read it through and put it back. It was over. She was exhausted, she had lived another lifetime.

She would walk a bit in the dead silence of the empty streets of the empty town.

There was enough light from the open door for Ria to see a car. Slowly, gracefully a tall man got out.

She walked uncertainly past him.

'You're late,' she said softly. 'Trop, tard, trop tard,' she made the words sing.

The man looked up at her as he flicked the lock shut and smiled.

An unexpected brilliance darting towards Ria in the quiet unearthly night. She shivered, frozen in her loneliness. Folding her arms around herself she crossed the road.

The man watched her unsteady progress along the bridge. His smile and its brightness followed her everywhere, those tiny fragments glittered holding his reflection.

There would be scraps of Bruno everywhere. Her home was filled with him. Now she had followed him down the years. She knew too much, had seen too much and forever he would follow her. A shadow, a tone of voice, a tilt of a head and he would come walking back as if he had never been away. She would live out her life beside him in some parallel existence.

The trees stood lifeless and no wind stirred the branches. The moon bathed in the satin water of the river.

Ria picked up a stone and threw it into the water, watching her own reflection disintegrate in the brilliance of the rippling silver circles of the moon.

THE BRIDGE

'Grandad wants a bridge,' Donny answered his father's musings about what to get Grandad for his birthday.

'He never seems to want anything these days – always says "don't bother – it's just another year",' Andy, his father, said.

'He wants a bridge,' ten-year-old Donny said again.

'Why?' his older brother Josh asked quite reasonably. 'He doesn't have a pond or anything.'

'I dunno,' said Donny. At that moment Darren his friend from around the corner turned up and they both disappeared off on their bikes to the park.

'I'll call him before he goes to see his sister.'

'Wish I was going with him to Minnesota. I'd love to go to America.' Josh looked wistful.

'I wish you were going with him to Minnesota, but we can't have you off school for so long. I wish *I* was going with him. I'm not happy about him going all that way on his own. His eyes aren't what they used to be. I'm afraid he'll end up in Hawaii!'

'I've booked his flights, but he has to change planes – Heaven knows what will happen. I've asked for passenger assistance, but whether he'll accept it's another matter – you know how he is! I'll take time off and take him to the airport to make sure he has help.'

* * * * *

Later, Andy phoned his Dad. After checking on his progress with packing and making sure he understood about changing planes and that he must ask at the desk for assistance he finally got around to asking about the bridge.

'Donny says you want a bridge. Is that right?'

'Yes, when I get back I'll do something about it. I can only think about one thing at a time. I'll deal with that later.'

Andy knew his father and knew he was right he could only deal with one thing at a time so he dropped the subject. 'Well, I'll pick you up on Thursday Dad and make sure you are all checked in.'

'Thanks son and don't forget about watering the garden. At least once a week or I'll come home to a dreadful mess.'

'Okay Dad.' Andy knew his father's garden was his pride and joy and the whole family would have to be involved in keeping it up to some kind of scratch while he was away.'

Once he had ascertained that his father was not floating around lost in America, but safe and sound with his sister, Andy marshalled his family to drive to the nearby village where his Dad lived on the outskirts.

Jen, his wife, had brought some lunch. 'We'll make a picnic of it,' she said, not completely happy about the loss of her precious Saturday morning. Now she had a job at the town hall her weekends were taken up with sorting out the house. Andy was not bad at helping out, but mysteriously, his helping out always involved complications and more work for her!

Anyway Jen was happy to pitch in and do some cutting, snipping and dead-heading for a little while. *But not every week,* she had privately decided.

'I wonder where Gramps wants this bridge?'

Josh looked around the garden which was fairly large and terraced with rockeries, flower beds, a veggie patch for tomatoes and lettuce this year. There was a well-tended lawn edged with rather unruly marigolds and several beautiful Weeping Willows at the end of the garden, sweeping gracefully along the boundary of the garden in front of a stream.

Years ago, Grandad had discreetly annexed a little of the common land so he could enjoy the trees along the towpath as part of his own garden. The stream had been pacified by some kind of engineering upriver and flowed sufficiently and consistently all year.

Josh walked to the end of the garden and surveyed the terrain very seriously.

'You know, Grandad could mean he wants a bridge over this stream,' he called to his father. 'It would be handy to have a bridge.'

'Why?' Andy surveyed the terrain equally seriously. 'There's only woods opposite.'

'There's the towpath that leads to the shops on the other side of the stream. It cuts off loads. It would be easy for Gramps to walk to the centre of the village.'

'Oh I don't know about that.' Andy was dubious, he could see all kinds of pitfalls – including marauding revellers on 'Midsummer Green Man' night trampling into his father's garden.

'Well the stream is a kind of moat that protects Gramp's garden – we could build a kind of drawbridge that he could pull up at night or whenever.'

'Umm…' Andy thought about this. 'We'd need walls either side to fix it to, but that could be a good thing. I'll think about it Josh.'

* * * * *

The more they thought about it, the more they thought it was a good idea, so after several trips to various builders merchants all they needed was assembled. Andy and Josh had drawn up different plans for the bridge and settled on what they considered to be Norman walls with crenelated tops and square pillars to support the drawbridge. With assistance and advice from friends, Andy had arrived at a system for pulling up and lowering the drawbridge.

The family became entranced by the project and spent far more time at Grandad's house than they had originally intended. They got to know the locals who frequented the nearby pub and after a while they took to dropping in to check on progress and stand around and chew the fat.

'You know, when Grandad gets back we should hold a grand opening and invite everyone for a get together.'

Even Jen was enthusiastic. 'A few nibbles, beer and soft drinks should be easy to do.'

The day arrived and Grandad had safely managed to find his way home by himself 'without airport assistance' as he told them rather emphatically.

Andy brought him home from the airport and ushered him excitedly into the garden where the rest of the family were waiting eagerly to see Grandad's reaction to the bridge.

He stood for a while and looked distinctly puzzled. 'Well...well...it's novel, anyway son. Who gave you that idea?'

'Well you did. You said you wanted a bridge.'

'Did I? I don't remember. Well you're right it would be handy to take a short cut to the centre of the village I s'pose. You'll have to show me how the contraption works. Well, now you're all here let's have a drink.'

Grandad was pleased his garden looked very good – much better than he expected.

Jen had been keen to show it to its best when the neighbours came for her little soiree, so she had weeded and planted a few extras that made a good show.

It had been a very nice surprise. Weeks passed and Grandad got used to taking his little short cut, when one day a rather ominous letter arrived from the Council.

In unnecessarily menacing language it roughly said that Grandad had contravened several bylaws and had to remove the bridge or be liable for a hefty fine. Grandad was very upset about this and fumed. 'If only everyone including Andy had just minded their own business…'

Andy discovered the news of the bridge had spread around the village and some righteous busybody had reported it to the Council who had taken a highhanded attitude to the whole affair. Andy and Jen were furious.

Jen enquired of her colleagues which department had sent the offending letter – it was town planning, but then of course there were different committees and different departments committees and legal eagles to contend with. And so it went on.

'Take no notice – tear the letter up,' said Josh.

'Er, no. I'll write and say to get in touch with our solicitor. You know old Tich, he owes me one – he'll look in to it.' Andy picked up his phone.

Well Old Tich did his very best but after some research he could not come up with very much to help the situation.

'It's complicated. No one actually knows who owns the land the stream runs through. It's probably common land – I believe that belongs to the crown…I'm not sure. But how the Council can make threats of huge fines is very dubious. I think they are trying it on.'

They all repaired to the pub where the discussion continued and the locals put in their two penn'orth.

It was near closing time when old Seb came in. As the oldest inhabitant everyone turned to him for his take on the subject of the bridge.

He laughed…'Oohh we're goin' back now…ooh…that land don't belong to the Council or to the Crown. That's part of, as was, Lord Cholmondly Burghley's estate. Long story…' Seb looked around expectantly.

Andy caught on quickly. 'A pint Seb?'

'That's mighty gracious of you. Well I would suggest if you visit the local museum in Bichester you might find out a lot about that land and about Graveny 'All.'

Graveny Hall was the once stately home high up on Graveny Hill but was now a clinic for soldiers recovering from serious injury.

'They're doin' a local history project up at the museum. They asked me and Rose Hipps as the oldies around here to take any photos and mem…memor…stuff we had and tell stories into a recorder of what we remember of them times. I get a bit muddled – go and see them they'll tell you. They've got hundreds of computers and filum whatnots and are digging up there too.'

Andy was delighted. 'Thanks Seb. another pint?'

'Don't mind if I do.'

* * * * *

So it came about that a small deputation arrived at the Bichester Museum with the letter from the Council. The young and eager staff smiled, sniggered and generally pooh-poohed the allegation.

'Hmph!' Mr Smithson the director of the museum also harrumphed over the letter. 'The Council doesn't own any of the land around that area.'

Andy had phoned Mr Smithson the curator, so he was prepared for the visitation and had many documents, photos, letters and little mementoes arranged on large tables for them to peruse.

'It's an interesting story. To begin with Lord Cholmondly Burghley was not a Lord. His father had been a very successful industrialist and made lots of money in the middle of the eighteen forties. He was only called Lord as you would "the Lord of the Manor". Which is all to the good for your family.'

Andy, Josh, Jen, Donny and Grandad were all eyes and ears. Mr Smithson continued.

'What you need to know is that Lord C.B. lost both his sons at the Somme in WWI. He was devastated and went into complete decline. The estate became neglected and no longer developed as a working estate with farms and piggeries etc. His wife had no idea how to deal with the situation and threw herself into the life of the roaring twenties – often staying in London for long periods.

'Lord C.B. agreed to having a cottage built on the estate where she could discreetly pursue her own life – a bit *Lady Chatterley* if you know what I mean on the understanding that she would be at home with him more often. She agreed and it was your family that built the cottage your father lives in now.' Mr Smithson looked at Grandad.

'Yes I know,' Grandad said.

Andy frowned at his father. 'You never said.'

'You never asked.'

'Anyway to get on: when he died, because he was not a real Lord, part of the aristocracy, his wife Edwina and her surviving son could inherit the estate. Then came the Second World War and Graveny Hall was commandeered by the MOD and it became a home for wounded soldiers. The family never really came back. Edwina's son went to America and she died. In her will she gifted the cottage and many acres of land to your family – including the land where the Council estate is now built.

'There was no one to properly oversee the will and everything at that time was very confused. Of course the Council claimed the land from the MOD as they wanted to build more houses after the war. There might be an issue of inheritance tax, but at the moment I can't see that being a problem, as so many people have financially benefitted and it would take years to unravel all the ins and outs of the case. There's a lot more to tell you, but we can have another session another time – it's all so fascinating!'

When they came out of the Museum, they were quiet and a little dazed.

'So much to think about,' Jen muttered. 'Anyway the bridge will not be a problem and if the Council get difficult, we'll threaten them with years of back rent for the land they are using now! Can't believe it – it will take a while to get my head around it.'

'Well I must be off,' Grandad said.

'Where are you going Dad?'

'The dentist – I want a bridge put in. It's as well I don't have to pay huge fines as this is going to cost me a packet.'

Donny grinned and piped up, 'Told you he wanted a bridge.'

LEAVING HOME

It would have been painful obviously, but for the note. Such a small, slightly scruffy piece of paper, she had almost missed it.

The kitchen dresser was always crammed with letters, newspapers, unwanted handouts, empty packets of various kinds – the usual clutter of family life.

Bebe looked at the note again and looked around the kitchen. 'We are not a family any more, we haven't been for a long time.'

She read the words on the note again. So he had finally made a decision.

It was curious because so had she. *Strange how things work out*, she thought.

He had finally decided he was going back to Australia to his first wife.

Well, Bebe reflected, his only wife. The rest of us have been what the papers refer to as 'wifelets'.

He was a charmer of course, or she would not have put up with him for so long, which was why it would have been painful to tell him that enough was enough.

She screwed up the piece of paper and was about to throw it in the bin – then she changed her mind and smoothed it out again to keep somewhere safe. Charmers have a habit of turning up again. She wrote the date on the top of the letter.

Bebe fell to mindless tidying up, if her body was busy it stopped her thinking too much.

Money was not a problem – she had been supporting him for years.

She pondered on whether to ring her son Jem at University. She decided to leave it until later when she had things more settled in her own mind.

A nagging ripple of doubt ran through her – supposing he chose to live with his father? The loss of Martin could be overcome, but if Jem went too, that would be devastating.

Bebe had tried to shield Jem from his fathers 'outside activities' as she referred to it to her friends. Maybe as he got older she should have given him a few hints. But it was too late now.

There was a ring at the door. Bebe did not want to talk to anyone, so she ignored it and went upstairs. A few minutes later she heard a scuffling sound in the hall.

'Is that you Jem?' she called knowing full well it was not him. She called again as she walked very carefully downstairs. 'Is that you?' her voice getting louder. She furtively looked around for a heavy object in case she needed to defend herself.

As she reached the hall the scuffling had turned to definite sobbing followed by bursts of heart-rending crying.

Bebe followed the sound into the living room.

On the floor in a crumpled heap was Mavis. 'Oh it's you,' Bebe said as she attempted to pick her up.

'Have you had a note too?' Mavis would not move. A muffled assent was all Bebe could hear through a mane of tear-soaked chestnut curls.

'Come on Mavis –get up.' But she remained in a heap on the floor.

At that moment the phone rang. It was June.

More sobbing and bosom heaving, thought Bebe.

'You might as well come over, you can all get it off your chest together – ring Rosie and Tracey.'

The evening was crowded. Bebe was dispensing coffee, red wine and chocolate biscuits at regular intervals.

The mood around the sobbing and bosom-heaving was changing to resentment and in Rose's case to a full blown outbursts of rage.

'Just get it off your chests girls. It's over. It's been fun while it lasted.'

Mavis swore very loudly over the hubbub in the room.

'Fun!! – Fun!! What about my £30,000?!?'

Rose joined in. 'And my £250,000?'

' My £50,000?' Tracey added.

'Well I suppose he has taken it all back with him to Australia.'

Bebe looked at them gently, reproachfully. 'You were silly girls, why did you give him so much money?'

'I loved him,' Mavis and Rose wailed in unison.

'I loved him so much,' Tracey positively howled.

'Do you think you ought to go to the police and report it?'

An unnatural silence settled on the room.

'I don't think that would be a good idea.' Mavis said rather lamely.

'Why?' Bebe's eyes opened really wide. 'If Martin has robbed you all then it is obviously the only thing to do.'

The women shuffled uncomfortably.

Bebe was obviously bewildered as to why there was a problem, but suddenly she had a thought. 'Where did the money come from?'

The unnatural silence deepened.

'Oh this and that,' muttered Tracey miserably.

Bebe just raised her eyebrows.

'Oh I hadn't thought of that.'

Bebe pursed her lips, 'So I suppose there's not much chance of the police helping out?'

'Don't you go near the police either,' said Rose a little aggressively.

'What about you Bebe? What did he get away with from you?'

'Oh the house,' she said airily, 'years ago, but as you all said. We loved him so much and we would have done anything for him. Do any of you want to stay the night?'

'No,' they muttered and mumbled among themselves. 'Not really, too many bad memories.

'I need to phone my son,' Bebe said, 'see yourselves out.'

'Hi Jem, glad I've caught you. How's your IT course going? Yes I know you're a Whizz kid. Did you manage to do that "little thing" I asked you? No problems? Oh splendid! What a clever little hacker you are. And how much do we have in our off somewhere-or-another account? Oh Wow!! As much as that? By the way Martin has gone. Oh you knew?'

Bebe listened as her son explained that he had always known what his father was like.

'Oh! I thought you were especially enthusiastic about the "little thing" I asked you to do.'

———— ⟨⟨◦⟩⟩ ————

LIFE AS A SONG

Lionel leaned forward, nearly toppling off his interview room chair.

'Well you know how it is...It Was Just One of those Things.'

'Stick to the point, Mr Caplan.' The officer tapped the desk hard with two fingers – it hurt and he tried not to wince.

'Oh, oh – okay, okay,' Lionel put his hands out in a gesture of surrender.

'I was looking for the Good Life – and she was a Poor Little Rich Girl...So I thought well Anything Goes...'

'Mr Caplan...' the officer warned him again. 'Stay on track.'

'It's easy for you to say...for me there were so many tracks...'

'Carry on Mr Caplan – then what?'

'Well this girl...can't remember her name – maybe Nancy With the Laughing Face? Who knows? She was wild! Oh Boy!'

Lionel threw back his head and looked at the newly decorated ceiling as if her face was looking down at him. Suddenly he sat up straight and pushed his face closer to the policeman.

'You know she wanted me to Fly Her to the Moon!! Can you believe that?'

'No! Enough!!' The officer spoke to the mic, 'Interview terminated at 4.47 p.m.'

* * * * *

The inspector and the constable left the room allowing Lionel time to sit alone and ponder on his situation. How had he got himself into this mess?

He tried to re-trace his movements in his head, which did not feel like his own.

He had been sitting alone in a bar – In the Wee Small Hours of the Morning.

He did not notice her come in.

'Set 'em up Joe.'

It was her voice – like treacle over gravel – a Play Misty for Me voice – fur-lined, perfume drenched, enticing as a longed for caress.

Lionel turned and there she was. He tried not to stare at the long legs that were a Stairway to the Stars and the mouth that Made him Feel so Young – Irish Eyes Smiling straight through him.

In that instant Lionel's heart left his body. 'Please, please, For Once In My Life, For Once in my Life – Oh Lord!' Tentatively he smiled back at her praying The Best was yet to Come.

He couldn't move, she had Put a Spell on Him.

'Don't you remember me?' She glided towards him along the bar. 'When we were very Young? – When we were Young Last Night?'

Lionel moved away slightly, confused and with a bubble of disappointment welling up in him.

'I think you must be mixing me up with someone else.'

'I know It's the Wrong time and the Wrong place, though Your Face is Lovely it's the Wrong face – It's not His Face, but it's a Lovely Face, so it's alright with Me.'

She cupped his cheek with the palm of her hand. Lionel's breath had been coming in short gasps, now he felt he might pass out.

'The Nearness of You,' he wanted to whisper in her ear.

'Are you okay?' he said eventually – immediately wishing he hadn't – it sounded so trite. Up close her face was washed out and empty almost pleading.

'Who Can I Turn to? Maybe You on a New Day? Who Can I turn to when Love slips Away?'

Lionel instinctively stood up put out both his hands to her.

'Smile Though Your Heart is Aching, Smile even though it's Breaking. One Day the Sun will come Shining Through.'

Lionel had some difficulty remembering what happened after that.

He was holding both her hands – when Wham! Bam! Azzakaszam!!

That was the last thing Lionel remembered and it wasn't Wonderful You Walking By, he thought later.

The officers had been gone a long time and Lionel thought he had heard raised voices and a heated argument going on outside the door.

The officers came back into the room. Lionel touched the back of his head. He could feel a dressing and a very sore and tender patch.

'Well Mr Caplan, is there anything else you can tell us about what happened this morning? There was a large amount of criminal damage and an unlawful affray. There will be a huge bill to pay – to say nothing of the dozen or so people in hospital!'

'Hang On!'

Lionel scratched his chin and pondered. 'I'd driven Mr Barnett to his hotel – parked the car – ready for tomorrow and then decided to have a quick nightcap before turning in. The bar was almost empty…who are all these people in hospital?'

The young constable squirmed, sweating slightly. The Inspector pursed his lips.

'Quite a lot of them are police officers,' was all he was prepared to say, looking as if a truck had rolled over him.

'Where did they come from?' Lionel inquired puzzled, 'They weren't there when I came in.'

'Actually they were.'

'Well I didn't see them.' Lionel stuck to his guns.

'That was the whole idea.' The Inspector looked even more glum.

There was a deafening sound of pennies dropping in Lionel's head.

'Oh I get it! They were waiting for...Who? Not me I didn't know I was going to that bar. I just happened to be there.'

'Did you just happen? Didn't Mr Barnett send you?'

'No! He's Christadelphian! He's speaking at County Hall tomorrow,' he looked at his watch, 'today – I'm driving him there. He doesn't drink. '

The officers left the room again. Lionel was alone once more in the interview room, reflecting on the smell of the newly painted walls. The officers came back quite quickly.

'Yes, Mr Barnett corroborates your story, but what about Tallulah?'

'Who's Tallulah?'

'Oh come Mr Caplan, you had Lipstick on your Collar and all over your face!'

'I did!' Lionel beamed from ear to ear. 'Did I?' Lionel felt His Living had not been in Vain.

The young constable spoke quietly to his superior. 'Tallulah was upset when DC Jones hit Mr Caplan on the head and she tried to bring him round and give him mouth to mouth.'

'That was what the Flying to the Moon was all about and Playing among the Stars.'

A ribbon of memory floated back to Lionel.

'Then mayhem broke out – I'm getting a vague memory.'

'I was the Wrong man in the Wrong Place – Though my face was Lovely it was the Wrong Face…' Lionel sang to them.

'Don't start all that again,' the Inspector said wearily.

'Come on…Life is a Song…' Then he stopped, 'But what did Tallulah have to do with all this?'

'She sings in the lounge bar of the Grenadier Hotel where Mr Barnett is staying. He knows her and asked her to tell you his talk at County Hall had been cancelled tomorrow? Today. Apparently they knew which bar you frequented.'

'Oh, did they? But why were the police there?'

There was a strained silence.

'Ah, ah, Ummm…Now that is a very good question. You may be needed as a witness for an internal police investigation. ' The Inspector was anxious now to leave the uncomfortable subject. 'I think that will be all, Mr Caplan.'

Relieved and cheerful Lionel waved to them as he left. 'So I'll be Seeing You…'

Lionel went down the stairs avoiding some still wet paint. As he passed the desk – the sergeant called him back.

'Mr Caplan, there's a young lady waiting for you in the witness suite.'

'Thanks,' Lionel wondered who it could be and followed the officer into a light and airy room. A rather slight young woman with red hair came towards him.

'Oh Mr Caplan, I am so sorry for this – it's all my fault, I got kind of carried away. It was late and I'd had a few drinks…'

'What's all your fault?'

'You here and all that…it wasn't because of you, it was because of me!'

'So you're Tallulah!'

'Not really, that's my stage name.'

Lionel glanced down at her overstuffed bag. He could see a familiar hairpiece and the stylish clothes he remembered.

'Ah these Foolish Things Remind me of You…' He looked at her inquiringly.

'My name's Maisie.'

'Let's get out of here and have breakfast Maisie – I think we have a lot to talk about.'

LOST AND FOUND

'So you were lovers?'

Dee looked thoughtfully at the policeman.

'Umm…I suppose we were. We didn't use that word in those days. Only people in films and books were lovers…a fling, a bit of an affair was how I thought of it. We lived different lives then – more relaxed about things – many of my friends were musicians, artists, dancers, it was kind of normal.'

'How long did it last?'

'A couple of years I suppose. He seemed lot younger than me, but he wasn't. I was young too.'

'Where was your husband?'

'He was abroad, an engineer, was often away for long periods, working on bridges, dams even oil rigs.'

There was a silence.

'It was different then – we had an arrangement – no questions: "What happens in Vegas…" you know what I mean.'

Dee looked at the paintings and drawings the policeman had given her and smiled at her memories.

'He was a Geordie – used to call his trousers "trews" or his "Keks". He had a slightly fey charm. He was comforting when I needed it. Somehow lovers suggests something hot and heady…it wasn't like that. We weren't in bed all the time!' Dee laughed to herself.

'He would come for the weekend or stay for a few days, we had family dinners and took the children on the tops of buses – they were just tots – sometimes to the park or on a boat on the lake.' Dee was talking to herself.

'It was all a bit "Cathy come Home".' She stood up.

'Would you like a cup of tea?'

'Thanks that would be nice.' The policeman was in no hurry and had no intention of rushing back to the crises of the station.

The room was pleasant, light and comfortable. For a moment he could imagine a rather rootless artist might enjoy a few home comforts.

'How did it end?' The policeman bit into his ginger biscuit with a snap.

'Nothing dramatic: my husband came back and G got a good commission in Newcastle – I don't know what…I think it was the murals in the Eden shopping centre, but I'm guessing.'

'You kept the paintings and sketches.'

'Of course – they are of me – and incredibly good. He was never one of the Brit Pack, but he was one of the leading artists of the North East.' There was a certain pride in her voice. 'I went to his Exhibitions at the Royal Academy and later the very spectacular one at Tate Modern linking his work to the history of the industrial north…Amazing!'

Dee leafed through the pictures studying them intently.

'I learned a lot from G.' She looked back at the policeman, her smile, her eyes alight with pleasure. 'Even though he was young and I was married with two children, he…' She didn't finish her sentence.

'Didn't you miss him?'

'Yes, dreadfully.'

'You know these painting and drawings are worth a lot of money.' The policeman reminded her of why he was here.

'I suppose so, but I will never sell them.'

'What did your husband think of them?'

Dee giggled. 'I could hardly put them up on the wall. I put them away safely – I thought – but when we moved house...Where were they found?'

'In a big haul of paintings, sculptures and other art stuff in a disused warehouse. There was a big fire and loads of it went up in smoke but a few things were saved. In the investigation by the fine arts boys they found you on a list of people who had reported items stolen.'

'That's how you got my address?'

'Your original report was never followed up.'

'It was difficult for me to pop in and out of the police station then, it's okay now.'

'Did you see the photographs? They're in that white envelope.' The policeman pointed to a white package on the table.

'Looks very official.' Dee picked up the white quarto envelope.

'That's how we knew the pictures belonged to you. I recognised him and both your names are on the back.' He paused. 'You met him again didn't you? You're both older in the pictures.'

'Yes.' Dee closed her eyes briefly. 'Yes, we met again.'

There was another long pause. The policeman waited and helped himself to another ginger biscuit.

'Yes,' she leaned forward. 'It was funny – extraordinary really – I was on the underground, when there was an announcement over the tannoy. There had been a terrorist attack and the trains would finish at Liverpool Street, the next stop. They tipped us all out – it was such a scrimmage! Crowds of people milling about like headless chickens. I'm tired, after work and half asleep. I had just about managed to get on a bus, when a man sat next to me and said my name. He'd seen me in the crowd and had elbowed his way through "wrestling a few old ladies to the floor!" as he put it. It was George. I was thunderstruck!'

'He's dead isn't he?' the policeman said bluntly.

'Yes,' Dee picked up a photograph and put it against her face, tremors of sadness hovering around her mouth. 'Umm…It was so quick – the shock! Liver cancer…he was only forty-two,' she whispered. 'We were going to…we talked of…'

The policeman wasn't listening, he was looking at the family photos on the mantelpiece. 'I see you have three children.'

'A late baby – Gina – she's an Art student.' Dee smiled proudly and picked up another photo to show the policeman.

'She's incredibly talented and funny.'

'Like her father?' said the policeman.

'Umm…' Dee nodded then she turned and looked directly into the man's eyes for the first time.

'Exactly like her father,' she said definitely and her smile broadened and grew until it filled the whole room.

———— ∞∞∞ ————

MATTERS TEMPORAL

After centuries of various fires, floods, bombing and finally an earthquake, the roof of the Santo Paolo Abbey wearily collapsed into the chancel and finally the Catholic authorities decided that perhaps it was time to take a radical approach to their beloved ancient Abbey and seminary.

No one was entirely sure who actually owned the building or the land.

The Catholic Land Commission obviously insisted there was no question it was church land and had been since the Abbey was built in the Middle Ages.

Signor Piccolito, the Grand Seigneur of the village and all the surrounding land had other ideas. He was quite certain it belonged to his family that could be traced back to long before the Renaissance and well into Roman times. He maintained his Ducal ancestor had ordered the Abbey to be built for the moral and spiritual guidance of the villagers and the outlying farmers and winegrowers' families.

He declared, at the emergency meeting, at the Municipio that he had all the relevant documents, even scrolls, safely stored in vaults in his cathedral of a house high up above the village and also in banks in Rome.

'Of course!' sniffed the Abbott, I suppose he is going to tell us that he is related to St. Peter!'

'We are living in the twenty first century.' The Mayor, who was feeling a little under the weather, was relatively new to the area, having only lived there for a mere twenty years.

'We can't keep living in the ancient past – there is a pressing need for the building to be either demolished or restored or renovated. I propose we consider all the obvious ways of raising money from the Historical Society and various Catholic trusts, as well as applying for the government grant from the department of land and ancient sites.

The assembly of clergy and civic dignitaries hummed and hawed and muttered among themselves, but generally agreed with the Mayors proposal. As long as they were not asked to put their hands into their own pockets, they were happy to accept money from anyone anywhere.

The recent earthquake had confounded them all and to see their beloved Santo Paolo Abbey in ruins was a local catastrophe.

The remaining monks had been rehoused fairly easily as their cloisters, called Monastero Castello, were nowhere near as badly damaged as the Abbey or other hillside villages.

Signor Piccolito was not happy; he had his own ideas and plans, but it was not a good idea to say too much at this time.

'Signore's,' he stood up, 'this is all very good and reasonable, but I think you should wait until I have had a chance to investigate my own claims to the property and land before going ahead, or you may find yourselves in the tricky position of having accepted a lot of money for a venture that you have no legal right to be undertaking.' He sat down.

A hush fell on the room as the members of the Municipio ruminated on his words.

The Abbott hissed to his cure 'Piffle.' He stood up. 'Gentlemen, I have every confidence that our holy father in Rome will personally take a great interest in the restoration of our beloved Abbey and will refer our case to the legal department of the Vatican.'

Signor Piccolito snapped, 'Oh I see, you think our Holy Father will be happy to rob St Peter to pay for St Paul!'

'I wouldn't put it quite like that.' The Mayor could feel the temperature of the room rising and wanted to call the meeting to a close. Arguments and counter arguments had been exchanged and it was getting late.

'Perhaps we will finish this meeting today and resume on Thursday at 9 p.m. We are all a little tired now and need time to think things over.'

The Abbott stood up, performed the blessing and they all crossed themselves and gratefully made their way to the great door of the Municipio.

As the Mayor trundled slowly up the narrow, cobble-stoned street to his imposing four storey, five-hundred-year-old house, he puffed a little, but was fairly pleased with himself. He could tell his wife he had taken the bull by the horns and had acquitted himself well.

His wife was a still pretty, round cheeked woman – softly plump and good-natured.

'I am sure you were magnifico,' she said to her husband, as she took his supper out of the oven.

'Well...' Even Gino had moments of modesty. 'Perhaps not magnifico, but certainly...' he searched for the exact word...'Effectivo!'

'Exactly,' beamed his wife and they turned their attention to their gnocchi with spinach.

They were ready to settle down for the evening when there was a knock at the door. The treasurer from the consiglio comunale let himself into the room. He was carrying a large briefcase. He kissed them both and 'come staaed' as he sat down at the table accepting the small glass of Limoncello that the Mayor offered him.

'Was made by my uncle from his own lemons,' he said, as he had said a hundred times before.

The treasurer opened his bag and laid out a range of documents. The two men pored over them.

'That seems fine,' said the Mayor. The treasurer nodded and they smiled conspiratorially at each other.

The government's compulsory purchase of the land and the building went through last year with Vatican approval, and permission to restore part of the building as a chapel, but the major project was to be a large hotel, with swimming pool and gardens and a conference centre for the promotion of Catholic values in the twenty first century.

All the funding was in place and a large proportion of that money would flow into the Mayor's office for his control and approval.

The two men smiled at each other again.

'"Control and approval", music to my ears,' said the Mayor.

'They've approved the scheme – in every detail.'

'Well,' the treasurer poured himself another Limoncello and sat back in his chair.

'You know what they say not all bad things are bad…I felt it wise not to mention recent legislation regarding the unsafe nature of the region. We will leave that in the hands of Santo Paolo and God and rely on his goodness and mercy.'

The two men put their hands together in private intercession.

And the Signora crossed herself, sending her own private prayer to thank the good Lord that at last she would have a shiny new modern kitchen.

My Heroes

It always fell to my lot as the 'drama' bod on the staff to put on the school concert. I was young and foolish – did not know my own limitations – and recklessly threw myself into the task. My drama background was extensive and in my spare time I was so often on courses here and there, soaking up all kinds of ideas to use in school.

My partner in crime was either the Music teacher or a friend of like mind. Where we lived was not far from Stratford East Theatre and also E15 Drama School. Stratford East was a gold mine for incredible ideas – we haunted the place.

I remember one fantastic production of the 'Lone Ranger', which was hysterically funny and had the main character (on his horse!) bobbing up from all kinds of places on the huge and extraordinary set. A wonderful idea! You can have several people playing the same part!! All dressed the same and the mask and big hat meant they all looked identical. To add to the joke as the performance went on and the audience got the idea, the character began to change – get taller, get smaller, grow a beard – go grey, wear a dress…It was such a fantastic idea and so easy to use in a junior school.

I mention that as an example. At that time the whole era exuded bright ideas and innovation. So, the school play became less and less formal and more and more peculiar. Everybody loved it – the sky was the limit you could do anything. We had no stage – no problem. The lower school hall was very big and contained loads of gym equipment and mats etc., which were all brought into service for many and various reasons.

The particular event I am thinking about was after I had been on a lighting course and was clutching my 'stificate' of competence. From my budget I had bought a wondrous lighting board that could produce all sorts of (for that era) magical effects. I was itching to use it. We never built scenery – except the odd moveable item. We used the gym stuff and screens and a few boxes as a dais. From other shows I had built up a comprehensive wardrobe, a full range of sound effects on cassettes and other sundry useful items that parents donated regularly. A team of small children had helped me to position all the lamps with their required gels – me swinging from the top of precarious ladders – they holding on for dear life to stop me falling off.

For my sins the eventually chosen title for this particular show was 'Jungle Fever'.

The head always liked the whole school to be involved, it was a group 7 – a big school! hundreds of children! – a feat of extraordinary lateral thinking on its own. So in the after school drama and music sessions, my buddy and myself heaved together a framework for an hour and a half concert. The bulk of the children were all in animal costumes in a raised choir that provided the links to a series of little scenes. A loose story ran through it about spies and gangsters – don't ask!

We always plundered the talent of the school. Lots of children went to the local dance school and many went to Stagecoach the local stage school. There was also a little musical group who played recorder, violin, piano etc. Then there were the natural comedians, who I have to say often came from my class. Kids who could do impressions, play local characters (or teachers) and had a fund of jokes. And then my gym club provided the acrobatics – they were very busy, as this was about being in the jungle, swinging on the ropes and showing off their back flips.

The songs and the music were a curious mix of the Jungle Book film songs, James Bond, 1920's Buster Keaton chase type music and popular themes and pop songs of the day and somehow 'When I'm cleaning winders' crept in. A popular request from the parents.

Who mentioned the word copyright? Sorry a bit deaf – oh dear never mind!

Of course, not all the children were enthralled at the prospect of being expected to wear silly costumes and sing or perform on stage. I did not believe in press-ganging kids or other teachers into doing things they were not happy doing. I always wanted a happy and eager gang around me. So those not keen to take part were absolutely okay to do other things, like front of house jobs, giving out programmes (very necessary if you were to have a clue what was going on), or to help with costumes, makeup etc.

My backstage 'crew' were a couple of girls doing sound effects and back projection – absolutely vital as it set the scenes. And a very enthusiastic bunch of slightly nerdy, skinny kids with glasses, who were my techies. They would not be seen dead on stage, but as backroom boys they were in their element. They were in charge of the lighting – the brand new lighting board – and of course, ensuring the whole show went on smoothly, easily and with no hiccups. (If in doubt – blackout! The golden rule!)

They were brilliant and really got the hang of how a lighting plot works. They also provided the bangs and bumps and percussion noises. You know the boom, boom noises. They just loved having 'technical rehearsals' and took their responsibilities very seriously. It was not long before they were using all the backstage jargon like veterans.

'Bond needs a follow spot, Miss.'

'Okay.'

'What about some uplighting for the dancers?'

'Okay, if you think so.'

There were no entrances and exits the whole school stayed in their places for the entire show. The children just walked out of their seats and did their bit and went back and sat down – hence the linking choir, music and jokes etc.

It's a recipe for disaster having children hanging around in classrooms used as dressing rooms. That goes for parents as well! Keep them where you can see them.

Well, we were due to give three performances. The first one went swimmingly. The parents helped enormously, singing the songs as they dressed their offspring which gave a jolly atmosphere. I was pleased that my draconian organisation had worked. A good plan coming together – like the A Team.

Then, disaster. I was running to the bakers in the lunchtime and slipped on the wet crossing and tore a muscle, not a huge problem in itself. BUT that night, silly, silly billy I was, I tried to give my leg some heat treatment at home using Jim's ancient infrared lamp. And FORGOT to wear any sunglasses.

That night I was in agony and ended up in A&E with a flash burn to my eyes, which put paid to me being at my post the following night directing operations for the show. I was desperate, as you can imagine, but there was nothing I could do. I was swaddled in bandages around my eyes – couldn't see a thing, terrified I would go blind. It was a while before I returned to school as you can imagine.

'How did it go?' The first thing I wanted to know, 'Did they cancel the show?'

People looked at me blankly. 'No, why would they? It was great – a howling success!'

No one seemed to have noticed I was not there for the last two nights.

My little crew of 10/11 year olds mobbed me.

'You alright? You alright? We did it for you Miss – everything – no one knew you weren't there. We didn't tell anyone. We just carried on and did everything like normal. The music Miss asked if we needed any help and we said, "no we're fine".'

I was dumbstruck and at the same time ridiculously proud of them and myself. It was probably one of my greatest achievements in teaching and I wasn't even there!

Being in charge of an entire show with all the various light and sound cues and checking on props and performers is very complicated. And they had worked as a team and pulled it off miraculously.

Those kids were my heroes and they were not yet twelve years old – astonishing! They had saved the day. I remember them with such affection. There were loads of photos and I am not in any of them. But I still enjoy looking at my little heroes grinning from ear to ear and so proud of themselves.

―∞―

The Sacrifice

'The Anatolian Turk has never been conquered.'

The professor made his statement with all the assurance of the eminent academic.

'That is his misfortune.'

Timothy Bosworth stretched his long legs into a more comfortable position. Even his thin shorts were now damp and beginning to chafe.

On the low, carpeted bolsters that passed for settees, Tim sat awkwardly. Around him the men reclined, leaning comfortable on their arms. Dressed in trousers, shirts, ties, they seemed undisturbed by the heavy closeness of the room.

'Their misfortune?' Tim politely queried this statement. In his white socks and sandals he felt stripped of his manhood. In spite of, or because of, his added height he felt a gangling boy scout.

'Of course.' Leaning forward the professor sipped his apple tea with obvious pleasure. 'Delightful, delightful,' he muttered his appreciation to himself.

'Think of the Romans.' He was warming to his theme.

'All of Europe has grown from seeds the Romans scattered. Much of it from even more ancient cultures and dynasties: Judaic, Greek, Egyptian, any number.'

Timothy, an engineer, nodded enthusiastically. 'Oh yes, roads, water cisterns, that kind of thing.'

The professor laughed heartily in his jovial manner. Sitting amongst his uncles he was indulged, the clever one of the family – used to being the life and soul of the party. Everyone laughed when he laughed, basking in his presence. He waved his hands to acknowledge this approval.

'Just little things, you know, like systems of government, language, mathematics, physics and other incidentals. Almost ninety per cent of Turkey is Asian and the Eastern Anatolian is in direct line of descent from the hordes that followed Genghis Khan – nomadic tribes from the steppes that swept westwards. And still, today, many of them have a mentality that is straight out of the tent.'

'But Istanbul?' Timothy interrupted. 'The superb mosques, Topkapi Palace?

'Ah, you speak of Istanbul. Remember, it was once Byzantium then Constantinople. Here where we sit is the European side of the city. Once the centre of the Eastern Roman Empire. The European Turk is a different creature.' He gestured to his uncles. 'Here we have more of the Balkan, perhaps even of ancient Greek descent. My uncles have a European realism.'

The uncles nodded approvingly, as their youngest professor spread his arms to include them in a conversation they had no means of understanding.

'Still Islamic, but in its most liberal sense, like the Arab.'

Timothy was becoming uncomfortable.

'I thought Islam was the same everywhere.'

'Great Heavens, no!'

The professor rocked and held his belly. The last syllable of his resonant voice hurled high, gathered into the conical ceiling, funnelling into a small chimney. There it was lost through a tiny square window at the very top, where the only light in the room straggled listlessly downward.

'No, no, Islam in the hands of the Ottoman Turks was a quite different thing. When the Khan said kill, they killed, no questions asked. You know of Conan?'

Timothy nodded, but really only remembering lurid films. The twists and turns of the professor's trains of thought surprising him again.

'There you have it. A man designed to kill.'

'But the Turks are a friendly people,' Timothy tried again.

'True, friendly and charming, but do not get on the wrong side of him or he will slit your throat. What I am saying is that at bottom you have the tradition of the clan. Obedience to the tribe. The Arab on the other hand retained his intellectual freedom. Yes, they follow the five pillars, but they never lost their independence of thought, their system of abstract thinking. For four hundred years the Arab civilisations kept the torch of learning alight and guarded a store of knowledge, which would otherwise have been lost forever. Ottoman Turks had no real philosophy, little creative energy before they embraced Islam. One form of despotism replaced another. A slave mentality, a people who knew nothing else, but to follow the commands of their Khan or chief. Religion is always very closely stitched into the fabric of a society, because it controls every aspect of a person's life, but most especially his thinking.'

Timothy felt emboldened by what seemed to be an obviously wrong conclusion. 'I hardly think Saudi Arabia could be described as liberal. They are so traditional in their way of life.'

'The social code, yes.' The professor was no longer smiling. 'Dress, position of women and so forth, yes, but think what they did to their country as soon as they realised what riches lay beneath the sand. A monumental leap forward technologically. A result, I suggest of the influence of the European Empires.

'The Ottoman Empire declined because it was too inward looking. The Sultan attempted reforms, but the people…would you believe it? The people!' He emphasised the word with incredulity. 'The people would not change. Everything must remain. The tradition must be upheld – and so it was for centuries.'

'I could not help comparing Topkapi palace with its 17th century equivalent.' Timothy had at last made some contribution to this dissertation. 'It struck me that it was really the same as living in a tent. They exchanged canvas for ornate stone, but apart from that they lived in the same way.'

'Exactly so. Exactly so, my point precisely!' said the professor.

Timothy was pleased with himself.

'It was not until Atatürk that Turkey made even the smallest move to make contact with the rest of the world. The first attempt at dragging Turkey by the scruff of the neck into the twentieth century.'

By now, Timothy had lost count of how many cups of apple tea he had sipped so carefully. The Bulgarian professor was beginning to gleam as highly as the polished brasses that surrounded him.

The uncles smiled, rather shy modest smiles. 'A fellow you know of your Oxford University – the youngest ever…' their faces seemed to say.

'Very good,' said Timothy.

'Well my dear it's high time the theory of the noble savage was demolished. There has to be more to be said for civilised living and learning.

'I do so agree with you.' The men shook hands warmly like old friends.

'Next time you come to the University we must play a few rubbers. Bring some friends. We can have a nice time.'

Tim nodded and murmured vague assent. Gathering his papers together, he tucked them securely inside his document case. He zipped it with a satisfying snap. Men of the world – people who knew about the rise and fall of empires and building the future. Tim had enjoyed the conversation, he had found it most stimulating and unexpected.

Outside in the street, the bright light stung his eyes, the traffic jangled, unaccountably faster and louder than before, bugling horns played one to another.

Tim looked at his watch. It had been a decent sort of afternoon. The geological reports he and the professor had discussed endorsed and underwritten the original findings of his company and the first government survey. He was happy, the project could continue without further hold-up. The site for the dam was much further inland, closer to the capital. Tim pondered their discussion of the geological structure of the area.

It was the largest project he had been associated with so far. Responsibility weighed heavily on his shoulders as he thought of the huge sums of money involved. If the deadline was met with no serious setbacks he would be made, he could write his own ticket from then on. In his mind's eye the great dam soared into a radiant blue sky, holding and controlling millions of tons of water so badly needed by this slowly developing nation. A major achievement, a monument to man's extraordinary intelligence and technological development. Factories, schools, hospitals, shops, offices, residential zones could now all mushroom around the great plain. Beyond the flooded valley.

Tim headed a sizeable team of engineers, surveyors, geologists, analysts and he was keen to maintain smooth working relations. To keep all channels of communication open, he made himself available almost all the time. Ready to discuss any problem as it arose.

I suppose it's a bit hard on Jan, Tim thought.

Jannine, his wife, was a deceptively slight woman, some years younger than himself. She'd already accompanied him to several remote parts of the world and proved herself to be resourceful and fairly well able to cope with the demands of Tim's job.

At first, she had been a bit difficult, but he soon made it clear to her that this was his life and she could like it or lump it. Now she seemed well able to occupy herself and of course there was the child, their seven-year-old son Peter, now at the International school in the city. But he didn't have time to think about that.

He hailed a taxi. The professor's insistence on Tim meeting his family had been kind, but rather upset his tight schedule. The professor talked of progress and civilisation, but he was as Turkish as the next man. To sit and drink tea with his family and hold endless conversations was his idea of time well spent.

Traffic was locked together tightly on the main road to the Atatürk Bridge. It appeared not one vehicle could move in any direction. Tim wound down the window as far as it would go and stretched out his head to see what was causing the hold up. But the haze of heat, fumes and yellow dust blurred all outlines into an indistinct wobbling morass. Only the sheep on the roadside remained clear and in any kind of sharp focus. Sheep on one side and the gypsies on the other.

Dirty brown, once white sheep, daubed with a smear of orange paint, huddled together outside the masons' stoneworks, beyond the cemetery. Their round grey noses touching each other, they clung in tight circles. A sort of comfort, being together, being close, they became one entity. All their feet gripping the harsh, soilless surface of the pitted ground that edged awkwardly into scraggy low hills.

Unshorn, their wool hung heavily around their bodies, overpoweringly luxuriant in the pitiless landscape. Tim knew these were the sheep that had escaped the sacrifice. One of the major festivals had just taken place and sheep were ritually slaughtered each day until the end of the celebration. Id, big Id with a capital letter had just ended. These nuzzling groups confiding secretly together had been spared.

Tim watched their ludicrous shape and filthy tottering rumps pushing and shoving against each other and yet each maintaining their position in the untidy circle.

Not one left behind, the smallest and weakest not pushed out, but carried along in the tightly held mass to the next patch of burned grass.

Close by, the gypsies' makeshift tents of sheets lashed to flimsy wooden staves flapped uncertainly in the hot breeze. Beneath the once brightly striped canopies, now bleached by sun and age, were planks held up by rocks heaped with all kinds of cheap goods. Crumpled clothes and plastic ornaments, large combs, bright scarves, cheap jewellery. Tim could not make out most of it, the piles looked trivial and nondescript.

This wayside market had an impromptu appearance, everything probably having emerged from the large bundles and could be crammed back into them at a moment's notice. Women and girls in long heavy clothes, wispy scarves wound around their heads, sat or squatted impassively beside their wares. While tin kettles steamed on an old 'samavesc' and old men brewed tea, ragged little boys played on small metal flutes, producing a mysteriously resonant, yet plaintive fugue.

There seemed to be few customers, but a liveliness and vitality pervaded the market. Young men called to each other, laughing and joking. Their voices rising above the music of radios that quivered with the oriental throb of Turkish music. Every so often they sang a few snatches, or raised their hands above their heads, dancing almost without realising they were.

Tim disliked the local music, as he thought it discordant and was profoundly thankful when at last the solid plug of traffic broke free and he was carried away from this squalid area of the city.

Janine loved Turkish music and, even more, she loved dancing.

Occasionally, if they went to a taverna, he would be dragged on to the floor where he felt clumsy and uncomfortable. Men frequently danced together! Timothy could not face it – to take a few steps with Jan was as much as he could manage. He did all he could to avoid celebrations. They'd had arguments about it.

'I am the handmaid of Shiva – Lord of the Dance, the life of the world.'

Jan twisted her hands into petal shapes around her face and shifted her head from one side of her neck to the other. It embarrassed him; it made her something different and foreign.

'Don't do that,' he said sharply, 'It's so stupid.'

Jan planted her hands heavily on the table and leaned towards him.

'Tim we've been married for ten years and lived in all sorts of places around the world. Did you think I would remain forever that eager fresh-faced teenager from Barnstaple?'

There was a pause.

She continued more gently. 'Do you think I've lived in a plastic bag untouched by these ancient cultures and powerful influences around me?'

Tim did not reply, he continued steadily with what he was doing, which was tying his shoelaces into perfectly symmetrical bows.

'And you call me stupid?'

'Some people manage it,' he said eventually in resentful tones.

'Yes dear,' she smiled in sinister sweetness, 'and some people are as thick as shit. Some people wouldn't notice if God descended in the High Street in a chariot drawn by Seraphim and Cherubim!'

Tim was unclear what Seraphim and Cherubim were. He decided to drop the subject, not wanting a full-scale row, but aware he had touched a nerve.

She spoke her mind so forcefully these days. When she was young, and they'd first met, she had been so careful not to annoy him. Nowadays when he was sharp and irritable, she made no attempt to soothe him with hugs and soft words, but instead flung his roughness back at him.

Again, Tim looked at his watch – he was due to meet his site manager. If the taxi driver stepped on it, he wouldn't be late.

Des Winrush was not married and preferred a hotel room to anything more permanent. He was sitting in the bar when Tim walked in. Des was Australian, not as tall as Tim, but a man who took up a lot of space and like many of his countrymen enjoyed his beer.

Jan sometimes teased him to the point of rudeness. 'Other men are painters, plumbers or mechanics, but Australians are Australians. Just being Australian is a sort of life's work.'

'No,' he chided her, 'it's more of an Art Form! It takes constant practice and dedication.'

Although Des had great difficulty in keeping his clothes on his back in any organised fashion and most conversations included a lot of Des' sweaty chest, both Tim and Jan liked him a good deal.

'You're a slob,' Jan would say and tidy him up before they went anywhere.

'I know. I need a good woman like you to look after me.'

Des grinned at Tim as he wound his long legs around a barstool.

'What'll it be?'

'I'll have whatever you're drinking. I'm parched, the traffic around the Mihrimah was jammed solid.' Des ordered another birra.

'How's your delectable wife Tim?'

Tim pulled a slight face. 'Not always so delectable.'

'Well, the girl's got spirit. Not many women could take what she does. I think you're a lucky man.'

'Well, she knew what she was getting into,' said Tim defensively.

'At eighteen?' Des raised one eyebrow at him over the top of his glass. 'What say the three of us do the town tonight?'

'Jan's not here.' Tim hesitated. 'She's...she's gone away for a bit. Staying in one of the firms holiday flats on the Black Sea.' He paused again. 'You see my parents have taken Peter to France for a couple of months. She said our flat would be too big for her on her own.'

Des frowned. 'She's going to be out there all by herself?'

'She'll be okay.' Tim was casual about his wife's unexpected departure. 'She's very friendly with the family who run the café next door to us. They've got a place down there. They go for weekends now and again, so she won't be completely alone.'

'And you could drive out there now and again – there's a good coast road,' suggested Des.

'Well, I suppose I could,' Tim sounded doubtful. 'But now that we've got the go-ahead I've worked so hard for I don't think I'll be able to spare the time. She'll be fine. It's a lot cooler than Istanbul this time of the year.'

'So, your little family is all spread out this summer?' Des ordered two more beers.

'Jan and Peter have started learning Turkish!' Tim looked contemptuous. 'I said what's the point of that? Who's ever going to need Turkish for God's sake? I decided it would be better for Peter to learn French while he was young.'

'It would be bloody useful for me, I can tell you,' Des said slowly. 'With the guys on the site I do what I can with bits of German, bits of French, bits of English...but...' He waved his hand despairingly.

'Who's teaching them?'

'Oh some cousin or nephew of some sort – name's Tekim, I think he's up at the University. Serves in the café sometimes for a bit of extra cash.'

'So she pays him,' Des finished for Tim.

'God no! I scotched that. It was bad enough when I discovered she helped out when the café was busy. Now they've some kind of arrangement. She helps him improve his English and he helps them with a bit of Turkish.'

Des looked thoughtful.

Tim suddenly had had enough of talking about his family. Strange how he always found himself telling Des all kind of things he never spoke of to anyone else.

Des was easy going and good-natured, people trusted him. His job was enormously difficult, with so many different aspects of the project to tie up. There were so many people to deal with: highly skilled technicians, temperamental academics, company executives, foremen and a huge labour force. All the problems came to him and passed through the site office. He kept his team close around him and he had a nose for what he needed to know.

Tim was pleased to be working with him, but he didn't know how this rather slow untidy man was so good at his job. Somehow everyone felt that if Des was there everything was alright.

'Let's eat,' suggested Tim. 'I've got a few things to go over before we get into top gear.'

'Sure, where do you want to go?'

'I'll leave that to you. I'm sure you know more about the watering holes in this city than I do.'

'Trouble with you Tim is that you're an eat on the run man. Plays hell with the digestion and your sex life!'

The restaurant was a long narrow room inappropriately panelled in heavy wood. Its curiously Gothic appearance was relieved by over-bright chandeliers that illuminated every crack and crevice. Long, narrow tables were covered in gingham tablecloths.

There was plenty of room, so Tim and Des spread themselves out on a table intended for six people. Tim laid his documents out.

The waiter took their order and soon they settled into a satisfying discussion of the details that consumed their attention in their working days. Both men had a deep knowledge and interest in their work and soon the conversation turned to the wider implications of their immediate operation. They talked of the Company, its financial status, and government decisions pertinent to their particular field. And by the time they were working through the bowl of fruit, they were ready to speculate and philosophise about the future of developing nations and the implications of the world's technology.

'We're the thin red line, you know,' Tim said leaning back in his chair, looking ponderous. 'Modern day Empire builders – maybe it's a different battle with different things at stake. But it's a battle just the same. Without us, countries like this would still be back in the dark ages. The Swiss built the bridge over the Bosphorus and I think the Japs are strong contenders for the next.'

The steamy heat was beginning to trouble both men. Tim refused the lemon cologne always proffered to refresh diners at the end of a meal. They paid the bill, went to the Gents then stepped out into the relative cool of a sultry Istanbul night.

'I need a shower – I'm ringing wet,' said Tim. 'I think I'll take a taxi back.'

'Okay mate, catch you later.' Des touched Tim's arm by way of farewell, then he turned to him, as an idea occurred.

'Look you don't have to be back for a couple of days. Why don't you spend the time with Jan? Be good for the pair of you, a bit of time on your own.' Des rolled his eyes suggestively performing odd skipping movements as he sang in a croaky baritone, 'By the light of the silvery moon…'

'Sod off!' Tim said roughly, feeling awkward as he raised his hand and called back over his shoulder. 'I'll see how things go.'

Black silence greeted Tim as he walked through the door of the house. He had never seen it like this before.

He fumbled around the wall to find the light switch. The light was reluctant to give its best, but it finally came on fully. All the services were a bit hit and miss. It was Jan that coped with these little inconveniences. The drapery of tangled wires had been tamed into bundles and polite scallops across the walls. Tim only occasionally caught the daily drama of toilets not flushing or brown water coming out of the taps.

'God, this bloody country!' Tim fumed, but surprisingly Jan defended it.

'It's because it's off the main drag. If we were nearer the centre it wouldn't happen so often. It's the price we pay for being somewhere quieter.'

Tim had to agree it was a small price to pay to avoid the hullabaloo of the city. Although Jan now settled quite easily more or less everywhere she went, she seemed especially contented here, judging by the number of friends she had made. Tim was forever tripping over new ones.

Jan explained. 'I need to get know a country from the inside, not just from books, plans and statistics. And people round here are so kind! I often need a little help, or company when you're not here. Like the time Peter came off his bike. If it hadn't been for Tekim rushing us off to hospital I don't know what I'd have done. We'd only been here two days and I didn't have a clue where anything was! He came streaking out of the café and before I knew what was happening everything was being taken care of and Peter was the proud possessor of ten stitches in his head. Since then, we've been adopted by the whole Bisouri family – and you too,' she added as an afterthought, 'when you're here.'

'When you're here,' Jan's words whispered to him in the empty living room.

'When you're here.' Her words tiptoed after him up the stairs as he took his shower in an unnaturally clean and tidy bathroom.

He opened the wardrobe. Most of Jan's clothes were still there. Very little was gone. Tim remembered something she'd said to Des.

'We're nomads. We travel light. Find our pleasures where we may and make the best of life in any way we can.'

'But wouldn't you like a nice little semi-detatched like most women?'

'Um...yes, I would have once. Not now though, I've learned to live differently. I've found there is more to life than immaculate plumbing and three-piece suites.'

In the bedroom, Jan seemed to smile at him from the mirror where she often brushed her hair – no longer short neat curls around her head. It was past her shoulders now. Sometimes Tim hardly recognised her, she looked well – really well, she and Peter.

'Good enough to eat,' Des had said as he planted a smacking kiss on her cheek.

'Do you like my hair long?' she'd asked Tim one night. 'It's the heat, it makes it thicker and grow more.'

'It's nothing to do with me.' Tim always distanced himself from any enquiry of this sort. 'You do your hair any way you like.'

She always looked good – she was fine, she was all right, she was okay. Why was there any need to go on about it?

'The Turks have beautiful hair, haven't they?'

'I suppose they must. That's why women have to cover their heads. Hair in the Islamic culture is considered to be erotic.' Tim aired another of his pieces of knowledge.

'Well, some women cover their heads, but loads don't,' she corrected him. 'Anyway, I was thinking about the men.'

Tim fingered his own thinning sandy head. 'Well, you know what they say about grass and busy streets...' but she had stopped listening.

'Can you hear them singing outside?' She leaned out of the window. 'It's some chaps in the café.' She hummed along with them.

The air hung quite still and the sound of the singing – the strange yearning that had no beginning and no end – and an insistent penetrating rhythm, wound itself around Tim getting tighter and tighter until he felt he would suffocate.

'For God's sake, shut that window! I can't bear that caterwauling a moment longer! We came here because we thought it would be quieter.'

Reluctantly Jan closed the window. 'I think it's beautiful,' she said quietly.

'It has a melancholy, an intensity and a passion about it. It reminds me of Flamenco. No!!' She put her hand out to stop him. 'Don't give me a lecture about roots and origins. You may know a lot but knowing is not the same as understanding.'

'There's a quality about this country, a beguiling, sweet, seductive quality that's nothing to do with facts and figures, but is to do with the place itself, the people, the music, the weather even, all kinds of things.'

Tim carefully dried and combed his remaining hair with no clothes on, as he always did. Carefully patting the sides into exactly the position he wanted.

He went over to the basket to throw in his dirty clothes, when he noticed a wallet of photos on the bedside table.

Sitting on the bed he spread them out. The Bisouri family beamed back at him. Granddads, Aunties, Nanas, cousins, uncles, Mums, babies, children, Dads.

Jan and Peter were in many of them. Apparently, they were pictures of family outings to different places. Tim recognised the little playground at the edge of the Golden Horn and Tekim and Peter taking huge bites out of great red melons. Jan and Muguet – big hats and pin-up poses. The family eating in an outdoor restaurant. The family eating again on a beach, several children splashing in the sea. It looked like one of the little holiday resorts along the Bosphorus.

Tekim and Jan in a motorboat, both their hands on the steering wheel. Tekim and Jan dancing, this one taken at night in a taverna he didn't recognise. The beach again, cousins and nieces sunbathing or lying under umbrellas. Tekim with Peter on his shoulders and Jan beside him.

Tim looked through the photos for a second time, then he looked in the wardrobe again. A twinge of distress beginning to sound in his mind.

Why had she taken so few clothes? This was an Islamic country. He looked at the photos again. He looked at the women and girls stretched out in their bikinis. They looked like any family anywhere.

Tim started to get dressed. Perhaps he would drive down there for a couple of days after all. It was late, the road would be very dark, but fairly empty, he could get there by the early hours.

As he drove along the silent winding coast road overhanging bushes and trees seemed to peer at him through the windows as though he didn't belong there.

He felt out of place. Branches slapped the side of the car, almost pushing him out of the way. The road wound this way and that. Driving was difficult in such darkness. Outcrops of ugly shapes and patterns, a cruel pastiche of nature rose all around the beam of the headlights, threatening to crush the small car, but it was something to cling on to. Junctions presented themselves, he was unsure which to take, afraid of going miles inland. Wind was beginning to buffet him, nagging and taunting.

Vaguely he remembered it was said that this coast was very windy.

For no reason, he thought of pirates and corsaires shipwrecked in storms. Several times he had to break hard to avoid going off the cliff edge. He felt himself being pushed and pulled in all directions.

Wishing he had never started this journey, his mind travelled back to the photos spread over the bed. Those smiles, the way in which they sat or stood or leaned were so relaxed and natural. They belonged. It looked so easy and Jan too.

What forced his mind over and over the images was not seeing Jan and Peter in the centre – the subject of the pictures – it was in the groups, in a restaurant, caught in profile in mid-sentence. Those smiles, so responsive. Fingers opened, arms raised, alive and vivacious. Sharing some private joke or precious memory.

Tim realised he had looked at people he did not know, who went to places he did not know, who talked of things he knew nothing about. Tekim – Tim had met him, perhaps twice. He was Anatolian, not very tall, but strongly built like the men who worked on the dam, no spare flesh, their muscles defined in the way of a body that is used to lifting and carrying heavy things from a young age. Tim had seen small boys constantly in and out of the water swimming almost from babies. Kicking a ball around on any piece of waste ground. Lifting crates and boxes as big as themselves for all family businesses that sustained so many people. Tekim, slightly smiling, holding Peter as securely, the child's hands stroking his thick black hair. Jan and Peter deeply tanned, but paled beside his rich depth of colour.

The appalling sense of belonging in all the pictures made Tim wince. His stomach turned over, he was hot, his hands sweated and slipped on the steering wheel. They were dancing together,

Tekim and Jan. Not touching at all. Their arms raised above their heads. She was leaning slightly backwards, he leaning slightly over her, looking at each other. The natural curve of their bodies from one to another were part of the same line, her hair hanging almost to her waist – dancing figures in a frieze.

Finding the place was easier than he had expected, there were so few buildings. Tim drove slowly and quietly along an unmade road and parked at the edge of the new complex of holiday apartments. The numbers were clearly marked. Tim had no key he remembered, but the number on Jan's note said a ground floor flat.

He stepped carefully around the heavy clay of the unmade area, soon to be a terrace. Glass doors at the back slid open silently. He stepped into an almost bare living room. Sharp clear moonlight sliced the room like the blade of a sword. A table showed signs of a late dinner. Glasses, plates and dishes had all been left. Wrapping paper, coloured ribbon and some boxes lay in a pile on a chair.

'Oh Christ!' Tim stood absolutely still. It was Jan's birthday. He'd promised to phone, but he'd been so busy, he'd had so much to do, he'd had so much to think about. Anyway, she'd think he'd remembered and driven out all this way after a late meeting.

He tried a couple of doors, at last finding the bedroom.

Back on the winding road, in the now muddy dawn, Tim drove without thinking, his body empty.

At first, he'd wanted to throw furniture, break windows, hit out, attack them, drag them across the floor, make them grovel with guilt and remorse – make them beg for forgiveness. But he couldn't, he knew he could do none of those things.

It wasn't fair! It just wasn't fair! Why him? He worked so hard. He gave all his precious skill, his expensive education to the country.

He was a good man and he only wanted what was good for other people. He just wanted Peter to have the benefit of the same education as himself. He never did anything wrong. He had just done as he was told all his life, believed in the right things – it was just so unfair!

Above all he wanted to cry. He wanted this terrible pain to pour out of him. He felt the torment of tears piling up inside him unable to escape. Locked in, pent up, like the dam. But Tim was driven by a mechanism so precise, so finely sprung, there was no accommodating any other beat or any change of pace.

Outside of time now, he had fallen into some slipstream of consciousness, slithering helplessly. The ticking of his mind had stopped. Carried along by some unrecognisable current, he freewheeled, and the road took him as its plaything and kicked him this way and that until it tired of its own game.

They had looked so unbearably peaceful. Their faces so close, lips almost touching. Tangled across the pillow her hair, threads of dark gold, the spiteful moonlight glossing his to a high sheen.

Under the covers, their outline made one shape, their bodies folding into each other so naturally and their breathing came slowly and gently in the same rhythm of the wind and the waves that grumbled at Tim for his simplicity.

MY OLDER SISTER

'My, my, dear how you've grown and so smart. How old are you now dear?'

Sandra had not seen her Aunt Lulu since she was a child. It seemed so quaint to be spoken to as if she was ten years old again. She replied politely.

'Twenty-eight – well twenty-nine next week.' I feel about a hundred, she thought.

'Oh well you're fairly young, you still have time dear.'

Sandra knew exactly what she meant: time to find a husband. Sandra felt cold suddenly – Lulu had put her right back into the straight jacket of her childhood. A childhood she felt she had left forever. She had come home for her father's funeral.

Moving away from the aura of discomfort that Aunt Lulu had engendered, Sandra decided she was hungry and would eat something before she started the long drive back to Highgate. Apart from the family there were several people she did not know who had come back to the house after the service at the crematorium.

She put out her hand to take a plate when she was distracted by her niece, known as 'Dolly', with the perfectly good real name of Susan.

She took the plate as a voice said, 'Sorry but I think that's my plate – I just put it down to take seconds.'

'Oh I'm so sorry – I wasn't looking.'

Dolly tugged on the arm of a young man Sandra had never seen before. 'Uncle Barnacle can I have some ice cream?'

'Of course babe.'

Sandra smiled a grown-up smile at the man, but her eyes grinned at him, as she stocked up on the substantial sandwiches and sausage rolls – to fortify her for the journey home. He did not look like the kind of man who would be called 'Barnacle' or refer to girls as Babe. He appeared suited and booted to the manner born. His discreetly dark suit had not been dredged from the back of a wardrobe for its only outing in ten years.

Sandra left him to satisfy the whims and fancies of Dolly. She looked at her watch. If she was to get within striking distance of home before it got too dark she would have to leave now. She looked for her sister, her brother-in-law and her mother to say goodbye. They hugged and kissed warmly with promises of phone calls and visits in the coming months.

'Oh, by the way could you give Bertie a lift back to London? These train strikes are such a pain. I think he's staying near you.'

Sandra's sister's 'near you' could mean anything from Central London to Brixton She had no idea about geography or the size of London. Sandra's face registered doubt.

'Well I'll take him to the nearest underground station, I don't drive in the centre of London – Congestion Charge?' She raised her eyebrows.

'Oh yes of course,' her sister replied vaguely, not having the slightest idea what Sandra meant.

The man in the very nice suit presented himself to Sandra. 'I hope this is not too much of an inconvenience for you,' he said very politely.

'No, no of course not...' Sandra lied valiantly, then thought to herself, 'It might be nice to have some company.'

She led him to the car, and they settled themselves into their seat belts. She was quite proud of her car – she had not done the usual thing many women do, which is to buy a dinky car – she had gone for the larger, more comfortable model.

'Before we start, I think I should tell you I am Sandra – Mr Forster's youngest daughter.'

The man proffered his hand, Sandra took it and they shook hands rather formally – which Sandra found oddly comforting. 'okay Bertie let's be off.'

'My name is not Bertie…'

Sandra interrupted – 'Sorry, Barnacle…'

The man interrupted her. 'No, no….' he chuckled. 'My name is Kay.'

They both laughed.

'Why do they call you Bertie?'

'I have no idea I think it is perhaps a curious English custom?' He spoke English almost perfectly with only a trace of an accent.

'Now I come to think about it, you could be right. I know loads of people who are christened one thing and for the rest of their lives called something else. Well my father is really Arthur – always known as Alan…I have no idea why??' They both laughed again. 'Crazy!'

Sandra found herself feeling comfortable with this stranger. He had a good sense of humour and was easy to be with.

They swapped information about themselves. It turned out that Kay had worked for six months at Sandra's father's firm when he was a student and the pair of them had often played golf together. 'You don't know this? Your father never mentioned me?'

'No, but I would have been busy at the time. We were not close.'

'He was very good to me and helped me a lot.'

'Well, you were probably the son he never had. I think my mother knew you?'

'Oh yes very well. A very friendly and welcoming lady.'

'Yes, she is – always has been – she kept me going for years.'

'You and your father…'

'No we weren't close.'

Kay said nothing not wanting to seem intrusive.

But somehow the car – the small space, the warmth, the rhythm of the engine – invited confidences.

'I was not quite what my father wanted. I didn't come up to scratch. Now I'm older I kind of know why. I'm not like my sister. She's bubbly and fluffy and makes everyone feel good. I was rather studious – good at school – opinionated and maybe a bit of a feminist. My father hated that. He always made a point of showing me clearly my faults and failures. I was fond of him – your Dad's your Dad after all– but after I went to university the gap between us seemed to grow. I did well but I was not allowed to enjoy it. It was just "Of course you did well it's no more than we would expect. Perhaps you can pay me back soon".'

'Thanks Dad.' So, I busted a gut to get good jobs and climb the ladder and now I'm an executive secretary to Lord Atherton – head of Atherton International Carriers. I am boasting to you because I can! It makes me feel good.'

'Good for you!' Kay applauded her, but not in a sarcastic English way. He made her feel as if it was fine to speak of one's achievements.

'How about you? You look as if you have done well too.'

'Yes, I have – but with lots of help from my Papa. He is always there and Mama. Perhaps I have been spoiled a little.'

'Do you work in the City?'

'No, I am a veterinarian, an animal doctor and I am here to work at a centre for research and development of animal medicine. My father has horses and when he was young, he worked at the Spanish Riding School with their famous Lipizzaner horses. You may have heard of them? He loved it and it encouraged him to buy a stables and keep horses himself – which is where I grew up – surrounded by animals of all kinds as well as horses. It was a very good childhood.'

'It's a daft question but I take it you can ride.'

Kay laughed and laughed 'Of course I can, from a very young age – perhaps five years.'

'You mentioned Vienna – I took it you were German.'

'No no, no – I am Austrian,' he said proudly.

'I am not entirely sure of the difference,' Sandra confessed.

'Oh yes there is a big, big difference. Austria was a major country in Europe before Germany was unified in the nineteenth century. The Austro-Hungarian Empire and all of that. Not always a glorious history.' Kay made a face.

Sandra laughed sympathetically. 'Ditto the British Empire, so we are all in the doghouse together.'

'Yes we are and we have to make the best of it.'

'My father would not agree with either of us – he was very much fly the flag and beat the drum. A different generation! You know when I come to think of it that was one of the things that kept us apart – he came from a different world to me. Education can be a terrible thing! My sister and my Mum were blessedly unaware of so many things so they never clashed with Dad.'

Sandra began to concentrate on the traffic, which was piling up in all directions.

'I don't like the look of this – I'll have a look at road conditions.'

'I can do that on my phone – you are driving.'

He frowned and turned to Sandra. 'It is not good news – there has been a major power failure up ahead and all traffic has been stationary for two hours.'

'Oh no! I did wonder, as it's a Bank holiday Friday as well, when the roads are always jammed with people wanting to make a quick getaway.'

'I can see some cars are turning and driving onto the hard shoulder to get off the motorway.'

Sandra looked very dubious. 'I don't think I could do that.'

'Would you be very offended if I drove?' Kay asked politely.

'Not at all be my guest – and it's getting dark.'

'We find a suitable place where we can stop for a second and we change places.' He looked around at the traffic. 'Right now, everything's slowing down.' Kay was quick to take the moment.

Sandra did as she was told. 'I am not sure where I am,' she said.

Kay fiddled with the sat nav – 'We're near a village' and he named one Sandra had vaguely heard of or seen on signposts. He followed other cars that were bumping their way down what looked like a cart track. They went on some way on very unpromising terrain when it opened up to the back of a farm with straggly farm buildings scattered all over the place. Someone knew what was going on as a makeshift sign had been put up pointing towards a track to the village.

'That was good of them.' Kay was concentrating hard. 'I hope you don't mind a rather long round and round journey to find our way back, but it is better than sitting for hours and hours stuck on a motorway. I can't stand that.'

'Definitely!' Sandra was sure of that. 'I did fill up before we left Mum's – which is something – the mileage is good in this car.'

Kay looked at her wryly. 'That is as well! We could have an interesting journey.'

Sandra felt herself to be in good hands, so different from Lorenzo. Kay was very much a man who took the imitative and concentrated on solving the problem and not on making a petulant drama out of the situation – which is what she had lived with for several years.

'Are you hungry?'

'Yes perhaps.'

'I've got those sausages rolls in the back and sandwiches – I'll rummage around for a bottle of water – I usually have one somewhere.'

They found a small entrance to some kind of big house and stopped. It was slightly eerie: a mist was just beginning to settle on the fields and trees. Sandra shared out the food and they both drank from the bottle of water.

'I'm sure you don't have "foot and mouth",' Kay laughed.

'I am the man who would know what to do if I did!' He smiled wryly.

Sandra noticed for the first time he had a lovely smile and very surprising, blue, blue eyes.

'I think I'll change my clothes – my jeans will be more comfortable for the Grand Tour of the English countryside.' She fished around on the back seat for a bag.

'I meant to change before we left – but I was distracted…'

'By me, I think. I will do the same.' Kay took off his jacket and carefully folded it into a neat pile. They both got out of the car and in the thickening gloom Sandra took her clothes off and wriggled into a pair of stretch jeans and a warm fleece.

Kay could not help but see her. 'Ah now I know where I have seen you before!' He looked at her admiringly.

He also had a bag and produced a more casual pair of trousers. They both could not help giggling in the slight embarrassment of the moment.

'This would look so bad if anyone came along now…Very ooh, la, la!' Kay zipped up his trousers and grinned like a schoolboy.

They were no longer strangers. Sandra felt as if she had known him all her life.

'Aah that's better.' They both relaxed back into the warmth of the car.

'What did you mean when you said "I know where I have seen you before?"' Sandra was curious.

'Your sister showed me some photos of you.' He did not elaborate. He did not need to. 'Oh no!!' Sandra put her head in her hands. 'Not those!'

'Yes, I am afraid it was those photos.' Kay grinned even more widely than before. 'Please don't be upset – you look wonderful in them – a lovely figure and fantastic legs, I thought.'

'It's not your fault – my sister!' Sandra looked despairing. 'You know what families are like – no respect!'

'Indeed, I do – I have some pictures of me with no clothes riding bareback like an American Indian and my father insists on showing them to people I do not know!'

'I take it you've known my sister for a while."

'We kept in touch when I went back to Austria – we were a similar age and I liked her.'

'Umm that I understand. My sister is a nice person and always friendly. Is that an overnight bag? On the back seat.'

'Yes…I was going to stay overnight with them when she told me you had offered to take me back to London.'

'I did not offer, she asked me if I would give you a lift.'

They looked at each other.

'We've been set up!'

Neither of them spoke for a while.

'Do you mind?' Kay cautiously enquired.

'I don't,' he said definitely.

So many things went through Sandra's head, past mistakes and romantic disasters. She was not quite sure what to say.

'I've got a map and probably a torch in the boot. I don't trust the sat nav. I'm a regular boy scout like that It's what makes me dull and sensible and not much of a 'fun loving clubber', but my boss thinks I'm the best thing since sliced bread.' She sounded suddenly a bit sad.

'You did not answer the question. Do you mind us being set up?' Kay gently pushed her soft long hair away from her face so he could see her more clearly. The question hung in the air of the car.

Sandra took a deep breath. 'You seem very nice and I like you. You're far too attractive for someone like me…' She muttered the words so quickly Kay almost didn't hear them.

He took her hand and put it to his lips. 'I think you are a very beautiful woman. I hate clubs they are noisy and unpleasant, with terrible music. I am an Austrian and of course very musical.' He waved his hands in the air like a conductor.

'I love all the composers of my country and the best fun for me is to go to a concert of classical music.'

'Do you really?' Sandra was astounded. 'I don't know anyone of my age who likes classical music! I had music lessons for years and play several brass instruments. People think it weird. There is a story to those photos. My sister started me off as a cheerleader at local fetes and charity events – then she "joined me" in a marching band – hence the revealing costumes of the photos,' she said with heavy emphasis. 'It was to attract a bigger audience. And oh boy, did it! In my lessons I found I loved all kinds of music – classical, jazz, swing, world music – all sorts.'

'Tomorrow you and I go to a concert or something musical. I will look on the internet, there will be something on in London on a Saturday evening I am sure. We will have an amazing time.' Kay was getting excited.

'I know you, I do – I have always known you – we just did not meet yet. I think we have both been with the wrong people for too many years.' Kay took her both her hands and kissed them.

Sandra felt overwhelmed. But ever practical, she said, 'Don't you think we ought to find our way home first.'

'Of course, of course,' Kay put on his seat belt.

Neither of them had any real idea of where they were, so they concentrated on the sat nav and prayed it knew how to get the car back to Sandra's house by itself.

Inevitably the instructions were sabotaged by roadworks, new roundabouts and all kinds of diversions. Kay and Sandra shared a common exasperation with the situation. Kay found a lay-by and stopped again. He took out the map and they put their heads together as they fully opened it out on their laps.

'Hang on, hang on…I think we just passed a sign with that name on it. I'll walk back along the lane and have a look.' Sandra hopped out of the car.

Kay felt suddenly concerned about her it was very dark on the winding country lane. He took the torch and shone it along the lane to keep her in view. He called to her 'Sondra, Sondra….'

She had taken out an envelope from her pocket and was writing down the names of the villages and towns. 'I'm coming,' she called.

Back in the car they studied the map again.

'Ah-hah...I can see where we are now if we take the–' and she said the numbers of the various roads, '–that will get us to the closest town. Once we get there, there will be streetlights and pubs where we can ask for directions.'

'I can see why your boss thinks so well of you,' Kay said.

'It's a bit late but do you want a stop at a pub for a drink?' Sandra asked.

'I love English pubs, but I think another time would be best. There will be another time, I hope, lots of time for us liebling,' he said quietly.

After a few more wrong turns they reached the edge of London. Things began to look familiar to Sandra and she managed to direct Kay to her house. He parked on the small off-street parking area in front of the house.

'It's so late now Kay.' He locked the car and she opened the front door. 'I thought...I thought...' he closed the door behind her and put his arms around her.

She stood on tiptoes and kissed him.

'It has been a long day, but it has been our little adventure,' he whispered into her hair. 'As it's so late...as it's so late...we're both tired...'

Sandra took the plunge. 'I thought you might like to stay the night?'

Eighteen months later at the very nice wedding that Sandra's sister and brother-in-law had organised, her sister took the mic at the reception, her hands outstretched to embrace the assembled company, her voice filled with glee.

'I take all the credit for this occasion and for this beautiful love affair. There will be another ceremony in Austria to which everyone is invited – as Bertie's family have loads of room at their farm and want you all come over and have a smashing time.'

Sandra shook her head laughing from ear to ear. 'My sister!!! What can you do with her Kay?'

ALL SET

'Do you come here often?' Jack Beale smiled.

Loretta stubbed out a cigarette. 'Too often,' she drawled. 'How many takes does this guy need? We must have done thirty already!' Loretta pushed her hand through her thick brown wavy hair.

'Do I dare take off this hat?' Jack adjusted the brim that had been knocked out of place in the slight scuffle that had taken place in the scene. He smoothed the crease in the felt material and looked at the extras leaning back in their chairs trying to relax a little after an arduous morning.

The set was cold and rather dusty, they looked at their watches praying for the magic words 'We'll break for lunch now.'

'This coat is rather nice,' said Loretta. 'I wonder if they will let me keep it'?'

'They might.' Jack settled himself on a barstool. 'I wouldn't be seen dead in this suit.'

'Well, they are vintage aren't they?' said Loretta. 'They're not always easy to get hold of.'

'George looks a bit frayed around the edges under that hat.'

Jack watched the leading actor as he slumped in a chair with his name on.

'Well wouldn't you be'? Loretta said. 'It was a bad accident.'

'If it was an accident,' said Jack doubtfully. 'He drinks like a fish.'

'Don't we all?' said Loretta.

'Not like George – it's his profession, his life's work!'

'How's Beanie taking all the "hoo haa"?' Loretta sat down her high heels were killing her.

'Well they were on the verge of divorce,' said Jack, 'But now she seems – at least according to the gossip that wafts around the film crew – she's standing by him.'

'She's okay is Beanie,' said Loretta.

'It was the lifestyle that got to her,' Loretta continued. 'She never knew where she stood. It was hard on the kids too.'

'Yeah.' Jack was non-committal.

A loud grinding noise of old machinery drowned any conversation.

The director and his various producers had decided to bring in some extra scenery.

The director spoke to his cast through his loud hailer. 'We'll try that scene again, but I'm wanting to make it tighter and more awkward and claustrophobic .'

'Oh boy!' said Jack 'I'm likely to lose more than my hat this time.'

'Positions please, Ladies and Gentlemen. Use the same chalk marks and work around the extra scenery,' The director's voice echoed authoritatively around the film set.

'How can I do that?' Loretta stepped forward. 'That new wall and banister is right on my chalk mark!'

'Use some imagination darling, you're an actress. Where do you think Helen would stand if she was waiting for Gary?'

Loretta felt sufficiently stung into silence and decided to stand at the bottom of the stairs, her beautifully manicured hands evident on the banister rail. She turned and faced the camera.

'There you are darling, I knew you could do it if you really tried.'

Loretta raised one eyebrow.

'Perfect! Keep it in,' shouted the producer.

'Now George you turn around and the smoke from her cigarette swirls around both of you. I want it intimate – sensual.'

George went over his lines again and arrived at his appointed place.

Loretta blew a sizable plume of smoke from her cigarette. George coughed and spluttered.

'Cut! Cut'! shouted the director. 'We're not making a "Carry On" film – Loretta, gently!'

'I don't smoke,' Loretta defended herself. 'No one does these days – I don't know how to…'

The director sighed deeply and audibly.

'Okay, okay,' Loretta continued. 'I'm an actor I should be able to manage it!' She muttered to Jack, 'They'll be giving smoking lessons at Drama College soon.'

Jack was more preoccupied with how he was going to get to his part of the scene now that another wall had been added to the set. 'And I'm going to have to learn to walk through walls,' he hissed at Loretta.

They both smiled winningly at the director, both remembering how illustrious a director he was and if he said you could walk on water, that was what you did.

Jack insinuated himself around the wall as if there was a door there. The camera rolled closer on to his face as he approached Loretta at the bottom of the stairs. Harshly and crudely he barked his lines at George.

George swung round to push him out of the way, but Jack was too quick and landed him a heavy punch on the mouth.

George reeled back into the arms of several extras, obviously caught unawares and shocked by the blow.

'That's it! That's it! Much better!' The director sounded jubilant. 'That's what I want. Put 'em on edge, change things,' he said to the producers.

'Don't let 'em get too comfortable or complacent. I want that look of shock – pain makes good movies! We'll do it once more,' he bellowed.

'Oh my God,' groaned George, who by now had a cold flannel over his eye. 'It's meant to be a film Otto, not real life!'

'There's no difference,' the director shouted, 'next time I want blood!'

Jack and Loretta smiled. 'Poor George, another accident...a black eye is going to make a great picture in the press.'

'Divorces, accidents, black eyes – how much more publicity does this film need?' Loretta wondered.

The cameras were back in position. The extras were back on their barstools.

'Pull the set in even tighter!' The director was beginning to feel a sense of anxiety and edginess in all of his cast.

'Angle that wall more obliquely!' His orders came thick and fast.

He could see at last he just might have a film on his hands!

My Sons, My Boys...
My Life

David was sitting in the refectory. He had been with the others to the Holocaust Memorial service. The experience had made a great impression on him. He needed to be quiet and by himself for a while.

Of course he had always known about the camps and the 'final solution', but it had happened years ago and he was a modern teenager from a very mildly orthodox family that was bustling and busy like any other family. It was just mentioned in passing, as if it was something he already knew about.

His grandfather went to the synagogue regularly and on a sunny day in May he rang David to say, 'They are asking for students to help out at the Jewish Holiday School. Why don't you go along my boy you will find it interesting and you will learn a lot about your people.'

'Your people.' The words grated a little on David, he wanted to say Grandpa, 'Everyone is/are my people.' But he didn't.

Grandpa had mentioned it to his father. 'I think it is a good idea, you will meet more people like yourself.'

'Dad, I already meet people like myself, every time I go to school, or in my music lessons or when I go to Judo.'

'Yes, yes that's true, but this would be different, and I agree with Gramps it would be interesting for you. Something useful to do in the holidays and you would meet other students – to get a better idea of what it will be like when you go to Bristol in September.' His father referred to his place at the University's Medical department.'

'But I wanted to work in Tesco's – they pay quite well for the holidays.' He and his sister had always resisted being heavily identified as being 'Jewish'. They didn't really know why, it was just a feeling, almost an instinct.

'Gramps said he had suggested you for your music and singing and being sporty in a different way. You have a lot to offer.'

David felt he had been backed into a corner. 'okay,' he said a few days later.

He wasn't particularly looking forward to it. He was taken to meet the organisers who were very jolly and reassured him somewhat.

'There are lots of other young people coming, you'll enjoy it.' He also really liked the food they had prepared for he and his family.

'It was really yummy.'

'Well at least we know you won't starve when you are there! Dad will drive you down.'

David packed his rucksack and took a couple of the instruments he played and wished his sister and Mother goodbye.

'Darling – do phone.'

'Yes, Mum, don't fuss. I'll be fine.'

The other students were bubbly, lively and very friendly, but he did find it strange. He nearly caused a major incident by not realising the significance of having a milk kitchen and a meat kitchen and that dishes and plates had to be returned to the right kitchen or a rabbi might have to be called to rectify things. He began to learn the prayer at the beginning of all meals and that he must do nothing on the Sabbath, not even small things.

He found all of them, children, helpers and organisers extraordinarily talented and willing to pitch in with everything. He enjoyed the campfires at night and singing and playing for everyone. He became very interested in the stories of those who had been brought up on a kibbutz. A word he did not know. The stories and the life sounded exciting and dangerous at the same time. He met Tasha who gave him another new word 'sabra'.

There was so much to take in and he was drawing deep drafts of this new experience.

There were a few much older people there too. One afternoon when it was raining and he was not needed elsewhere, he went over to talk to them. He asked them about themselves.

'We come every year, it is for us a holiday.' The people had a slight accent.

He asked them where they came from. 'Potters Bar.'

'And before that?' David pressed them.

They looked at each other and shrugged, and very slight smiles passed between them.

'We are not sure. We were very small children when we were brought here after the war. No one knew exactly where we came from.'

'What language did you speak.'

'Oh several, a little of Polish, Russian, German. We had lost our country and our mother tongue.'

David felt a shiver of fear run through him. 'And your parents?'

'Oh, they died in the camps, we don't remember them.'

The old man rolled up his sleeve and showed David a number tattooed on his arm, 'This was my number – Mother show him yours.'

His wife rolled up her sleeve and she too had a number tattooed on her forearm.

David looked at them and said nothing. Words seemed pointless, he felt himself shrink and that anything he said would be trite and meaningless.

The old man laughed, trying to fill the conversation gap. 'We were not alone – of course – we had many friends who went through the same thing. So many stories.'

His wife interrupted him. 'Oh Manny, Manny, not those stories again. He is a young man, he does not need to know all of that.'

David frowned. 'I do, I know so little.'

'Well maybe just one, a little one...I had a friend Reuben who was older than me – now sadly passed, and he told me of what happened to him. He and his small brother managed to stay together in the camp. Their parents were gassed almost as soon as they arrived at the concentration camp. So the boys only had each other. Reuben was quite strong and well built so he was useful to the Nazis; he could work near twenty-four hours a day and still stay on his feet. His brother Aaron, was younger and weaker so the man called Ishmael, who shared their bunk where they slept did his best to keep him out of sight of the guards. He would hide him under piles of rags and the boy only came out to eat and when it was safe. But he grew weaker and it became obvious he had T.B.

'The word got around that the Germans were near to collapse and Reuben did his best to help Aaron stay alive. The camp was humming with rumours and counter rumours of the Allied forces on the march towards them and when they saw and heard the welcome noise of Allied planes roaring overhead they knew liberation was very near. The guards began to disappear – rats deserting a sinking ship, including the Commandant! Reuben and many others ransacked the guards quarters for anything of use…mainly boots and warm clothes or anything they might be able to sell. So much of what they found belonged to the prisoners anyway: the guards and those in charge even took the gold fillings from their teeth and also hair from the women.'

The old man held his wife's hand tightly and could not continue for a while.

David sat quietly and waited.

'It is beyond description the depravity of those so-called human beings. Reuben had found a case and tried to prepare for their eventual release.

'He tried so hard to keep his brother alive. "They're coming, they're coming, my little brother – remember what father said to us…You are my sons, my boys…you are my life." We must stay alive for him and for mother…We must keep them alive in memory for all the generations to come.

'Ishmael their friend and companion held Aaron in his arms. He knew the boy had died, but could not tell Reuben for a long time. Eventually Reuben realised and no one said anything.

'Eventually he said. "I am not going to let my brother be put into a mass grave – I am not going to leave him in this cess pit of pure evil. I shall take him back to our homeland and put him where I can tend him and talk to him when I want." He did not cry – I can tell you by then all our tears were dried hard to rage, despair, or a kind of dreadful nothingness as if we no longer existed at all.

'The Allies came and were stunned into silence at what they found and shocked for the rest of their lives. The gates were opened and big American trucks arrived to take people away in relays. Reuben waited his turn and when he climbed into the back of the truck he whistled and smiled a cheerfully grim smile. No one ever guessed he had a corpse in his suitcase.'

'Did Reuben take his brother home to be buried in his own land?' David was gripped by this terrible yet strangely wonderful story.

'He did. He travelled on barges and down many rivers until he arrived back in Holland and to the day he died he went to his brother's resting place regularly with his own family and talked to Aaron all the time. They hold on tightly to that link and the chain of memories of a lost family and all those lost families.'

'Well how was it?' David's dad wanted the full low-down on how David had got on in six weeks at the Holiday School.

After a short pause David said, 'It was absolutely great...So different. I made loads of friends and will stay in touch with them all! Especially Tasha who has invited me to stay with her family in Tel Aviv...I really want to go to Israel, I kind of need to.'

Dad was pleased that the stay had been a good experience.

As they got out of the car, David suddenly put his arms around his father. 'I love you Dad, I never knew how much until now.'

His father was astounded as David bounded into the house and swept his mother up off her feet. 'I love you Mum and thanks for...you know...just everything!!'

David's parents looked at each other in astonishment and wondered if he was 'on' something. David even hugged his sister, who looked equally astonished. Their open mouths looked like a fairground attraction.

'I met some amazing people that I will never ever forget. I feel...' he tapped his chest. 'Somehow different inside.'

'Yes, I expect you're hungry,' his mother said.

NEXT OF KIN

'It's Gillian,' Mimi called to her mother, waving the telephone in the air towards her.

'Ask her to hang on for a minute,' Jan mouthed to her daughter.

'Wonder what she wants this time?' she muttered as she took the phone. 'Hello Dear – you okay?' She used a particular tone of voice to speak to her sister that Mimi referred to as the 'Gillian' voice.

Mimi leaned on the bannisters and listened to her mother's side of the conversation.

'Ummm...Yes...Oh dear.' A long pause. 'So who was your father?' Another long pause.

'Well I suppose...umm did you ask them? I'll have to cut you short Gillian – sorry about this – someone at the door. Talk later...love you lots.' Jan put the phone down.

'What was all that about?' Mimi was all ears.

'Oh give me strength – some silly nonsense about being on a plane and meeting a couple who were sure they knew her father.'

'But isn't her father your father?' Mimi was even more intrigued.

'You would think so. I think so, Mum thought so. Where all this has come from I can't imagine.'

'And who are these people on the plane?' Mimi was fascinated.

'They were probably a perfectly ordinary husband and wife on holiday and Gillian has spun them a yarn and they have listened sympathetically.'

'Just as she seemed to be settling down.' Jan went back to what she was doing in the kitchen and sighed. She was tired of the inevitable Gillian crisis that reared its head every now and again. She was too busy with her own life to be drawn into another cock and bull story of Gillian's.

'It's a pity Grandad's dead or you could have had a DNA test done,' Mimi said a little unhelpfully as she helped herself to yet another large bowl of cornflakes.

'I'll have to dig out her birth certificate – I think I've still got it, or I can probably get a copy.'

'What about Grandma?' Mimi asked.

'Well,' Jan said doubtfully. 'She's a bit vague about where things are these days.'

'I didn't mean that, I meant couldn't she just say to Gillian that you two have the same Dad?'

Jan made a face. 'As I said she's a bit vague these days and after several marriages, she could confuse the issue.'

'But your Dad…wasn't that her first marriage?'

'Well, no, I think it was her second.'

'Who was the Grandad I knew?'

'He was my dad. Mum's third husband had skittled off by then.'

'Who was it who died years ago?'

'They both died two years ago,' Jan said.

'I'm losing the plot bit,' Mimi said.

'So, who was Grandma living with when she went a bit vague?'

'Oh, that was uncle Charlie and NO he was not eaten by cannibals!!'

Mimi sat down and stretched her legs on the sofa. 'I'm beginning to understand why Gillian isn't sure who's her dad.'

Jan put on her slippers and parked herself next to her daughter on the sofa. 'It's not that complicated really.'

'How do you know Grandad was your dad?'

'I do,' Jan said firmly.

'But are you sure?'

'Of course I'm sure.' Jan looked slightly uncomfortable.

'Anyway, it was all a long time ago – Gillian will forget about all this soon and move on to something else.'

The telephone rang again. Jan sighed and slowly picked up the phone. 'Hello,' she said in her Gillian voice. 'Oh Bill – nice to hear from you.' She relaxed.

'You'll be over later? Okay will you need feeding? Fine.' She put the phone down.

'That was your brother, he'll be over later – he needs a bed for the night.' And Jan got up to go upstairs.

'Oh drop everything for him,' Mimi said cuttingly. 'He can make up his own bed.'

'I know, I know...'

'You were exactly the same with Dad, and looked what happened there?' Mimi added.

'What do you mean?' Jan turned round frowning.

'Well, he ran off with a male model didn't he?'

Jan shook her head despairingly. 'That wasn't your father that was Gillian's father.'

'But you said you both had the same father.'

'Yes we were brought up by the same father.'

'So you're saying he may have not been your biological father? Aahhhh...maybe Gillian's not so nuts after all.'

There was a knock at the door. Mimi went into the hall and opened the door.

'Mum…there's a man at the door who says he's your father!!!'

Not Cricket

It was a perfect day in late summer. The kind of English summer day that is often remembered in old age as being before the war, either war, one or two...A time of lost youth, contentment and endless possibilities.

Nigel had been bowled out for a duck and was sent to deep field. But the day transported him to the furthest end of the cricket pitch where the grass was golden and the wildflowers nearly up to his thigh. Nigel lay down in the long grass and allowed himself to be hypnotised by the eternal blue of the sky, the summer hum of insects inspecting stamens and sepals and butterflies inspecting his own white shirt.

Nigel ruminated and chewed on a piece of long grass. He had never been as far as this, on what was known as the village green, but was in fact a little way from the village near a local wood called Adders Copse. He had only recently moved from the suburbs of Manchester to the middle of Northamptonshire. The rolling unspoilt countryside had encouraged he and his wife Maureen to retire early and buy a picturesque cottage with the requisite rambling rose around the door and a country pub within walking distance.

* * * * *

They were in the throes of settling in and getting to know the neighbours when one night in the Duck and Flowerpot the conversation with their new friends turned to the subject of cricket. Had Nigel ever played? Had he ever been in a cricket team? Was he interested in sport?

Maureen had sighed inwardly remembering that Nigel has spent most of his adult life propping up the bar at his local Sports club.

'Well, yes...' Nigel lied in his teeth. 'I follow the England team and all that kind of thing...the Ashes and whatnot – the Barmy Army,' he sniggered lamely, trying to get out of actually saying, 'No I have no interest in cricket whatsoever.'

But the words would not come and before he could finish his sixth pint of cider, he was pretty well signed up to play for the village team.

'You must be mad.' His wife looked at him witheringly. 'You're always trying to be something you're not...they'll soon find out you can't play.' She threw her hands up in resignation and went straight up to bed to watch re-runs of 'Friends'.

'I can always say I have an old war wound or sciatica, or ingrown toenails...whatever...and get out of it,' Nigel called up the stairs.

Nigel turned up as summoned at the Cricket Pavilion on the Tuesday night when they put up the roster for the coming Saturday and sure enough, he was put down to bat at number ten, which was a relief. He could scramble his way through the bowling – having been a bowler many years ago at school – so he actually knew how to bowl – but he was a hopeless batsman and at number ten not a lot would be expected of him. He looked around at the other team members and he was several years younger than most and many years younger than the membership of the Cricket club's social section.

Nigel could hear the gentle sounds of 'howszat?' and at least three people clapping softly far, far away. The perfect blue sky gently began to weigh heavily on his eyelids. He could feel himself drifting into a comfortable doze.

The match ended and the men strolled towards the clubhouse for a 'sundowner'. The team looked pleasantly expectant to the first beer of the evening. Low sun streamed across the cricket pitch with patches of deep shadow, as the trees seemed to bend low ready for nightfall.

'Where's Nigel?' a slow voice inquired with not much interest.

'Oh, he sloped off into the long grass ages ago – a bit of a shower if you ask me.'

'Well, you know these incomers.'

'Umm…' One of the older locals put his hand up to his forehead to shield him from the low sun and screwed his eyes up to see across the pitch into the far distance where the wood began.

'Has anyone told him?'

'Told him what?'

'You know…' the older man tapped his nose.

'Oh that.' There was a pause. The group were by now up the wooden steps and inside the clubhouse.

'We haven't had time – he's only been here a few weeks and besides it's been no trouble for years.' They joined the women who were sitting on stools at the bar.

'Come on you reprobates – you're not usually slow to the trough.'

'We were jest wondrin' about old Nigel. We've not seen him and...' the man looked around the clubhouse. 'And 'e doesn't seem to be 'ere either.'

'I expect he went home – his wife didn't come to the match I noticed,' one of the wives said tartly. 'My hubby says he's no loss – absolutely hopeless. We'll never win a match against Upper Hobstone if we can't find another decent player.'

They all nodded gloomily in unison.

'Oh come on let's have a drink, something will turn up.'

The group turned their attention to the burning topic of who would be the next captain now that old Fiddler had announced his attention of retiring as he was, after all, seventy-five.

As the conversation became a little heated with several disagreements about old Fiddler's successor Maureen walked into the clubhouse. 'Has Nigel finished playing?' she enquired pleasantly.

The group turned to her as one. ' 'e left hours ago – we thought he'd gorn home. Have you looked in the Duck and Flowerpot?'

'Well, they're not really open yet but I put my nose in and he wasn't there.'

'Oh.' There was another pause that developed into a silence.

A silence that went on for some time and was accompanied by slight fidgeting and coughing.

'What is it?'

'Well, we never knew 'e would go and lie down in the long grass 'e was supposed to be deep fielding.'

'Where is he?' Maureen could feel a cold clammy sensation creeping up her spine. 'Do you know where he is?' A nervous panic made her voice sound shrill and hectoring.

'We don't 'xactly know…But, but…'

'But what?!?' Maureen was definitely panicking now and hysteria was beginning to bubble.

''E could be in Adder Copse,' one brave soul blurted out what they were all thinking. 'No one got around to tellin' you – don't go into Adder Copse.'

'Why? Why?' Maureen was ready to put her hands around someone's throat if they did not tell her what was going on. 'Can you take me there?'

Cries and shouts of 'No!' and 'Not on your life!' filled the clubhouse.

Maureen felt sick. 'I'm going straight to the police and ask them to search the wood'. The assembled group in the clubhouse looked doubtful.

'I don't know if Seth will be on duty now.' One of the men looked at his watch.

'There must be someone!' Maureen was despairing. 'This is the twenty first century! A man is missing in what you say is a dangerous place.'

Maureen rushed back to her car and drove along a country lane to the village. She knew where the police station was – there were lights on and apparently signs of life.

She ran across the road and found a duty sergeant behind a desk.

'Thank God!' She panted as she put her head in her hands – her elbows resting on the old oak desk.

'How can I help you Mrs…'

'Mrs Winters – my husband is lost and the cricket team think he is in danger in Adder's Copse.' Her words came out all in a rush.

'Calm down Mrs Winters – what have that barmy cricket mob been telling you?'

'They say my husband went to lie down in the long grass on the edge of the wood and that something terrible has happened to him. They won't say what.'

'Of course they won't, it's jest an old wives tale that there are giant adders in the wood that eat people and turn themselves into stone trees, where they sleep for a hundred years and then multiply into a thousand more giant adders that roam the woods looking for more prey.'

'Oh My God!!' Maureen's face was drained of all colour as she sank to her knees.

The sergeant helped her on to a chair.

'They're rogues that cricket mob…. Always frightening people. Don't worry Mrs, your husband is probably in the pub or watching the football results at home. I'll get young Seth to run you home. If he's not there, then we will begin to make a few enquiries.'

The younger policeman took a shaking Maureen to the car and drove her home. All the lights in the house appeared to be on. Maureen looked even more panicky and upset.

She and the policeman walked down the path to the front door and called to Nigel.

'Oh hello dear,' a voice answered them.

Maureen went inside first and screamed a blood-curdling scream that could have been heard in the next town fifty miles away.

The policeman pushed past her to see what was going on. 'Oh my God, oh my God!' He couldn't stop saying, 'Oh my God, oh my God!'

The living room was filled with giant adders sitting on the settees, the chairs, the stools, the floor.

'They're hungry; it's been a hundred years since they had a decent meal,' Nigel said as he watched his wife disappear into the open throat of the first adder and the policeman disappear into the mouth of the second adder.

The snakes made disgusting belching noises as the satisfying meal made them drowsy and they began to nod off.

'Out, out, out!' Nigel shooed them all across the road into the dense wood opposite, where they instantly turned to stone.

Nigel was beginning to shed his own scaly skin and look like himself again.

'That's a relief,' he said to the one remaining adder who was also shedding its skin and a new Maureen was emerging.

She looked in the mirror. 'Oh, I wish we had more of a choice of how we emerge.'

'Well, we are twenty years younger…'

'Even so…I fancy a change. Also, I'm not keen on Northamptonshire…'

PUB CRAWL

Dorothy was a bit late. She bustled into what had once been the *Rose and Crown* but was now *Buster's Bistro*. Craning her neck around the room looking through the throng of diners she managed to see her friend Celia frantically waving to her.

'Over here...' Celia mouthed and took her coat off the seat beside her.

Dorothy beamed and scuffled her way to the table.

'I thought I'd better get a table, it was so busy when I came...We should have booked – didn't think. Anyway we're okay here in this corner.'

'Yes, very comfy!' Dorothy laughed 'Do you remember how it used to be?' She reminded her friend of the days when they had been drama students together and with the rest of the group had regularly fallen into the *Rose and Crown* for a drink after class.

'It's so different – I can't quite work out where the public bar used to be, or the snug.'

'Do you remember the railway carriages? And how we used to fight to get them all to ourselves?' They giggled together.

They had been doing a version of *Great Expectations* then. 'What larks Pip? What larks Pip?' Celia did her usual impression of Joe Gargery to amuse Dorothy.

'Those were the days – when a pub was a draughty uncomfortable place with bare wooden floors, church pews for seats and funeral parlour lighting. We didn't care though – we just trampled our way in and shoved up close to each other on wooden seats. It was always cosy in the snug. I preferred here to *The Woodman* or *The Flower Pot.* I couldn't get into the "real ale" obsession.'

'We weren't dedicated drinkers like the boys. A half of shandy lasted me until closing time.'

'We were more interested in the current burgeoning romance – who was interested in whom and the gossip about how ghastly the director was and the battle to make our costumes fit.' The waiter brought Dorothy back to the present. 'We'd better order or they will sling us out.'

They ordered, went to serve themselves at the salad bar and returned to their seats.

'Sorry for rabbiting on…how have you been Celia? Sorry I couldn't come to the funeral.'

'Oh that's okay there weren't many there anyway. It was quiet and discreet. Which was better.'

'It must have been a shock for you and the boys.' Dorothy added.

'Yes it was at the time, but strangely appropriate.'

Dorothy looked enquiringly at her friend.

'Oh, of course you don't know! George was playing squash and was hit over the head with his partner's racket, he fell, had a total stroke and died in minutes.'

'Oh my God!'

'He was declared dead before the ambulance arrived.' Celia looked quite matter of fact.

'How ghastly for you.' Dorothy was very sympathetic. 'You and the boys must miss him so much.'

'Not really, he was hardly ever there anyway. He was always at the club playing tennis or Squash and later in the bar, or at the Cricketers playing cards. He hardly saw the boys and they communicated through me. "Tell Dad…or say to Rob or Colin"…I felt like a pillar box.'

There was a bit of a silence. Dorothy didn't quite know what to say. 'But things were always fine between you?'

'Well, more or less, like any couple you accommodate and get on with life.'

They had finished their main course and were contemplating the dessert menu.

'How are the boys?'

'Oh they're fine – they argue of course – Rob always wanting to be the elder brother and in charge, gets on Colin's nerves. Just the usual family stuff. They both have nice girlfriends who change occasionally.' Celia grinned. 'I'm always upset when one of the girls goes…I get to know them and then I miss them.'

Celia looked rueful. 'Remember how we were? Falling in love with our juv leads? When I played Lady Macbeth – I adored Phil who was my MacBeth…we had quite a fling. And I remember you with your Romeo! That was hot and heavy.'

'Those were the days – as people our age say all the time! But times were different. It wasn't a big deal. I blame mobile phones and social media…too many noses poked into other people's private business. Do you ever see anything of the old crowd?'

'Funny you should ask that: just recently when I was with the boys in the *Royal Forest* and suddenly a voice behind me said '"Hello Celia" and it was Kit – remember him?'

'Lovely fella – remember him well – I see him sometimes on TV. Isn't he the face of Dilly Donka Doughnuts?'

'Yes he gets the odd part and often does adverts. We did laugh about his face grinning at us from the hole in a giant doughnut and singing barmy little jingles. He said he cries all the way to the bank! But he's mainly into antiques, so after a few drinks we told him that George had passed away and we had a houseful of antiques. George was very keen on them and had inherited a lot from his family. I always found them a pain – too big, too heavy and a bugger to clean. The boys were keen for Kit to come round and value them. Mercenary little souls as they are.'

'I expect you would like something more modern and easier to live with.'

'Absolutely! Also the boys want proper boys rooms with computers and modern stuff around them. The house is fine, we love it, but it needs seriously updating. Soooo…Kit came round and was pleasantly surprised at what we had. He said he could get them auctioned through his company and would do all the necessary. I breathed a sigh of relief – the prospect of sorting out lorries and delivery people or house clearance had been bothering me for ages. I just let him get on with it. He would take a fee of course, that was only right. Actually in the event he charged me nothing.'

'That's great.' Dorothy had a happy ending look on her face.

'There was just one small detail – in all the commotion about this and that – we had forgotten about George. '

'Forgotten about him? He was dead?'

'Well yes, but I had kept his ashes of course, somewhere, intending to have a scattering with the boys sometime. Now George had always kept the ashes of his family in various places, in the furniture, wardrobes, cupboards, drawers. There was Grandad, Grandma, Uncle Reg, Aunty Flo and others. I lost count and just forgot. They were nothing to do with me. It all happened so quickly. Kit and the boys shifted all the ghastly furniture and only later I realised my mistake. Kit was thrilled and came bouncing in with a cheque for several thousand. He had shipped them off to some potentate in Sumatra or Brunei – I can't remember. And then it hit me.'

'What hit you? Where were all the ashes?'

'Well, it was just a mistake.'

'Wait, what?'

'We had auctioned off George and all his family and they were now somewhere in the Philippines!'

'Well, you got a good price for them – fancy another coffee?'

'No let's go the *Sailors Rest* next door and have a real drink.'

───※───

SALAMANDER

Salamander was given his name when he was a very small boy living in the red-light district of Amsterdam.

He was technically an orphan but had been taken in by the gay community who kept an eye on him and kept him safe from the kind of predators that they knew only too well. His 'guardian' shared a kind of parenting with the ladies who sat in windows to attract clients.

A very strange childhood, but to Salamander it was home. The garish neon lights flashing on and off twenty-four hours a day outside his bedroom window was normal. Social Services, such as they were in those days, gave a nod to the arrangement and as he did go to school – most of the time and appeared well fed – they let things lie.

Salamander was never quite sure if he wanted to be a boy or a girl and, as he was perfectly free to dress in any way he chose, he did slowly understand that he was not very 'boyish or mannish'.

He enjoyed the company of his guardians who often wore make-up and beautiful underwear. He knew he was different and, as he became a teenager, revelled in the attention his amazing looks attracted.

Clients often took his photograph and it was not long before he was initiated into the lucrative world of snuff films and pornography. It was not an easy choice of profession and he made mistakes and suffered often-shocking consequences.

His guardians said to him, 'You've got to wise-up Sal or you won't survive. You must learn to be the one who calls the shots – not them.'

And so, in time Salamander took control of his situation. He met an extraordinary variety of people – often quite famous – until he came to the attention of Rossellini who was keen to make an art film around the making of snuff movies

It hit the headlines, coming in the wake of 'Last Tango in Paris' and Salamander became a household name almost overnight. He appeared at the Palme D'or in Cannes and the Venice Biennale.

He was not the same boy who had cuddled up and slept soundly with his drag queen guardians as a child. He had an edge. He was slick and had a razor-sharp wit. He knew how to entertain people with his wise cracking stand-up comic routines. He could also sing and dance a little. He came to be in great demand and was given a show of his own on T.V. In his life, lovers and partners had come and gone, often with recriminations and drama. He either rued their departure or was happy to be rid of them.

Until he met Renee. Renee was Swiss and a lot older than Sal. He was immensely wealthy in his own right. Money was often a bone of contention in Sal's love life. Sal made a lot of money, but he also spent a lot of money and was suspicious of relationships. 'It's just the money, just the money it's all you want,' was often the death knell of the latest affair.

Sal felt he could relax with Renee and simply enjoy his company; he was an astute businessman and chided Salamander about his casual attitude to his earnings. 'You throw money away Sal – you won't always be young and command the kind of fees you do now. What will you do when you are old and grey?'

'Die in the gutter!' Salamander said flippantly and waved a graceful hand through the air like a butterfly wing.

'You won't! I won't let you, my precious boy.'

Salamander kissed him tenderly on the top of his head. 'You're such a Daddy to me – I love it. How could I manage without you?'

Renee slowly took over the role of guide and mentor. He showed Salamander how to dress, weaned him off the flashy, brassy, over-revealing creations he favoured.

He showed him how to make-up so that he no longer looked like the result of a bad day in the beauty salon. He took him to nice places and Salamander soaked it all up. He felt loved, he felt cared for again.

When Renee died suddenly in a freak accident on the slopes of St. Moritz, Salamander sat in a chair in the sun room of the villa looking out at Lake Lugano for three days without moving or eating or sleeping.

The staff were devastated by both the loss of their beloved Renee but also by the condition of Salamander. They tried to shake him into some reaction. They called doctors and psychiatrists.

'It's shock,' was the verdict. He will take a while to come out of it.' They helped him into a daybed and eventually he fell asleep for three days.

When he woke, he was completely at a loss – he had no idea how to carry on with his life. He could hardly get out of bed or put one foot in front of the other. But he had no choice and the housekeeper and the secretary gently guided him into some kind of equilibrium.

It was a quiet funeral, close friends and staff. 'Such a loss,' was really all anyone could say. Twelve years Renee and Salamander had been together and pretty well everything was left to Salamander, who could not take it in.

'I have to get away from here,' he said to Francois the secretary cum P.R. cum site manager cum general factotum. 'Can I leave you to deal with everything?'

'Of course Sal – like normal.'

'I don't know where to go…' Salamander looked like an empty envelope.

'Well, Sal, Renee was booking flights for you both to look over the nightclub you have in Rome to see how things were being managed – the 'Conca Azzura'. You can stay in the apartment near the Trevi fountain. I will phone for the staff to make it ready for you and organise cars etc.'

Salamander did as he was bid with little enthusiasm for the journey.

When he arrived, the apartment seemed too big, too empty, too Italian.

'Why such huge furniture?' Sal sighed to himself.

Francois had travelled with him and was to stay for a few days. 'I'll have to settle him in,' he explained to the housekeeper in Lugano, 'or he will sit and stare at the wall all over again.'

Francois organised a car and a driver to help Sal with getting around Rome. 'You'll soon get the hang of where you are.'

'I am not staying long,' Sal replied.

'But I thought…' Francois stopped himself. It was no use reasoning with Sal: he was grieving, he didn't know what he was doing.

The driver turned out to be an older man who spoke English, very experienced in conveying the wealthy and the famous to anywhere they wished. Salamander spoke Dutch, French, English and some German, but his Italian was limited.

After a day Francois encouraged Sal to go for a drive and see something of Rome.

The driver favoured churches and of course St. Peter's. Sal dutifully traipsed around apparently not taking in very much until they came to a small chapel in some glorious cathedral.

Sal sat down in one of the pews. 'Just to take the weight off, love.' He sat and sat and sat.

'Do you want to move on sir.'

'No, I like it here – the peace, the peace is…where are we?'

'It is part of the Vatican – almost a private chapel.'

'Oh! is that good?' For the first time in ages, Sal showed some kind of interest in what was happening to him. 'I'll come here tomorrow.'

'What about tonight Signore?'

'Yes tonight…I have to visit my nightclub…the Conca Azzura – you know it?'

'Of course Signore – everyone has heard of it – it is very famous.'

'I suppose so…I had forgotten.'

* * * * *

The club was just off the Via Veneto the door was small and totally unremarkable with only a small neon sign

conca azzura

in blue letters.

Francois had phoned and alerted the staff to the arrival of the owner of the club. They were all hovering in anticipation at seeing Salamander in person.

Sal knew that nothing would be moving until late in the night – that was normal for a drag show, so he decided to arrive somewhat earlier to have an idea of how the club prepared for its visitors.

The driver rang a discreet bell.

The small door opened almost immediately and an American voice welcomed Sal down the rather plush stairs and into the main salon of the club. 'Good evening sir, it is such a pleasure to meet you and for you to join us at the Conca. My name is Hank and I am in overall charge of the business. Can I interest you in a drink from the bar?' He was as sleek, and smooth as a silver spoon as if he had just been brought back from the grooming parlour.

'Good evening Hank. I do hope it will be a pleasure for me too,' Sal said a little waspishly.

'I can promise you sir you will be very well looked after and you will see how popular the club is with all our guests.'

'If you say so. Francois tells me he has examined the books and he is very satisfied.'

'It will be a while before the main guests arrive, so I have organised a little 'something' – just aperitivos – so you can meet some people who are very keen to see you again. I hope I have not overstepped the mark.'

'Well you have, as I am not really ready to see people. But Renee would not want me to be rude after you have taken so much trouble – so I will see them.'

'Very gracious of you sir,' Hank said slightly condescendingly.

Sal could feel the unspoken 'who does he think he is?' and followed him into his private office and sitting room, his feathers ruffled. Sal was surprised and pleased to see the people waiting were friends from his film and TV days. A couple were his back-stage buddies who he'd leaned on very heavily in his early days in the business. He'd laughed and cried on their shoulders, slept on their sofas, worn their clothes, eaten their food, got drunk with them, ignored their advice on people who later turned out to be bastards.

'Sandra! Charlie!' Sal was surprised how pleased he was to see them. He felt his legs almost give way from under him. Tears poured down his cheeks and he did nothing to stop them.

Sandra did what she had always done and gave him her handkerchief. 'Lovely to see you Sal, sorry about...' She squeezed his arm.

'Are you going to give us a turn tonight?' Charlie asked.

Hank looked at him expectantly. He said nothing, but his eyes pleaded like a Spaniel.

'Give me the grand tour of the place – show me the dressings rooms.' Sal wiped his face delicately.

The smell was so familiar, like a fox returning to its lair, Sal breathed in the pungent odours of deodorant, cheap perfume and stale sweat.

'Like old times Sal,' Charlie said. 'Hank runs everything very tightly and very "clean",' he said meaningfully.

Sal nodded in understanding. 'Like old times...' he murmured as he fingered the tulle, the satin and the feathers and the velvet basques. 'Leather?' he nodded. 'Those boots?' he marvelled. 'I thought I had long legs...what is this guy a giant?'

The performers began to arrive. Sal squeezed his way to the door put up his hands in acknowledged fellowship. 'Break a leg boys and girls and boy/girls – I'm looking forward to the show. '

'We have a table waiting for you Sir.' Hank could see that his strategy was working.

'For fuck's sake stop calling me "Sir", my name's Salamander or Sal as you well know.' He turned back to his friends. 'Sandra and Charlie, I hope you will join me.'

They hesitated and looked at Hank. 'We actually work here Sal,' Charlie replied.

'That's great – tonight you are my guests! And when the show is over I want to meet all the drag stars and get to know my people.'

The club began to buzz with the arrival of the clientele – all the tables were booked. Film stars, celebs, politicians, religious leaders, big businessmen, members of the military top brass – all dressed in wondrous clothes and startling make-up.

The band struck up, a spotlight fell on Sal's table and at a given signal the entire audience stood up and gave Salamander a round of applause.

The MC took the opportunity to say how delighted they were Sal was in the house. 'Welcome back to where the world is free, where there is no discrimination of any kind, race colour gender, sexuality, ability – all are welcome at the Conca!'

Three cardinals in their scarlet regalia stood up and blessed him. It was all a bit overwhelming for Sal.

'I think I might stay for a while, Francois. I am getting to know people. My cardinals tell me they can help me to have an audience with the Pope now I am becoming a Catholic.'

So that was how it came to be that Salamander, the legendary porn star, was waiting politely in the queue for his audience with Pope Francis when three cardinals their cassocks swishing gently approached the silent, politely waiting queue unaware this was the day Sal would be in the Vatican.

'Freddo, Georgio, Sergei!' Salamander's voice trilled like a parakeet pinging off the marble floors, the pillars and the ancient mosaics.

'Shh!' They approached him discreetly. 'Shh,' they whispered as softly as they could, taking him to one side.

'Salamander, this is not the club where there is no discrimination of any kind. Here in this place, it is the home, the bedrock of discrimination where bias and discrimination were invented and ruthlessly enforced.'

'Why are you here then?'

'Well, you never know, we might become Pope and change things!'

Salamander looked very sceptical. If that were the case, where would be the danger, the thrill, the living on the edge that he knew his clientele enjoyed?

———— ∞ ————

THE FIRST STEP

'Mrs Harding, Mrs Harding…Lucy…'

Consciousness came slowly, she did not want to wake up.

'We'll be landing soon.'

'Yes,' she answered automatically. 'Yes,' again.

She could still feel the soft wind tapping the side of her face, she could still see the anxious ragamuffin trees, their palms held out for pennies. Tiredness settled upon Lucy. In her dream she had been light, barefoot, scrambling down a cliff to the sea.

She shifted in her seat as best she could – pain in one hip, pain in one shoulder, she winced involuntarily.

Awkwardly she managed to get herself to her feet.

'Don't stand up Mrs Harding. We'll help you into the wheelchair.'

She was off the plane. Kindly stewards and airport staff dealt with everything: ramps, security, passports. Soon she was at the Arrivals door. The attendant waited a while as she was alone.

Lucy phoned her son Andrew.

'He's here – it's just the usual parking scrum. Can you take me outside? He's having trouble finding a space. If I wait by the road, he can just pick me up.'

Lucy fished the ready ten-pound note out of her bag. The attendant took it quickly, stuffing it into his top pocket. It was a busy day.

'Thank you so much for all your help...' she began, but he was gone, so she said it to the air. Help, help, that's all she did these days was thank people for help.

Lucy had observed over the last two years, that no one ever asked why she was in a wheelchair. She'd been absorbed into that amorphous group: the disabled.

She could not wait to get back into her own electric wheelchair.

Her son drove slowly towards her, she waved.

'Hi Mum, flight okay?'

Lucy got herself to her feet and Andy helped her to sit sideways and then together manoeuvred her legs into the car.

'That was good – miles better than when you went away Mum!'

They chatted in the car on the way home.

'I take it the treatment went well.'

'Yes, the place was fantastic – gyms, swimming baths, jacuzzi – loads of facilities. I had a lot of spa baths and back strengthening stuff. I want to keep it up. It was good.'

Her son looked straight at the road ahead. 'I think you enjoyed yourself.'

A remark that told her he knew.

Lucy smiled the hundred-yard smile Andy remembered as his Mum. 'Yeesss...' she elongated the vowel.

'Is it a secret?' her son probed further.

'Noooo...What have you heard?'

'Well, nothing really, except a few phone calls while you were away. Someone called Daniele? Didn't sound very German to me.'

'No, he's not. He's one of the physio guys.' Lucy smiled again.

Andy was a young army officer and had moved heaven and earth to get the best treatment for his mother. He remembered his

Mum as being energetic and sporty. When he was a child, she had been full of life, ready for anything: climbing mountains, water skiing, surfing. She had always been fit and strong with that outdoorsy attractiveness – she'd been good at her job working with troubled teenagers.

The accident had not only damaged her body, but also her spirit. For someone like her to be told she would never walk again, was a blow, but something for which she had the resources to recover.

But when his Dad told her bluntly he had not signed up for a wheel chair bound wife, he needed to 'move on', Lucy visibly shrank, disappearing inside herself.

Andy was happy to see his mother's proper smile. He'd hoped spending many weeks with Paralympians and badly wounded soldiers would help to raise her from the pit of despair she had, in some ways, created for herself.

In the following days Andy heard his mother on the phone. Something in her tone and almost, slightly teenagy manner told him it was Daniele. They chattered easily, obviously comfortable with each other, talking about all kinds of things.

'You like him, don't you Mum?'

'Ummm…he's…' she cast around for a nondescript word, '…he's nice.'

Andy would not be put off. 'Mum I mean you really like him.'

His mother turned her head away from him.

Her son took her arm rather firmly.

She pulled it away sharply, not wanting to prolong the subject.

Andy moved round, leaning down, looking at her intently, his gaze insisting on an answer.

'Alright, alright! Yes! Yes I do,' she said sulkily, defensive and spiky. 'What difference does it make?'

Andy frowned, not letting her move away. 'It makes a lot of difference – it makes all the difference!'

'It doesn't!' Lucy shouted. 'It makes no effing difference. I'm still a wheel-chair bound cripple!' Her words stung both of them.

'You're not! It's obvious this Daniele knows it and so do I!'

Mother and son glowered at each at each other.

Andy stood up. 'I only want…You know…' he began.

Lucy crumpled. 'I can't go through all that again!' Tears formed. 'He's a lovely man, a kind, funny Italian – what could he possibly want with me? He could have anyone!'

Andy was almost glad to see her so angry and upset. It was the stirring of life in her he'd hoped for.

He persisted. 'How did you two get on there? What did you do?'

Lucy looked at him and thought for a while.

'Of course you know – a lot of the guys – the soldiers are barely more than kids. There was an incident one night, one of the boys freaked out. Daniele and I sorted it, calmed it down, whatever. It kind of brought us together. I told him I had worked with stroppy kids for years.'

Lucy stopped and looked at her son. 'You know, being with those boys made me feel like a person again.'

'I can see you are much more like your old self. That's great! So why won't you give this guy a chance?'

Lucy chewed her thumb and looked at the pictures on the wall of her living room.

Andy waited.

'For so long, dreams have been my reality, where I'm comfortable and safe. Someone like Daniele coming along I could

only dream of. It scares me. I feel I don't know how to deal with it.
I don't know how to be a woman now I am in a wheelchair. I
didn't realise how my life would change forever. I thought I
would "soldier on" in the same way – just in a wheelchair.' She
shrugged.

'You've got to be brave Mum. Think of those kids back from
Afghan…They're in the same boat. Mending your body is one
thing but mending yourself and your life is the hardest thing you
will ever do. You could help them a lot you know!'

Lucy smiled. 'That's what Daniele said.'

Andy waved to someone outside the window. 'Well, you're
going over the top in about two minutes Mum. I gave Daniele
your address!'

Skinning Cats

'"Several excuses are always less convincing than one." I quote Aldous Huxley of course,' said Professor Janus. 'I don't personally adhere to the aphorism. I believe excuses should be harvested, winnowed, sieved, then baked into loaves and passed around as many people as possible.'

His students fidgeted. They'd heard it all before. They felt uncomfortable, as these words always presaged the work of some unfortunate soul being publicly vilified.

Professor Janus scanned the assembled students, taking in their various attitudes of slouch and the stunning array of extraordinary garments they were wearing.

He peered at them more closely.

'Aaahh,' he said. 'I can see you have all been at the bread bin today.' He waved several scripts in the air and his glasses slid even further down his nose.

'And these offerings are crumbs, ladies and gentlemen, crumbs that fall from a poor man's table!'

He swept the pile of scripts on to the floor.

There was an audible intake of breath from the assembled students.

This kind of behaviour from a teacher was totally unknown to them. They flinched. They trembled with resentment.

'Yes, I know your teachers have hung accolades around your necks for years – encouragement and pandering has abounded in your schools – fed by political correctness and parental indulgence.'

The students seemed smaller, shrivelled in their chairs. They had heard that Professor Janus was a tough cookie, but they had not expected quite such a full frontal assault so soon in the term.

Professor Janus wafted a hand over a large pile of books on the table in front of him. 'I do not want crumbs ladies and gentlemen. These are all to be read by next week for your assignment. I shall expect you to have mined the lower depths of this literature. There will be no plagiarising from the internet and no collaborative efforts passed off as individual work. The only place "success" comes before "work" is in the dictionary. Thank you and good morning.'

Martin and his friends breathed out and draped their arms around each other.

'Ouch! Not the blah blah doddle we thought this course would be.'

'Umm, umm,' his friends ummed several times searching for inspiration.

'So work first, inspiration later guys. I'm afraid we'll have to put the band on hold for a while until we have the measure of this guy.'

They had by their own assessment worked very hard to get to Uni and none of them wanted to mess it up – their families couldn't afford it. They dawdled out of the lecture room thoughtfully.

Dolly caught them up.

'Don't worry you'll get used to him,' she said.

'Don't you dare say he's a poppet.' Jake put his hand over his girl friend's mouth.

She removed the offending hand from her mouth and held it. 'No, I wasn't going to say that,' she looked into Jakes palm. 'It says on your lifeline: you either accept that you might learn a lot from him and do spectacularly well or it will require stealth and imagination to deal with him.'

'Not my strong suit – imagination,' muttered Martin and the others 'ummed' all over again.

'It looks like it's going to have to be work.'

Their faces seemed older suddenly. The mention of the word 'work' had put a weight on their shoulders.

'Well I'm going to the pub – this needs thinking about and guile can't be rushed.'

The group sauntered over to the Pig and Feathers and settled into their usual corner.

'It's your round Doll,' they said in unison.

'Chivalry is not quite dead,' she said with heavy irony. 'Well at least come and help me carry the drinks you layabouts.'

Silas from the Science group had wandered across to them.

'How's it going tossers?' he said jovially, bad language and rudeness being his idea of personal freedom and humour.

The group mumbled and complained about their professor.

'The truth is,' said Silas, 'that our race has survived ignorance – it's scientific genius that will do us in. Your professor is trying to tamper with your natural, God-given ignorance. He is trying to engineer your views and ideas to meet his own criteria. Is he right?' Silas persisted.

Uncertainty spread among them.

'You need to test him. Go to your next lecture armed and ready to throw a few cannon balls across his bows.'

'You're right,' said Doll. 'Maybe our collective minds might – actually should be a challenge.'

'Well it's an idea!' said Jake 'How shall we start?'

'Well, reading the ruddy books might be helpful!' said Doll.

S.M.S.

Sheila watched the rain coming down in stair rods and cheered and shouted and jumped around the kitchen. At last, after months of nothing more than the piffling occasional tear drops of water, the sky had finally broken open and rain hurled itself to the ground like the Gadarene swine.

The rain continued to pour for a week then another week and another. Sheila was delighted, the ground might finally turn from baked clay with gaping cracks growing wider each day, back to recognisable soil that would support life whatever that may be.

The dried up river bed at the bottom of the meadow had begun to become quite muddy again and birds had returned to drink and bathe.

Later that month the rain clouds softened fluffing themselves into pillows edged with blue ribbons. Sheila decided to go for a walk and see for herself whether the stream was flowing as it should. The overhanging branches still hung heavy with water and dripped musically into the stream.

Sheila breathed in the fresh clear air. It seemed as cool and crystalline as champagne after the recent heaviness of the atmosphere.

She was enjoying walking along the riverbank hearing the animals and watching for any movement in the water, which was flowing at some speed – this surprised her. The tributary seemed to be racing to join the mother river some miles away.

At first she ignored the Coca-Cola tin that floated past her, but as she walked on she felt mildly offended by its presence. It was ugly and belonged in a more brash environment, not in the natural world. She decided to follow it until she could find a suitable place where she could wade into the stream and fish it out.

The water was deeper than she had expected and as she reached for the can she lost her footing on the gravelly muddy riverbed. She fell into the water landing on her bottom with a soft thump.

Sheila scooped up the can, but in an effort to get back to the bank she fell again catching her denim jacket on a spiky thorn bush she hadn't noticed. She was flat on her back and soaked to the skin. Sheila floundered for a while but eventually managed to clamber up the bank and out of the water, grateful for a well-padded bottom and that no one was around to see her predicament.

Her romantic pastoral ramble by the stream had lost its appeal and all she wanted was to get back home as fast and as unobtrusively as possible.

Everything about her was heavy, dripping and cold. She squelched along the country lane leading to her house. The wretched can now scrunched in her pocket.

Next time I'll bring a net, she vowed, if there is a next time.

Of course, it was going to happen. Sheila passed the family from the Mill down the road. Mum, Dad and friends, with several children, eyed her peculiar condition with eager curiosity.

Sheila almost broke into a run. 'Hi can't stop – bit of an accident!' She sped up to get around the corner – at least she would be out of sight. No, there was Bobby the dog and Mr Selby.

'You been in the wars Sheila?'

'Yes just a bit!' And with that Sheila managed to reach her own gate and stagger to the back door that was, mercifully, wide open.

Sheila fell into the kitchen.

Her husband Neil looked her up and down. 'You're a bit wet, did it rain again?' he said to her departing back as she dragged off her clothes leaving a trail of dripping garments beached on the stairs.

Neil left them where they were. He would seriously have to think outside his box to know what to do with them. His every instinct shouted to leave them where they were.

Sheila came down sometime later warm from a bath and a hair wash.

On her way down she picked up all her wet clothes from the stairs and felt the Coca-Cola tin in her pocket. She cursed the tin and the company that made the offending object and threw it in the bin.

There was a gentle tapping on the back door.

'Who now?' thought Sheila.

A very small visitor with plaits, dressed in a red anorak and blue wellington boots stood on the mat under the back porch. She was holding some straggly wild flowers and something wrapped in kitchen paper.

'Hello!' Sheila smiled at her unexpected visitor.

'Mum says are you alright?' The little girl spoke quickly and very quietly and she put the flowers and wrapped kitchen paper into Sheila's hands.

'Thank you very much, I'm fine.' The paper fell open and a couple of slightly second hand looking chocolate biscuits fell out.

'Are these for me?' Sheila inquired gently.

'Yes,' the little girl almost whispered and nodded.

'You live at the Mill don't you?'

The little girl nodded.

'Would you like to come in an have an orange juice and share the biscuits?'

The little girl came in and stood by the sink, her head hardly reaching the top, holding on to the side as if she would fall.

'Come and sit here on a comfortable chair.' The little girl did as she was bid and almost disappeared inside Neil's favourite after-dinner armchair.

She just sat and looked at them and Neil and Sheila stood and looked at her.

'What's your name dear?' Neil spoke to her as if she was a cat or a dog.

'Jennifer.' She sat for a little while longer, then wriggled and looked around the room. Then she got up and went over to the bin and took out the Coca-Cola tin.

'Did you read the message?'

Sheila looked puzzled. 'No.'

'We put them in the tins.'

Neil took the tin from her hands and poked around inside. He hooked out a wet and dirty piece of paper. He opened it out and smoothed it flat on the kitchen table. Then he laughed, genuinely amused by what he read. The paper was a flyer for a business venture.

"'Jeffery's Superior Dry Cleaning Company. Personal service – door to door collection.'" Both Neil and Sheila laughed.

'How appropriate is that?'

The little girl laughed too. 'Tommy, he's my brother, thought it was funny.'

Neil and Sheila looked at her. The piece of paper was obviously not just an accident. They looked at Jennifer. 'Does your Mum know you're here?'

'No, Tommy sent me. He wanted to know if you had found one of the messages?'

Neil and Sheila looked at each other. The same thought crossing both their minds.

'How many of these have you put in the stream?' Sheila asked.

Jennifer smiled proudly. 'Hundreds, thousands, not all cans, sometimes Dad's beer bottles or Mum's fizzy water.'

The two adults open mouths nearly dropped to their chests.

'Why?'

'Well Tommy said it was good way to advertise Daddy's new business,' the little girl quoted her brother.

'But why?' It was Neil and Sheila's turn to look bewildered.

'Well, Tommy says that all the people who go and clean up in the countryside will get really, really dirty and need their clothes cleaned.' Jennifer's eyes got wider and wider. 'And Tommy says, now lots of people will go and collect the cans and bottles, as Tommy says we've put lots of them out everywhere.'

'What a little treasure you are sweetheart! Mummy and Daddy are going to be so proud of you and Tommy for trying to help out like this.' They laughed to each other somewhat ironically.

'What gave you the idea for this project?'

'Tommy fell in the pond in his best coat when he was trying to get out a rusty old bike and Daddy was cross and said "Now I'll have to dry clean your new coat".'

'A bright lad your brother. Create the market for your product...hmmm...I might just walk down with you to Mummy and Daddy's – I could do with some advice,' Neil said.

'Neil! And I'll be organising parties of clean up volunteers to save the countryside from people like you!' Sheila retorted.

Jennifer smiled, finished her orange juice and ate both chocolate biscuits.

Stage School

It's tricky. Nellie carried on with her ironing as her mind rambled around all kinds of scenarios, situations and solutions. Whoops! She almost dropped the iron.

'Concentrate Nellie,' she told herself, 'Try doing one thing at time – it might help.'

She was working in London some of the time, taking singing lessons some of the time, looking after Nana some of the time. teaching piano and singing at the Italia Rivera Stage School some of the time.

It's definitely tricky, she thought to herself again.

Her boyfriend Justin wanted to get married soon and she'd just had this extraordinary offer to sing with Bocelli in Verona at their famous outdoor concerts. The invitation hadn't come completely out of the blue – she'd met him at Italia Rivera when he was a guest judge several months ago.

Nellie had been detailed to 'look after his needs' which turned out to be few, as he had his own people who went everywhere with him.

Bocelli had charmed everyone and even sang for the students, a sudden impromptu performance and afterwards he had asked if anyone wanted to sing with him.

A chorus of 'Nellie! Nellie!' rippled enthusiastically around the auditorium.

The principle nudged Nellie on to the stage and introduced her as, 'A young lady who gives her time and her talent unstintingly to the school and the students.'

Quickly Bocelli and Nellie decided on a duet from one of Mozart's Figaro operas, which was light and amusing, but without accompaniment.

Nellie had taken a very deep breath and prayed. There were a few blips that most of the audience wouldn't notice, and it was greeted with enthusiastic applause.

The whole day had been a joy. When everyone made their final farewells it was agreed it had been a spanking success.

Nellie thought no more about it, she was too busy juggling her complicated life.

Justin was becoming more insistent: it would be better for both of them if they were married, it would be cheaper and more convenient.

Nellie had not even bothered to suggest that they move in with Nana.

Justin was a systems analyst and Nana privately wondered if he could ever settle down with an aspiring Opera singer. He seemed more suited to a comfortable semi in Carshalton with Nellie doing a little teaching at the local music school, or worse giving private lessons to fit in with the household arrangements.

Nellie had been named after Nellie Melba – it was almost her destiny to become a singer.

She had been adopted as a baby, but her parents had tragically drowned in a boating accident when she was very small. Nellie had never been sure quite why she lived with Nana. She wasn't even sure they were actually related.

Nana was musical and had lived a rather colourful life, according to the stories that had entertained Nellie as a child.

When the letter arrived Nana was overjoyed.

'You don't have to worry about me dear. I'll be fine. At sixty-two I'm not entirely ga ga yet – in fact I'll come with you – I can be your dresser!'

Nellie read and re-read the letter. There was no Pavarotti or Placido, but José Carreras was on the bill and an international cast of alarmingly well-known singers. Nellie was excited and very nervous.

A month in Italy would be fantastic – and well paid.

'It will look so good on my CV to have sung with such famous people. I will mainly be in the chorus, but I will be expected to give a concert performance of two supporting roles and understudy a well known soprano.'

Justin tried his best, but was only half-pleased for her. 'A whole month! And no guarantees it'll lead anywhere.'

'There are never any guarantees in theatre – you are only as good as your last performance or as employable,' she added. 'It's tricky. Do I give up my fairly well paid arrangements on one roll of the dice?'

For Nana there was no question.

'You must go – or you will regret it all of your life. It will be years of what ifs. You're freelance anyway and on short-term contracts. You can sort all that out.'

For Justin it was a threatening black cloud looming on his horizon. He also felt himself to be in a tricky position. If he said, 'Fine, Good Luck darling,' he could lose her, as she might swan off to major success. And if he said he didn't really want her to follow a singing career he would still lose her.

Nellie bit the bullet. 'You don't really want me to be an Opera singer do you? '

'It's not really that – I just can't see where I would fit into your life.'

'Why don't you come with me?' Nellie said impulsively, but in her heart she knew the answer.

'I can't take a month off. And besides, what would I do? You'd be rehearsing all day and performing at night.'

'Yes, it's tricky, but I suppose some people do manage – athletes for instance.' Nellie chewed her lip. 'But I suppose it's mainly the women who keep the home fires burning and wait for their men to return, legions of them, but I'm sure we can work something out.'

Nellie decided she was going.

Justin decided he would be kind and compassionate and let his wild bird out of her cage. Soon after, he accepted an interesting job offer in the government of Patagonia.

After a couple of years he returned.

It was coming down on the escalator that he first saw her picture. Nell Mckintyre starring in the critically acclaimed new musical by Andrew Lloyd Webber. He read the blurb in the advert in his newspaper.

> *Lloyd Webber has finally delivered his promise of*
> *being a superb classical composer in his new musical*
> *'Suffrage' a powerful and hugely imaginative opera.*
> *His new leading lady astonishes and amazes in the*
> *demanding role of Jenny a factory worker from Leeds.*

Nell's face seemed to be everywhere: on the *One Show*, on *Breakfast*, *Good Morning Britain* and so many interviews.

Eventually Justin booked himself a ticket to see the show and during the day he left a letter at the stage door. *Could he come back stage and see her?* He left his mobile number.

Yes, of course, she would be pleased to see him.

Justin didn't know what to expect as he looked up at the enormous picture of Nellie outside the theatre. Her performance had left him speechless: it was truly impressive in the range of her singing and the emotional depth she brought to the role.

With some trepidation he went backstage where he was met by a gopher and taken to her dressing room. It was the flurry of activity and the smell that he first noticed, musty, dusty, with a curiously pungent perfume. He knocked politely.

'Come in.'

Nellie was in a kind of dressing gown with her long hair neatly brushed. She looked much the same as when they had been together – fresh and young, as if she'd just got out of the bath.

They greeted each other warmly.

'It was fantastic that you could come,' she enthused.

They chatted and caught up on each other's news.

'A few of us are going to have supper at the Ivy – why don't you come with us?'

Justin felt the same familiar uncertainty – almost fear, tightening in his chest.

'No, no, I won't know anyone – I wouldn't know what to talk about.' He said his goodbyes and promises were made to keep in touch and they kissed each other several times.

* * * * *

Once outside in the street, the cool dark night revived him. He walked confidently towards Charing Cross road.

Justin was comfortable, the bright streetlights asking nothing of him. He was back on familiar territory.

He knew now that not placing any obstacles in Nellie's way and letting her go had been no sacrifice and had nothing to do with being a kind, compassionate man.

It was because he was a coward, who feared the unknown, the strange, the unfamiliar, the need to innovate and to live life with verve and imagination.

Talking to Tomatoes

'So you were talking to tomatoes?'

'Yes,' said George.

'And I suppose after you had given them the benefit of your opinions you moved on to the cabbages?'

'Yes,' said George.

'And after that you had a chat with the bananas?'

George looked at the supply teacher with contempt. 'Of course not, bananas don't talk!' He hesitated then continued, 'They do sing sometimes.'

'But this wasn't one of those times?' the teacher prompted George.

George was having none of it. '...It might have been.'

'Well did they, or didn't they?' the young teacher unwisely pushed the point.

'Bananas are very private, they don't like people talking about their business,' George said virtuously.

Having taken the moral high ground George decided the conversation was at an end and turned round to go back to his place.

The teacher returned to the board and, with chalk squealing with every stroke, he wrote *Midsummer Night's Dream*.

He turned to the class. 'This term, while I'm taking you, we will be looking at the characters and plot of this play.'

George put up his hand. 'Are there any tomatoes in it?' he asked.

'George – enough! We've finished with the subject of tomatoes. Let's concentrate on our work and get down to something sensible.'

Lorna put her hand up. 'Are there any bananas?'

The teacher was becoming impatient by now. He could see that his carefully prepared lesson was threatening to get out of hand. He tapped the desk with his pen. 'There are NO tomatoes or vegetables or bananas in Shakespeare's plays,' he said with an air of finality.

A slight sigh of disappointment rippled through the class. Boredom settled on the faces of his charges like sleep.

'Now that's a lot better,' said the teacher. 'Now we can all settle down.'

He turned back to the board and began to write: Hermia, Helena, Lysander and Demetrius.

'Copy these names into your books so you remember them, then write: "THE LOVERS" beside them in capital letters.'

A frisson ran across the class.

'We can't talk about vegetables, but we can talk about sex!'

Several of those around Tyler sniggered at the word sex.

'How do we know they're lovers?' asked George.

The teacher ignored it, he had had enough of George. He turned again to the board. 'Write this down: "TITANIA Queen of the Fairies" and "OBERON King of the fairies".'

Giggling and sniggering broke out among more of his charges and ribald comments rose above the low level of muttering.

The teacher frowned. He knew somewhere down the line he had led them down the wrong avenue of enquiry. He picked up a large poster he had brought with him of Titania fondling Bottom wearing his ass's head.

'This is Titania with Bottom,' he said encouragingly.

Shrieks of laughter swept across the room.

'Wow! So the Queen of the fairies is having it off with a donkey!'

The class could not believe its ears.

'Who's the King of the fairies shagging?'

The teacher thundered his fist on the desk. 'You are not taking this seriously,' he said sternly.

'Oh yes we are sir, we're taking this very seriously,' said Darren the loudest voice in the class.

'Who's the little green fella with no clothes and pointy ears?'

'That's Puck,' he explained.

The class exploded. 'Come again sir? I didn't quite catch that…'

Hoots and whoops nearly brought the ceiling down.

'We are taking this very seriously sir, I promise you.' Darren leered at Joanne who tossed a large amount of auburn hair in his face as she turned her back on him.

'And who's Puck when he's at home?' Ade was now conducting the class and he lingered on the first sound that just fell between an F and a P.

'He's one of the fairy kingdom who works for Oberon,' the teacher valiantly pressed on.

'We know what kind of work he does, don't we – nudge, nudge, wink, wink.'

By now the teacher knew he was a drowned man. 'Let's start again,' he said. 'Perhaps we'll read a little scene.'

'Yeah – can't wait!' A forest of hands waved at him.

'Who would like to read one of the Rude Mechanicals?'

Chants of 'Rude Boys, Rude Boys' ballooned around the room. Chaos reigned supreme. George left his seat and went up to the teacher's desk looking martyred.

'When I talk to tomatoes it's about manure and stuff – not this filf! And my bananas sing "What a Wonderful World"!'

The school bell shrilled – the sound of release and freedom. The class pushed and shoved their way out like cattle avoiding slaughter.

The young teacher sat at his desk, his eyes round and dry. 'George, can I join you and talk to the tomatoes?' he asked.

George looked doubtful. 'You have to believe,' he said.

'Oh, I promise you, I believe.'

George looked superior and took the teacher's hand. 'Come on, we'll leave that lot to the fairies!'

TEACHING PRACTICE

'No, no, it's fine – I'll be there.' Trudy reassured the other members of staff.

This was to be a whole school outing and they were rousting up as many willing helpers as they could muster.

'When I say "whole school", that sounds like hundreds,' Trudy said to her fellow students back in the common room at her college. 'The whole school is only on one floor of one of those ghastly ancient Victorian buildings in Bow. All stone steps and bilious green lavatory tiles halfway up every wall. "Abandon hope all ye who enter here" should be in neon lights around the door. That's another thing: there's no proper door, no school entrance. It's a poky little hole in the wall that we all kind of scuttle through.'

The students commiserated with each other on the horrors of their first teaching practice. One friend being detailed to the Isle of Dogs and another in Poplar – which sounded even worse! Huge high walls with barbed wire along the top. Was it to keep the inmates in or to stop them getting out?!

The students pondered on the matter.

'Oh and it has no playground, only a roof area that has been deemed too dangerous to use now. Mind you, there are a few I could happily smile at and say – "that's fine dear – you can play on the roof. I know it's got no railings round it, but don't worry –

when you fall off you'll bounce on the concrete only five floors down, no problem".'

They all laughed at their own wickedness.

There was in truth not much to laugh at; the children they discovered were a whole different breed from any they had encountered in their lives. Literally from different races, but it was the indigenous London children that ran them ragged.

So many stories of the terrors of the classroom were exchanged. Trudy herself was constantly vigilant for a favourite game, which was to cut off large lumps of a teacher's hair – she had long fair hair.

Putting their chairs on the table when they had had enough of anything was another ploy; stealing was mandatory, as was just walking out and disappearing for ages.

And then there was Bilal, who had killed his father when he was four defending his mother from a frenzied attack. Bilal was a law unto himself. Trips to the swimming baths usually resulted in him tying himself to the leg of the seats in the bus and help being sought from the burly caretaker to get him off the bus.

Treading a wary line between firmness and friendliness was a difficult skill to acquire, Trudy was discovering.

It was a typical half-nice, half-not English day in late May. The entire school was perhaps about 80 children all straggling along in an almost crocodile – sometimes a messy gaggle – as they were shepherded down to the underground station.

Trudy privately questioned the wisdom of taking them on the underground, but she was a lowly student and not in charge.

The platform, mercifully, was not crowded and Trudy found herself mainly dealing with the usual unruly elements hell-bent on throwing themselves onto the electric rails.

One particular child – even scruffier than the others was taking no notice of anyone.

Trudy grabbed his hand and said severely, 'You stay with me!'

He wriggled a bit, but the train was coming into the station and everyone's attention was taken up with making sure all the children were actually in the carriages and had not escaped.

'You sit next to me!' Trudy said fiercely to her miscreant, who said nothing and did as he was bid.

The train rattled and rolled along the tunnels and smiles and chatter broke out among the kids. They were happy to be out – anywhere – rather than school. They were fine and Trudy found them no problem as they piled off the train and trotted upstairs eventually spilling out at the Regent's Canal for their boat trip to London Zoo.

'Wicked Miss!' was the general consensus. Bob, Trudy's personal charge stayed with her obediently, but appeared to have no lunch, so Trudy gave him some money to buy what he liked at a kiosk by the snake house and they shared an ice cream, but could he keep the Toblerone for later? It was fine with Trudy and Bob seemed to be really enjoying himself – enraptured by Boa constrictors and Black Mambas.

'Could that snake eat you Miss?' He gave Trudy an old fashioned look.

She had no idea. 'We'll read the notice and then we'll know what to avoid.'

The afternoon went very quickly. The word went round it was time to gather them all up. Helpers counted heads and off they went, back to the underground and back to school. It had been a good day out all the staff agreed.

* * * * *

Outside the school's formidable high walls, Trudy turned to Bob. 'Is your Mum or your Dad or someone coming for you?'

He looked at her a bit blankly. 'No,' he finally managed, 'I don't go to this school.'

Trudy felt as if she had been hit on the head by a rock.

'You don't go to this school???' *My God*, she thought, *I've kidnapped a child!*

'But you must live round here,' she said desperately.

'No, Miss.'

'Where do you live?'

'I live in Clapham.'

It was miles away – south of the river.

Panic gripped Trudy. His mother might have called the police already. 'Umm…wait a minute, I'll take you home – do you know your address?'

'Yes Miss.'

So Trudy made hasty farewells to the staff and scooted herself and Bob back to the underground.

Bob became quite conversational. 'Love the underground – all those lines going all over the place underneath the pavement and the tunnels sing you know? They all have their own song. Listen! And they smell special.'

Trudy listened.

'Do you want a sandwich?' she asked him and they matily munched squashed tomato sandwiches together.

'You're not a teacher are you Miss?'

'No not yet.' And never likely to be, Trudy thought, if I get arrested for child abduction.

'I like you,' Bob said.

'I'm not very good in the classroom,' Trudy confessed.

'Don't worry Miss, you'll get the 'ang of it.' He was kindly and consoling.

After a long hike down a long dreary concrete road, Bob pointed to a forbidding looking set of filthy stone steps, crumbling brickwork and peeling paintwork.

'I live there,' Bob said.

Trudy braced herself for a grovelling apology to an irate or heartbroken mother.

There was no knocker, so she rapped with her knuckles on the door.

It seemed an age, but eventually she heard shuffling footsteps coming to the door.

It opened a fraction and a hand like a shovel grabbed Bob, by his collar.

'Get in you little git!'

And Bob disappeared into the cavernous hall as the door was slammed firmly shut in Trudy's face.

THE INTRUDER

The entire building was quiet. The offices on the top floor, the warehouse, the canteen were silent. Everyone had gone home.

Andreas Stastiades sat quietly in his office poring over some reports that he needed to present to the board the next day. A slight sound made him look up from what he was doing. He looked around, there was nothing. He looked out of the window. He could see only his own car. The factory building opposite still had lights on, but that was quite usual when there was a rush on.

He went back to what he was doing, maybe someone from the factory had brought a package over to the warehouse?

Andreas immersed himself in the report again.

Suddenly he felt a ferocious blow to the back of his head and knew nothing more.

The hospital was quiet and dimly lit when Andreas very slowly and groggily regained consciousness. Everything around him was blurry and far, far away.

I must be dead, was his first thought.

After a while a nurse came in. 'Mr Stastiades, Mr Stastiades, how are you? Time to wake up'.

He 'ummed' slightly for a while, his head hurt.

'Do you have any pain?' the nurse continued to try to coax him into wakefulness.

'Ummm...' Andreas nodded very slightly and the nurse manipulated the many drips and drains and tubes, to which he seemed to be attached.

Andreas drifted off again into a deep sleep.

'Well he's come out of the coma my dear, but he has had a nasty head wound and immediate surgery was necessary. We are keeping him very quiet for a while. You can see him through the window of the intensive care unit, but you won't be able to speak to him for a day or so. We are taking every care of him. Now don't worry my dear, you go home and get a good night's sleep. Phone in the morning and we will let you know when you can come and visit.'

Andreas' daughter was distraught. Her boyfriend comforted her as much as he could, but he really did not know what to say or do.

All Melina could say was, 'Why??Why??'

It had been getting late, there had been no call from Andreas so Melina had driven to his office and found him slumped over his desk with blood everywhere. She was still in shock.

Apparently nothing had been stolen, nothing had been touched, the computer still as Andreas had left it. No one could work out why the hard-working, unassuming, middle-aged man had been attacked. It was a mystery.

The police were mildly interested, but as they had found no one to question about the incident and no one could give them any information to follow up, they let the incident drop into the unsolved basket as soon as they could. They had concluded it had been a random intruder. The family could shed no light on the incident and everyone at the 'Amazing Shirt Company' were equally bemused.

* * * * *

Time passed and Andreas recovered very well. He was delighted when he could finally go home to his wife and children. They made an enormous fuss of him – even though they had been instructed to keep him calm and quiet for as long as possible.

The police questioned Andreas about what he remembered and all he could tell them was that he briefly saw a shadow on the frosted glass door of his office. Investigation revealed that it was probably his own shadow he had seen in the gathering evening light of dusk. It was a time when he was not usually at the office and did not know how the light changed the appearance of many things in the evening.

The company were sympathetic and insisted Andreas, a long standing employee, should take as much time off work as he needed to get properly well.

The family were keen for him to put in a complaint to the victim support agency and make a claim for criminal injury.

The immediate family were too concerned with Andreas to fully grasp that the police questioning of the staff was casting more and more suspicion on Andreas himself.

Why was there no physical evidence in the office? Why had no weapon been found? Why was nothing taken? They were coming more and more to the conclusion that Mr Stastiades was colluding with A-N-other in some scam to do with the running of the company.

The criminal injury section were of course holding fire on any claim that might not be valid as they had been instructed that Mr Stastiades might himself be implicated.

Any inquiry had reached a distressing and uncomfortable impasse.

* * * * *

Andreas' brother was incensed that Andreas should be implicated in a non-existent crime of which his brother was the victim.

He contacted the Victim Support Unit, who said there was little they could do, but on the Q.T. one of the officers recommended a particular private detective they had used very successfully before, who would be prepared to put in the hours and do some real digging.

The officer said a little wearily, 'An anonymous middle-aged man being hit on the head is not a top priority – if it had been a terrorist attack or if he'd died and it had been a murder case – it would be higher up the list.'

Georgio, Andreas' brother had made no bones about the cost. 'I am a very wealthy man I can afford the best.'

He was given an address and a telephone number that looked very unlikely in a suburban area that he knew was the bungalow belt of London. He had expected a seedy Soho office surrounded by bedsits where prostitutes plied their trade. Instead, he parked outside a neat and very well kept large front garden, with gnomes fishing in a silver pond.

It turned out to indeed be a bungalow. He looked for a bell, there was none, so he took hold of the curious looking heavy dragon that turned out to be the knocker. He knocked quite loudly.

A young man opened the door. 'Come in we've been expecting you – Mum is in the annexe. This way.'

Georgio was welcomed into a very neat and tidy office by a lady of uncertain years with a head of uncontrollable grey curly hair, wearing a rather stylish tweed trouser suit.

'Good morning Mr Stastiades, I am Mavis Davis.' The woman put out her hand and Georgio shook it firmly.

'I have many of the details of this case already. I have been in touch with the police who were called on the day of the attack. You're looking at me doubtfully, Mr Stastiades. Did the officer not give you an outline of my credentials?'

'No,' Georgio said feeling a bit remiss that he had not asked for any references.

'I am an early-retired CID officer with MI5 experience. My husband needed me in his last days, so I was offered early retirement.'

She was crisp and to the point which Georgio liked and that gave him confidence.

'Right, let's get started.'

The afternoon passed very quickly as Georgio outlined all his concerns to Mavis, who took copious notes and said very little, wanting to hear exactly what Georgio had to say.

'Well I can see immediately some glaring errors in the handling of this case. It's the usual – not important enough to pursue. What they perceive as apparently no evidence of any kind shrieks to me that something is definitely wrong, and it needs thorough investigation. No physical evidence or forensics? I doubt that. What did they say was the likely weapon your brother was attacked with?'

'They didn't say.'

'Exactly, it is not mentioned in any report. It is vital evidence. My first visit will be to the hospital to find out what they can tell me about the injury your brother had sustained when he was first brought into A&E. That can tell us a great deal. Also, it may be necessary for your brother to be examined by a forensic doctor. '

Georgio felt a sense of relief at last that someone was taking the incident seriously.

'I will also need to investigate the nature of your brother's work and the company's history and present status. As well, of course, as looking at the office and whole building where the attack took place, also the surrounding buildings and factory opposite and talk to members of staff. The idea that there was no evidence to follow up is quite ludicrous. A proper investigation will give you a great deal of important information.'

Mavis indicated that she had enough to work on at the moment and was eager to get started. She stood up and Georgio followed her lead and they shook hands again very enthusiastically.

'I will keep in close touch with you, Mr Stastiades and keep you informed of every development in the case.'

Georgio drove straight to his brother's house.

The family were relieved to hear what had transpired and Andreas himself perked up. He'd been getting depressed by the implication that somehow he was involved in his attack.

And because he could remember so little, he had no way of defending himself. It was like being attacked all over again.

A few days went by and Mavis phoned and asked to interview Andreas.

He and Mavis spent a long time together as he gave her as much information as he could about the report he had been preparing to present to the board.

Mavis had discovered that the current 'Amazing Shirt Company' was not the original. A few years previously it had been in financial difficulties and had accepted a merger with a Serbian company in order not to have to cut the work force, but they had retained the well-known name 'The Amazing Shirt Company' which had become a big brand name.

Over the years, things had changed. The shirts were no longer produced at the factory. The material and the basic cut of the shirts was produced in China and shipped over to the U.K. where the finishing took place and the unique motifs that had made the design so successful in the beginning were added. It was simply more economic for the company to operate this way. It was the start of other initiatives that involved materials being delivered by container lorry to a ground floor bay of the office building that had become a depot.

The report that Andreas was going to present had outlined that the company had been hard hit by the latest recession and would have to consider some kind of diversifying or downsizing. Mavis spent a lot of time organising a chart of the operations of the company. She felt that somehow the present status of the finances and the varied nature of the trading partners they had acquired was in some way connected to the attack.

She and Georgio, who was also a businessman, could see this was an avenue worth investigating. The implication of Andreas' report was that cut backs and redundancies might have to be considered. Maybe the attack was a bungled attempt to interfere with this situation?

Mavis requested a visit to the company to look at the building and talk to some employees. The company agreed very quickly as they were tired of this unsolved mystery hanging over their heads. It was not good publicity or good P.R.

'By all means feel free to poke around and speak to anyone you like,' the General Manager had told her.

Mavis pinned on her visitor's badge and looked at the list of people she wanted to speak to. She had been provided with a guide that she considered a bit of an impediment and also was not happy that this young man might report back any conversation to the management. She wanted the interviews to be free and frank.

'Let's start with the office where Mr Stastiades works.'

Mavis's eyes were like TV scanners – she missed nothing. She also took several photos.

There was a cupboard in one corner she was particularly interested in. Had the police considered that someone could hide in there? She made a note in large letters. She began to move boxes and files and sundry office equipment and tap on the back of the cupboard. Some of the shelves were very dusty – it was obviously a cupboard not used very often.

Then she noticed a couple of very small handprints – she asked her guide if she could see his hands and she looked at her own. No, it was not a small adult, it was definitely a couple of handprints of a child, probably under twelve.

'Have any children visited Mr Stastiades? Or have any one else's children been in here?'

'It is highly unlikely – Andry has no grandchildren and...' he looked around the drab office. 'Why would anyone want to bring a child in here and let them look in a boring cupboard? Doesn't make any sense...'

'Exactly. It makes no sense. Hitting "Andry" as you call him over the head also made no sense. Maybe we're getting somewhere.'

The guide looked puzzled. How could they be getting anywhere when nothing made sense?

Mavis took a lot of photos and poked around in the cupboard again. She also knocked on walls with the heel of her shoe. She made a note of the differing sounds and looked questioningly at her guide.

'How much do you know about this building?'

'Nothing really, except it's old, cold and has been knocked about a bit.'

'Is it possible to speak to any one who would know how the building was say ten to twenty years ago? Is there anyone on the staff who has worked here that long or maybe a retired employee? Or maybe I could look at some old architects plans of the building when it was built?'

'Well, there's a pretty old bloke in Import and Export – he might be able to help you.'

'Well lay on Macduff.'

'My names Duncan, not Macduff.'

'How very appropriate!' Mavis laughed and the young man looked at her oddly.

This woman is weird, Duncan thought.

Up several flights of stairs they found Mr Biggins who had worked for the company since the flood, as he told her, and was a very busy man.

'Always a problem – bills of lading go astray, invoices not paid on time, drivers going missing. Always been a mess since we hooked up with the Serbs. Paperwork has gone through the roof.'

Mavis was interested and listened carefully. 'How many countries supply 'Amazing'?'

'Bloody dozens, or at least it seems like that. We have to cope with all the different tariffs all the different tax situations – all the rules and regs of the E.U.'

'So it's mainly the E.U. countries now, not China any more?'

'That's right our biggest suppliers are the Czech Republic and Romania and they're all little back street factories who pay their workers tuppence-ha'penny! And then there are drivers!!!' Mr

Biggins threw up his hands. 'Spare me, half of them can't speak English and often get themselves into a right pickle.'

'Doesn't 'Amazing' use its own U.K. carriers?'

'Most of the time, but things get more complicated each year and more and more is farmed out to tender – like changing the suppliers – it's all about cost cutting, my dear lady.'

Mavis chose to ignore the slight put down. *His generation!* she said to herself and changed the subject. 'I am investigating the attack on Mr Stastiades.'

'Oh poor sod – that's what comes of being a bit deaf. Poor sod didn't hear anyone coming and couldn't duck.'

'Yes, I see from the hospital report that they found him a little deaf too.'

'I was going to ask you if you knew anything about how the building was before they knocked walls down and built others. Would there be such a thing as a plan of the original building?'

Mr Biggins thought long and hard: it was a peculiar question. 'Umm…there's some pictures in Holy Joe's office of the beginning of the company. He's very proud of them – he thinks it gives us "the dignity of longevity" to impress our customers. Hmm…' he sniffed cynically. 'I think there may also be a floor plan too, I vaguely remember.'

'Who is Holy Joe?'

'It's just a nickname for the Managing Director,' Mavis's young guide muttered.

'Well thank you Mr Biggins you have been extremely helpful and given me a lot to think about.'

'Have I? Oh well then…'

The phone rang. 'Yes? What is it now?' He listened for a few seconds. 'See? Just what I told you – one of the drivers, from who knows where, stopped at Dover,' he said to Mavis before returning to his phone. Mavis and her guide moved toward the door.

Mavis could still hear one side of the conversation.

'What's happened? Oh the usual, something in the back that Border Control are suspicious of...happens all the time.'

Mavis wanted to stay and hear exactly what the problem was, but she was ushered out of the office quickly by her guide.

'Where now?' her guide asked.

'Well I think it will be the General Manager's office to look at the photos and then I want to visit the basement.

'The basement! Oh, ooh – confront old Doddsie in his lair? The young man made hanging gestures with his tie.

'As bad as that!?' Mavis pursed her lips and nodded slightly.

'We may be calling the police to help us out.'

'We may indeed Duncan. That is a strong possibility.'

Duncan looked excited. 'Do you think you've cracked it?'

'Not yet, but I certainly have enough information to warrant another more thorough investigation by CID. Come on let's press on. By the way, I want to know if Mr Biggins has any more information about the driver held at Border Control.'

Duncan found the door to the basement and led Mavis down – he seemed rather nervous.

'What you doin' darn 'ere? No staff 'llowed in the basement – "Elf and safety!"' a very loud boorish voice shouted from below.

'Mrs Davis would like a look...' Duncan started.

Charlie Dodds drew himself and his overgrown belly up to its full height. 'And who's she when she's at 'ome? You ain't allowed darn 'ere,' he repeated.

'We have the permission of the Managing director Mr Dodds.' Mavis held up her phone. 'Would you like me to call him to verify what I have said? He will come himself if necessary; this is an inquiry into the attack on Mr Stastiades.'

Charlie Dodds continued to splutter. 'You ain't 'llowed darn 'ere.' He was obviously rattled.

Mavis and Duncan continued exploring the nooks, crannies and corners of the basement, even more deeply than before. They crawled behind the boilers, cobwebs clinging to their hair and clothes.

'Look, someone has been living down here!' Duncan turned to Mavis, who picked up a very small dirty red anorak and pointed to the makeshift bedding and what had once been a slice of pizza.

'Look how small everything is...' Alarm filled Mavis' whole body.

She picked up her phone and rang for the Security officer. 'There's no signal down here, Duncan!' she screamed, just as Charlie Dodds lunged towards her with a huge shovel, his great belly almost smothering her.

'Bitch! Bitch! Whore!'

Duncan, being the leading light of any Rugby team he had ever played for, launched himself at Dodds' ankles and up-ended him, heavily and painfully from behind. Unceremoniously he rammed him into the small space behind the boiler.

'I can't hold him for too long...There's an alarm over there Mavis...Quick! Press it and all hell will break loose!'

And it certainly did. Security guards came running from several directions and a very loud siren went off all over the 'Amazing' complex.

'Police...quickly...' Mavis puffed.

'The police will come anyway as that alarm is connected to the police station.'

When the police arrived in force and in body armour and helmets they were slightly disappointed to find that there was no armed raid in progress.

Mavis almost dragged the officer in charge to Mr Biggins' office – Mr Biggins having not left the building like the rest of the staff.

'Mr Biggins, phone Border Control and have them keep that driver in custody until the police arrive!'

She handed the phone to the officer. 'Tell them who you are and say you are the police.'

The policeman did as he was bid. Then he turned to Mavis. 'I don't understand what's going on.'

'I suspect that there are drivers who are people smugglers or worse – running an international Paedophile ring.'

Mr Biggins was just as anxious to speak to the police as Mavis.

'I was just coming down to tell you that the Border Control had taken the driver into custody, a small child had evidently crawled out of a packing case when the officers opened the back of the lorry to inspect the contents, having heard crying and shouting from inside. Unfortunately, the child was terrified, ran away and is now lost.'

'What a day!'

Georgio and Andreas had come to the police station, when Charlie Dodds was being interrogated.

Charlie's bravado collapsed quite quickly as soon as he realised that he was in big trouble and he spilled many, many beans indeed. He tried to say it was one of the children who had panicked and hit Andreas over the head.

Until the police reminded him that no other fingerprints were on the shovel and that the child would have had to be a budding Atlas to even to be able lift it up!

They were still puzzled by how Charlie and a small child got unnoticed into Andreas' office.

Mavis was called and she laid out all her documents, charts of driver's schedules, pictures of the building, reports in local papers and many other pieces of apparently indiscriminate nature.

'If the officers in the original investigation had looked more closely at the cupboard in Mr Stastiades office, they would have discovered that the cupboard had a false back and a door that led to a tiny forgotten corridor and hidden steps down to the basement. I found that out from the original plans of the building before it was renovated. I suspect the children were held there until their captors decided to whom and when the children would be sold and then they would be taken out of the basement at night.

'In the corridor outside Andreas's office was a little-used fire door only a few steps from his glass door. It took a matter of seconds to come out of the hidden door in the cupboard and reach the fire door. The usual health and safety rules and regs meant that it had to be left open. At night, security guards patrolled the building, but it was a simple matter to evade their regular timetable. That particular fire door is in a tiny corner of the building and never used – not even in fire drills.'

The inspector was impressed by Mavis' contribution to solving the case, but nonetheless the credit for the ultimate 'collar' was Thames Valley Police. He was a fair man and realised that Mavis might come in useful another time, so he made an appointment to see her the following week.

He asked Mavis to come into his office.

'I thought you might like to know we contacted Interpol and the children were almost all orphans, abducted from squalid children's homes in Romania and Albania. They were drugged to keep them quiet for the whole journey, but some died as the journey could be longer than intended. It was a lucky stroke that the child who got away must have had a weaker dose than the others. Being in a loose packing case, they could breathe okay, but Erdognan took his chance and ran. The local police picked him up in a Travellers camp. Men had been waiting outside the port to take the children away. So we had a good haul: the smugglers, the drivers and the gangs that farmed them out or sold them. You have been incredibly helpful. I would like to say "Thank you".'

'That's kind of you,' Mavis said graciously, 'but if your officers had looked more closely at the first incident, this case could have been closed months ago.'

'Yes, I do agree, but you know how it is, cuts, cuts, cuts...' The Chief Inspector looked weary and downtrodden.

'Same story everywhere,' Mavis said as she was being congratulated by the Andreas family and treated like a beloved family member.

'No cuts here!' Georgio wheeled in the biggest cake Mavis had ever seen.

'Wow! Big enough for me to jump out of!'

'This family is forever in your debt and we will never forget how hard you have worked for us. You have friends for life here Mavis.'

'Also, I will take a lot more notice of who works in the basement and not have my nose so close to the computer all the time!' Andreas added.

'Well, my job is not over yet. Now I must find the children, and I hope you, Georgio, will help me – it could take a while.'

THE QUEEN

In response to being asked to 'invent a legend'

If you look at a set of chess pieces you will find that the characters are all men except one: the queen – a white queen and a black queen.

The exact origins of the game are obscure. Several countries have claimed the invention of chess, but India seems to be the strongest claimant.

For many centuries the game had no female characters but during the Renaissance a queen was introduced. The Renaissance, as we know, was a time when the yokes and shackles of the middle ages were thrown off. A time of exploration and scientific advance. There was a huge resurgence of interest in antiquity. Its history, science, art, architecture and much more were rescued from obscurity and a great number of innovations and inventions were created. The movement was unstoppable and the entire history of Europe and later the world was changed forever.

At that time, in Italy, the queen was introduced into the game of chess. Her identity and origins are of course open to question and she has been attributed to many famous figures of antiquity – the Queen of Sheba, the Virgin Mary, Cleopatra, Aphrodite.

The queen is a very powerful piece in the game of chess, as she can move anywhere on the board and in any direction. Which gave rise to the belief she had supernatural powers.

In some parts of the world she came to be known as Queen Lachryma – the Queen of Sorrows or the Queen of Tears.

To this day, Queen Lachryma is revered and remembered in many small villages and towns across Syria, Jordan and as far away as Armenia, the Crimea and Georgia. Flowers can be seen placed beside beautifully decorated ewers of holy water and statues in out of the way places.

It is said Queen Lachryma lived around the time of the fall of the Roman Empire. A time of chaos and uncertainty when many invasions took place and small principalities came into being. Her name is linked to the Empire of Trebizond. The legend says she was famed for her beauty and when her land was invaded she was captured by the self-styled Emperor of Trebizond and forced into marriage. A marriage she resisted with all her strength and courage.

Queen Lachryma was also clever and managed to acquire a powerful hold over the Emperor. In those years she freed hundreds of slaves from many countries and sent them back to their homelands. She became much loved by the people, including those of Trebizond and beyond, but it was not to last.

Once more the regions around her were at war. Trebizond was taken and because of her reputation, Lachryma was imprisoned, tortured, then sent to the capital of Anatolia where she was beheaded by the Mamluks.

Her legend centred around the river Etalita which had not existed in her lifetime. Country people mourned her death and told the story of water gushing from a cleft in the rock and pouring down hillsides of the Ai Petri Mountains in the Crimea at the very moment the Scimitar severed her head from her shoulders. This water became the river Etalita that flowed into the Black Sea. Local people attributed healing properties to the spring and called it the tears of Lachryma. From then on she was known as the Queen of Sorrows – the Queen of Tears.

In later centuries the Genoese and the Venetians controlled several trading ports along the coast of the Black Sea. The story of Lachryma was well established by then and hills and valleys around the river were named after her.

In her lifetime she had become associated with the colour purple, which she had worn as a symbol of respect for the gods of Spring and to remember the re-awakening of the dead in the next world.

It is believed that the stories of Lachryma were taken by traders to Italy during the Renaissance and the appearance of the Queen on the chessboard was linked to her legend – a power behind the throne.

In February 1945 in Yalta, a well-known Black Sea port, the Conference of Yalta took place.

President Roosevelt, Churchill and Stalin met to try to come to an agreement on what would be the new world order. Agreements were made – and as we know – broken.

The world leaders arrived the night before the conference at the Livadia Palace with its splendid Florentine tower and Italian courtyard. A place once much loved by the Russian aristocracy.

A meal, as splendid as it could be in those times, had been provided. The three men enjoyed the style and comparative opulence of the dinner. After years of austerity, that had left no one untouched, it was a pleasure. At the end of the meal Churchill was happy to retire to a comfortable drawing room to smoke his customary cigars and enjoy several brandies. Roosevelt was not a well man and he opted to go to his room and relax. Churchill and Stalin had little in common socially, so Churchill suggested a game of chess to lighten the atmosphere.

Stalin had only a rudimentary understanding of the intricacies of the game and approached it rather as a bull at a gate, so Churchill won easily.

As he knocked down his Queen on the board, he laughed in his familiar slightly barking style and said, 'Mr Stalin, you must remember the Queen is a powerful force in this game, she can move in any direction. She is like democracy fluid and flexible – the will of the people may change and democracy can move with them – embrace change and justice. That which cannot bend must break. I try to remember it is not always force that wins the game.'

'You are drunk Mr Churchill,' Stalin said, waving away the wreaths of smoke enveloping him from Churchill's cigar.

'We are both drunk Joseph, me on Brandy you on Vodka – but I hope we can both make very sober decisions in the morning.'

In his room Churchill smiled to himself as he spoke to his batman.

'I never like to repeat myself, but I wanted to say that I will be sober in the morning Mr Stalin, but your regime will still be very ugly indeed.'

Outside the window there seemed to be a commotion in the town.

'Are they celebrating our arrival?' Churchill enquired.

His batman looked out of the window.

'Not exactly. There is a huge crowd in national costume and carrying purple banners, torches and burning brands – the whole mountain range seems to be alight.'

'Like the blitz? Oh well, as long as I can sleep through it,' said Churchill and he heaved himself into bed.

The following morning in the breakfast room there was news. The whole of the local population had been out that night following the return of the water to the dried up riverbed of the Etalita river. Overnight it had become a torrent flowing into the sea.

'Were they celebrating?' Roosevelt inquired.

'No sir, they were mourning. For according to legend the river is the tears of Queen Lachryma, the Queen of Sorrows. They are mourning for what has passed and for what is to come.'

Churchill nodded slightly. Saying nothing, he just looked over his glasses at Roosevelt.

THE RIVER

Part I

It had been a while since Connie had travelled on this train.

When she was at Art College she had come into central London every day. She remembered the race along the platform to get a seat on the way home, where she collapsed and often fell asleep until she came to the end of the line. They had been busy days when life happened at break-neck speed.

She had managed to get a seat by the window and, as the train neared Liverpool Street, it slowed enough for Connie to look more carefully at the little streets and old Victorian houses tucked between the Sixties tower blocks. Some old pubs were still standing. Imposing architecture in their hey day, now overshadowed by the sharp cornered blocks of flats. The small stations still looked uncared for – dirty, dark and shabby. The underpasses and bridges appeared slightly menacing.

Connie made her way up the stairs to the station gallery where there were shops, cafes and small restaurants. She bought herself a coffee and sat in the window where she could be seen and waited. Simon had said he would meet her at ten.

She could see the big clock – it seemed to taunt her. Good timekeeping was evidently not one of his strong points. She went to Smiths next door and bought a paper.

He's not coming, Connie decided eventually.

Connie paid for her drinks and made her way out of the station into the familiar streets of the City of London. They were due to go to a photographic exhibition in the old County Hall on the South Bank. It was a bit of a walk, but the weather was nice and she enjoyed being on the City streets again. She walked towards St. Paul's. The road beside the Cathedral seemed huge and filled with heavy traffic. Even finding the right traffic lights to cross the maze of roads was a herculean task. It was a relief when she finally reached the pedestrianised area and the tranquillity of the steps leading down to the river.

Before Connie walked across the Millennium Bridge to Tate Modern, she stood on the parapet of one of the office buildings and leaned against the thick wall looking along the riverside to Tower Bridge, the Tower of London and the art gallery opposite. Connie felt a feeling of sudden relaxation to be completely outside what had become her life.

She watched the pleasure boats, the barges, the river patrol boats. She thought of the incredible history of the river. Her attention was caught by the movement of the water as it fluttered against the side of boats and the shoreline and concrete walls. Its whisper lost in the slight breeze of the pleasant day. She was reluctant to move away.

The river just keeps going, she thought. My life used to be like that, now my river has dried up.

* * * * *

Connie had no idea what to expect, or where to go when she arrived at County Hall.

She had not been bothered that Simon had not turned up as she had privately decided that her visit would be short. Perhaps Simon had felt the same.

She knew he had the same mixed feelings about the exhibition as herself.

Connie had even left behind her invitation to the private showing – almost hoping they would not let her in. As she came closer to the entrance, she could see the huge banners advertising the event, similar to those on the underground stations. It was a much bigger affair than she had imagined. Her heart sank.

No wonder Simon didn't turn up, Connie thought.

She tried to shuffle unnoticed into the large entrance hall, but someone came up by the side of her. 'Ah, Mrs Burton, very nice to see you and happy you could come.'

Connie straightened up. 'I wasn't sure where to go,' she murmured.

'That's fine, we're here to see you're okay'

'Thanks, yeah, I'm fine,' she lied valiantly.

'Simon Hunt is here – he said he missed you at the station.'

Connie smiled slightly. 'It is a bigger affair than I imagined.' she looked around.

All she could see were walls filled with blown up photographs – some she recognised – but many were new to her. The name Todd Burton and his life history filled a large area of one wall.

'I wonder what Toddy would have thought of all this?' she mused.

Simon spoke behind her. 'He would have loved it for a while…then he would have been off on some new adventure. You knew him better than anyone.'

Together they walked slowly around the rooms packed with photographs.

Connie found herself looking intently at many of them seeing so much more in them than she ever had.

'He was a real artist Simon,' she said after a long silence.

'He didn't just take pictures – every one is a split second caught forever and filled with so much insight and imagination…and a kind of prophesy, I suppose. They remind me of the paintings of what they call the Old Masters, especially those Venetian ones crowded with people. They tell a story, they ask questions? Some have a kind of mystery about them.'

Connie stopped and leaned against a table.

'You know Simon,' Connie shoulders dropped for the first time in ages, 'I never really knew him. I think you knew him better than I did – you were there with him most of the time.'

'Ah…ah…I don't think so…I just toted along the sound equipment – there were no deep meaningful conversations. We more concerned about where the next meal came from or if we could get our stuff up to some ridiculous place to get a good shot! He could be a bloody nightmare.'

Connie nodded in agreement. 'I was more concerned with racing about pretending to be an artist and most of what I did was trash. Toddy used to say to me "Look. Look, then see. You're just pleasing teachers, tutors, critics, trends. You have to see for yourself. I never really knew what he meant.'

They continued in silence looking at the pictures, the videos and T.V. footage.

'I thought you wouldn't come.' Simon stopped in front of a montage of the accident. He put out his hand to keep her away. The violent images of a train crashing down a mountainside to the bottom of a ravine with other pictures of people injured, dying, screaming.

'I didn't want...this is why. Why? Why did they have to do this?' Connie waved her hands angrily and walked away from the terrifying images.

'I knew they would do this!!!'

'Come on Con, let's get out of this room.'

'Wasn't it enough to have it all over the TV for days? How much blood and gore do they think the public wants? It's become almost like watching Roman gladiators fight to the death in the arena!'

'You will say a few words Mrs Burton?' The organiser took her elbow and guided her to a private space where they were filming interviews.

'I don't think so – Toddy's pictures are quite brilliant, but they are to be looked at not talked about.'

'But what about your reaction to his death and the accident?'

Connie just looked at the organiser, her face beginning to set like concrete.

Simon intervened. 'She was thrilled!' he said sarcastically. 'We both were! That's all you're getting. Come on Con.'

Connie was looking murderous. 'This exhibition is about Toddy – my husband's work. It is not a parade ground for you to wring our grief out of us, spill our tears like blood for public entertainment! It was bad enough when it happened. That's it...no chance we're going to fall for that again. All over the TV News it was...'

Connie poked the organiser in the chest hard with her forefinger several times. He wriggled and winced uncomfortably.

'Not nice is it? Being a fish on a hook?!'

Simon took her arm and they headed for the huge door and the sanctuary of the river.

Part II

Connie took out a large file of newspaper cuttings.

'I am going to burn them,' she said to her mother, who said nothing.

It had been a dreary few weeks for all of them since the exhibition.

'It opened old wounds,' her Mum said in a private conversation with Stan, her soon-to-be-husband.

'I don't want to cramp your style Mum,' Connie had said. 'I'll move back into the house. I've been here too long anyway. It's about time I moved on.'

'There is no rush sweetie,' her Mum said more out of politeness than anything else.

Connie continued packing things in boxes.

'I've got some money now from the sale of Toddy's pictures and various other things, that were still in copyright. I never understood the finance side of his life, but my solicitor tells me that I will be fine for a long time. I knew he had an agent – like everyone who works for TV. I'll still stay on at the Library for now. Then, who knows?'

'Won't the house be too big for you? You were lucky to get it and it was fine when you were both needing space to work.' Her mother thought about it and looked regretful. 'It does have a lovely walled garden, though. But you'll be rattling around like a pea in a tin on your own! Why don't you sell it?'

Connie continued packing boxes and said nothing.

* * * * *

Simon had rung a few times, he was about to become a Dad. He'd blossomed and looked his happiest since the accident.

'Life goes on.' The counselling had done its job and he no longer felt responsible for having missed the train that he and Todd were booked on, to leave Peru.

'Have you ever thought of going back to that village?' he asked Connie.

'Well, when you and I went for the funeral with all the other people, I found it harrowing and swore it was a terrible place for me – I never wanted to see again.'

'Just a thought.'

Simon went on to talk about cots and buggies and how Eve was progressing.

'Happy to hear you so happy Simon. And loads love to Eve.'

Connie felt that somehow the impending baby had been the push to get her to start making some kind of life for herself.

The day by the river had caught Connie's imagination in a completely different way than anything else. Unexpectedly, she found herself thinking about it, even dreaming of being in the water and not knowing where the current would take her.

The library where she worked had asked her to paint a mural for the children's reading corner.

'Umm...I haven't painted for a while...' I'm making myself consciously obscure to make myself seem modern and with it, she thought.

The river came back into her mind.

'Okay,' Connie said finally.

For a couple of weekends Connie made herself a picnic, took her sketch pad and a camera, and scoured various corners of the river. Places she hadn't visited before: Wapping, Woolwich, East India Dock. She found them all a treasure trove of inspiration. Greenwich was spectacular and the fact that one spot on a hill in the park was the epicentre of all of the time in the world left her mind spinning in all the directions of the compass.

Connie rummaged through her workroom for materials and for the first time in ages she phoned friends, friends who were delighted to hear from her. Especially Cisco, who was the one who had kept in touch with her all the time. He was keen for them to meet somewhere, anywhere.

Cisco had been working on a site near where the accident had happened. He had been as devastated by Todd's death as Connie. He and Todd had been friends and Todd had helped him tremendously when he was a student working on his archaeology PhD.

He was now a professor. His family were so proud of him, especially as he had a 'such a good position' at the British Museum. He had dual nationality: Brazillian and British as his mother was Welsh and he had been born in the U.K. His father had been working as a doctor and his mother was a nurse.

But Cisco had always been fascinated by the ancient civilisations of South America and it had become his specialist field.

When Connie told him of her new venture he was delighted and insisted on driving her around to wherever she needed to go.

Sometimes the weather was traditionally English and they took shelter in quaint pubs and strange quirky cafes. They had known each other for a long time, but now they grew closer and realised they had a strong, almost psychic bond between them.

Cisco (short for Francisco) was by nature expansive, enthusiastic, laughed easily, was full of ideas, supposes and maybes. His eye for detail amazed her.

'I am an archaeologist!'

'Yes...' Connie laughed and they both intoned together, 'I leave no stone unturned!' It had become their private little joke.

Connie felt lifted out of a dark world, brought to the surface into the light. He was no longer a polite friend who kept his distance. He teased her, challenged her ideas and she did the same. They found they wanted to tell each other things and get the other's opinion on everything in their lives. She enjoyed his physical presence, his warmth, the touch of his hands on her body, the nearness of him, the way he looked at her.

Connie had always fancied the pants off Cisco but had felt it was some kind of betrayal to feel such powerful feelings, so she had kept her distance. Cisco had felt much the same.

'You're seeing someone.' Connie's Mum began to gush. 'That's good! Who, who, who ?'

'Mum give us a break...' she warded off her mother's enthusiasm and curiosity. Then she thought, 'I think you may have met Cisco at our place a few years ago. '

Connie's mother thought deeply, then her eyes opened as wide as a dustbin lids. 'You don't mean that dishy Brazillian?' she gaped.

'Yep, that's the one!'

She watched her daughter smile, her real hundred watt smile for the first time in eons. 'You know I asked him then if he had a girlfriend...'

'Mum, you're awful!'

'And he said he was always too busy, but he would never be too busy for you. He phoned when you were really down and said the same thing. He would never be too busy for you – I think he's been waiting for you.'

'Oh Mum,' Connie said, but she hoped it was true.

Connie's creative life had been revived and after the mural for the Library she began work on one huge painting after another.

Several panels of wood, hinged so that they could be placed at different angles for different effects, the past juxtaposed with the present. She painted both sides, so the work was free standing. It was of the river: water bringing life, the ancient past, the recent history, the present and the future, crowded with people and activity. The gentle subtle colours of the sunsets and early mornings seemed to drift as the day went by, it enhanced a subtle effect of time passing.

'I have to go to Edinburgh next week – I have been invited to hold a seminar. Why don't you come with me? Do you know Edinburgh? I know it's a long way, but they pay me well.' Cisco leaned towards her across the table and, looking intently into her eyes, took both her hands. 'Please, please say yes…'

Connie thought about it. 'I've never been to Edinburgh.'

Cisco came round to her side of the table, putting his arm around her shoulders, kneeling beside her, his eagerness wrapping itself around her like a shawl. 'It will be wonderful Carina – it is a beautiful city!' With his hands he carved out the shape of the castle on a hill. 'You will love it. Let me tell the organisers there will be two of us, Chuchu!'

His excitement was infectious and Connie was caught up in the deepening pool of his brown eyes, swayed by his sheer joy at the prospect.

'Now I work part-time, I can change my days more easily.'

* * * * *

The university had provided accommodation for them. When they arrived, the Bursar showed them to their room.

'I think you and your wife will be comfortable in here.'

They had both assumed they would have a small room each in a student block, but the room was light and spacious with a huge bed in the middle.

Cisco looked at her waiting for her reaction. 'Is it okay?' he said quietly into her ear.

Connie took his face in both of her hands and kissed him. His mouth was warm and soft. 'It's perfect,' she whispered.

'Dinner will be served at seven in the refectory.' The Bursar waited discreetly and hopefully for a tip, then silently closed the door behind him.

As soon as the door was closed Cisco held Connie close to him. 'You are sure?'

Connie gave his jacket a slight pull and it slipped off his shoulders to the floor and she began to undo the buttons of his shirt, allowing her fingers to explore his dark skin. She put her face against his chest enjoying the scent of him. He pulled her sweater over her head.

Soon shoes, tights, socks, underwear were scattered all over the room.

Cisco picked her up putting her legs around his waist and carried her to the bathroom.

They kissed and caressed as the water from the shower poured over them, but the space was small and the awkwardness made them both giggle.

'Let's go to the bed – making love in the shower is not as easy as it looks in the films!' They both laughed as they just about dried themselves and began to find the full use of the size of the bed.

'We are like starving animals Carina – we have waited so long for this. Tell me what you like Chuchu…' Cisco murmured.

'You,' was all she could say.

They were late for dinner.

A professional associate of Cisco's approached them. 'Oh, there you are Francisco. I can see a few changes have occurred in your life. Good evening Mrs Burton. I read in the *Guardian* your husband's exhibition was a great success, as was the Panorama programme on his life and work. How did you feel about it?'

Cisco tightened his hand in hers. Connie squeezed it reassuringly in return.

'It's okay.' She turned to what was, to her, a strange man. 'It was all good and very gratifying that Toddy was so well thought of.'

Someone came over to talk to the Professor. He made his apologies and walked away from them. 'I had not thought of people knowing who I was, Cisco…it never occurred to me.'

'I did not think either, but you don't mind them asking do you?'

'Darling, I can handle it now. I just try to keep everything as short as possible. I don't like it when they press me, nobody would – it's intrusive. People will soon forget.'

'Do you want to come to the seminar, Chuchu?'

'Yes – I wouldn't miss it for anything. It's nice to be able to be a part of something in your life. Not all the time obviously, but quite often.' She did not add what was going through her mind, *I don't want to make the same mistake I made with Toddy…*

* * * * *

The lecture hall seemed enormous to Connie, but Cisco was quite at home in his surroundings. He took the stage and dominated it with wit, charm and aplomb!

His smile, his charisma, his good looks, as well as his knowledge and experience and fund of stories were all part of the performance.

Connie realised that this was a side of him she knew nothing about. It made her slightly nervous. She reasoned with herself: Toddy was different in his films than in his own life – it's normal.

The lecture came to an end to tumultuous applause. The students almost mobbed him in their efforts to get him to sign his book they had carefully studied. The young girls flirted with him outrageously, which he definitely enjoyed. They were so pretty, young and fresh.

Connie, at thirty-five felt like a dowager among debutantes. She was uncomfortable, her joyous bubble had been pricked somewhat.

Oh grow up woman, she told herself, but she was experiencing an emotion she had never known before. Slowly it came to her it was jealousy.

In a very short time, more of Ciso's clothes were living in Connie's wardrobe, his shoes, his coats and papers and laptop. And as his flat was afflicted by the 'dreaded cladding' it seemed only natural that he give up his tenancy and move in with Connie.

They talked and talked – in a way Connie never had before. She had reached a high tide in her mind that overflowed into her paintings.

At night they slept close and talked about themselves.

'You seemed a bit quiet after my seminar in Edinburgh, Chuchu.'

Connie took a breath then confessed. It was easier to say in the dark. 'All those lovely young girls flocking around you, I was a bit jealous – I felt old and past it.'

Cisco sat up and looked very serious. 'Connie...' He hesitated, unsure of how she would take what he had to say.

'That is a particular tree I have climbed and fallen from with a couple of broken limbs. All the attention is not real – the flirting is a game. It's not about me, it is about my picture on the posters, my name in my books. They are just butterflies who move on very quickly to the next bright flower. It was a hard lesson, but I learned it is all empty flummery, to use an old English word. At first I was flattered, until I fell in love with you. You are so different, you ask for so little and give so much.'

'I feel it is the other way around.'

Cisco kissed her gently. 'No it is not. Toddy lived his life, loved his life – and you accepted him as the person he was and never tried to change him or stop him doing the thing he loved. You took it for granted you would be there when he came home.'

'You make me sound too saintly – I was doing my thing as well.'

'Yes, but you didn't expect him to change to suit you. You are unusual, you never play emotional games and have no agenda that drives you. There must have been times when you were lonely and missed him, but you just got on with things.'

'I suppose it's because my art is important to me that I understood Toddy.'

'With you, Carina, I feel safe. We give each other what we need to live our lives – that is very grown up.' They held each other more tightly and kissed for a long time.

'Darling why do you call me "Chuchu"?'

Cisco laughed 'It is Portuguese, like "darling" or "sweetie". The whole word is "chuchuzinho". I just make it shorter and "carina" is Spanish for a similar thing.'

'It's a whole lot better than "babe"!' Connie giggled and they both gently fell asleep.

Cisco encouraged her to submit her work for the Summer Exhibition at the Royal Academy.

Stan borrowed a large van and took them to the entrance in Piccadilly. When they arrived, there was a hushed surprise at the sheer size of the work. The panels had to be assembled and fixed together. Connie felt a sense of dubious amazement all around her.

'Well, it will be considered and in due course we will let you know if you have been successful.'

Connie was doubtful. 'It will need so much room – they usually have hundreds of paintings crammed together on the walls.'

An invitation had arrived to attend an anniversary memorial service in Peru for those who had died in the train crash.

'Why don't we go back together?' Cisco suggested.

'Okay.'

Connie and Cisco stood with their arms around each other facing the monolithic stone memorial near the crash site. They had brought flowers, but there were all kinds of offerings: clothes, shoes, food, even clay pots and pans.

'It is to help those carry on with their journey in the next world. Ancient beliefs that go back for thousands of years still flourish in these mountains. You and I are here together with Todd and I know he is pleased. We will carry on together.'

'Yes, I can feel it – like in the river nothing ends. It reminds me of a quotation from Buddha: "Our life is shaped by our mind and we become what we think". My paintings are my mind.'

Connie stopped and looked up at the hills, looked at the emerging and dissolving colours that created an almost translucent outline.

'You know Cisco, it's strange but I feel I know Toddy now in a way I never did when he was alive. If something draws me into a scene, it's as if he's with me and I am looking through his mind, through his eyes.'

Cisco kissed Connie warmly, lovingly and deeply. 'I love you so much.' Then he grinned mischievously 'We have done so much thinking and now I am very hungry my darling.'

'So am I.'

Connie's phone signalled a text. 'Oooooooooh!! Mum says the letter has come and my work has been accepted!'

They hugged each other excitedly.

'I never doubted it! I too believe it is Todd we have to thank...'

Cisco looked up at the sky as if he could see his spirit. He opened out his arms held them high.

Connie followed his lead and in some kind of ritual oblation together they embraced the air, the golden rim of the sun and the shimmering distant hills.

—∞∞∞—

THE SIREN CALL

For once in his life Montmorency was quite speechless. He knew he should make a flustered retreat and apologise, but he stood there and all good intentions to politely leave evaporated into the warm air.

His short life, of twenty-four years, flashed before him like a drowning man: his prep school, his all-male boarding school, his good job at Coutts bank in the high street, all coalesced into chintz and uncut moquette, doiliires and Assam tea on Sunday afternoons.

He was unexpectedly walking along this towpath of the river because there was some kind of emergency at the bank and as a lowly clerk he had been sent home. It was a glorious Saturday he had been given to do with as he pleased – and it pleased him to come down to the river, enjoy the sunshine, the blue sky and hear the birds sing especially for him. Montmorency stood still to take in the scene before him.

A voice called to him. 'You look like a nice lad, why don't you come in and join us?'

Plump, cushioned, wonderfully proportioned ladies with no clothes on beckoned to him. He had detected a slight country accent which made the voice even more appealing. St Albans had never before seemed like the most enchanting place on earth.

'Why don't you take a dip with us lad? It's very nice and soothing.'

'Yes, yes, I'm sure.' Montmorency hesitated. 'I don't have any swimming t-trunks,' he stuttered. 'Or a towel.' His excuses sounded pathetic even to himself. 'Also I'm not a very good swimmer.'

The ladies swam closer to his side of the riverbank. 'That's no matter.'

One of the girls stood up – the water was only waist deep. 'It's not so deep,' she said encouragingly.

Montmorency tried to suppress his instinct to splutter and gasp at the breathtaking vision that held a hand out to him, so close to his own hand.

'Mr Crowther…Mr Crowther!' another voice that was unmistakably that of Doctor Fearnley his local rector called to him from behind. 'I shall expect you at choir practice this evening as usual, Mr Crowther!'

The rector was complete in his biretta and gaiters ready for his usual visit to the Bishop. He looked at Montmorency fixedly over his silver rimmed glasses 'Mr Crowther, I urge you not to be led into temptation by these wayward creatures. I have to come here every Saturday to do the Lord's work and dissuade young men from the path of unrighteousness.'

The women giggled. 'Father it's nineteen ten not the middle ages! And besides, you'd come here even if there was no young man whose soul needed saving.'

The rector chose to ignore this last remark. It was beneath him to dignify it with a response.

Now two hands were stretched out to Montmorency, one from the rector and one from the voluptuous young woman. Habit and social training decided for him and he took the rector's hand and allowed him to pull him up the bank from the river's edge.

'That's right my boy, you know it is the right thing to do.'

'Who are those ladies?' Montmorency enquired.

The rector sniffed. 'Ladies! If you want to call them that. But I must be charitable. You ask where they come from. They are not local of course. One of these new fangled artist's communities has been established by Lady Braithewaite at Thrush Croft Manor – I blame the pre-Raphaelites!'

The rector waved his hands feebly. 'I despair of our society. New Edwardians they call themselves. I blame the poor example of King Edward as Prince of Wales – all his gallivanting around the south of France and his *Lady friends* if you get my meaning.' The rector pursed his lips, his face assuming that 'knowing' expression he often wore.

'Well, I will see you this evening my boy – happy to have been of service.' With that the rector waddled off down the road to the Bishop's residence.

Montmorency felt rather deflated, his euphoric morning had turned into nothing more than a touch of dyspepsia. He wandered down the lane to where he had lived with his aunt for most of his life.

Aunty Glady was a kindly soul and had taken in Montmorency when his parents took a sea voyage to India and subsequently drowned in the Indian Ocean. It was a long time ago and Aunty Gladys had been a comfort to the orphaned Montmorency. She always called him 'Monty' – 'They could have given you a shorter name dear – it would have been so much easier.'

Montmorency found his aunt in a fawn apron with her hair a trifle dishevelled struggling with a too hot plate of meringues straight from the oven. He picked up a tea towel and rescued them from her before they careered all over the kitchen.

'Thank you sweetheart,' she panted slightly. 'You know how dreadful I am at making cakes. But I could not escape it this week as it's my turn to provide the refreshments for the Mother's Union meeting.' Aunty Glady sank down on to a kitchen chair and wiped the beads of sweat from her brow with her apron.

'How was your morning Monty?'

Montmorency hesitated for a second and then decided to tell his aunt what had happened. Her eyes twinkled at him.

'Well, you're a good-looking boy – no, young man now. I am not surprised the girls are making eyes at you. You were a bit of a late starter, but all that rowing has built you up nicely.'

Montmorency remembered his late start. He had been a small, rather puny boy, a slightly spotty teenager, and did not grow to his full height until he was over twenty-one. A sudden growth spurt surprised everyone and he was now a full six feet tall.

He was never inclined towards cricket or rugby and was treated as a wimp by his P.T. teachers, but his friends in the rowing club eventually press-ganged him into joining the crew and he found he was a very good oarsman. He never looked back. He had lied to the ladies in the river, he was in fact a strong swimmer and loved anything to do with boats and water generally. The rowing had built him up quite nicely, as his aunt had said.

'You're a fine figure of a chap now Monty. You turn heads.'

To Montmorency it was all rather new and flattering, but mildly embarrassing, he didn't quite know what to say so he changed the subject.

'There was some kind of emergency at the bank _ I think a small fire somewhere, so we were sent home. I'm rowing this afternoon Mimsy.' He used his pet name for his aunt. 'By the way have you heard of any art colony that's just started up round here?' He tried to sound casual.

'Oooohhhh, yes, it was the talk of the Mother's Union! It's the project of Lady Braithewaite up at the Manor. They're running Art appreciation classes too. I thought I might put my nose in and see what they're like.'

'Mimsy! Isn't that a bit racy for you?'

'Well, it may all be a storm in a tea cup.'

Later that day when Montmorency returned from his rowing practice he found high tea laid out on the table and he remembered it was the Social at the church hall that evening.

'There'll be refreshments love,' his aunt reminded him. 'I've just done you eggs on toast. Do you fancy looking in at the Social, Monty? It's a long time since some of our friends have seen you...'

Montmorency thought about it. 'Oh well, I might – as you say it's been a long time. Not since I went to college.' He thought of the neighbours and the girls he'd grown up with – it might be nice to see them again. He'd had a shower at the clubhouse, but he checked to see if he needed a shave.

Perhaps a little scrape, he thought and he took out his flannel trousers, his striped blazer and a crisp clean white shirt. With his rowing club tie and his summer boater, he hoped he would look a little snazzy although he was not quite sure what that meant.

Aunty Glady was delighted to have the opportunity to show off her nephew to her friends from church, the glee club and the Mother's Union.

The church and the church hall were only a short walk away so they arrived on time to find the hall richly decorated with ferns, giant daisies, marigolds, lupins – all donated from people's gardens. Montmorency had brought some roses that he had nurtured from cuttings.

The small three-piece orchestra was already set up and benches were arranged around the walls. Montmorency spied the refreshments. It was a veritable feast and looked so appetising that small children trying to sneak a pie or sausage roll before the official time to eat received smacked hands and ears.

Montmorency watched from the side of the hall as the girls he had known when he was young began to arrive: Beattie, Rose, Bertha, Gertie. They had been pretty, flirty, sweet, funny, or plain, he remembered and he greeted them politely. He discovered some others he didn't remember were already married, several engaged and Gertie had two children.

'Goodness where has the time gone?'

'And you Monty, I wouldn't have known you – so tall!'

The hall was quite full when a slight commotion caused the crowd to part and Montmorency caught sight of Lady Braithewaite. He was surprised, as were others, and the collective sharp intake of breath was almost audible. With her were several of the ladies Montmorency recognised from the river. He watched with interest as they approached the rector with a loosely tied, rather bulky parcel and Lady Braithewaite went on the stage and announced that it was a gift to St. Cuthberts and the clergy and congregation.

The rector was persuaded to open the parcel. Inside the copious amount of wrapping paper was a magnificently embroidered silk altar cloth. He valiantly managed to suppress all his prejudices and reservations about what went on at the Manor, feeling he had somehow been out-flanked.

'Well, well…I don't quite know what to say – what generosity!'

'The artists at the Manor have been working on this for a long time and, now it is finished, we would like to see it in the church on the altar,' Lady Braithewaite said to the assembled company. 'It will give you an idea of the beautiful pieces that the artists are creating at the Manor.'

Montmorency was only half listening. The girl from the river was with the group – and so close – he could see her smiling at him. He could not stop looking at her. All he could see was that she had chestnut eyes and her tumble of almost auburn hair was only partially tamed by combs either side of her head. Even with her clothes on, she looked incredible. He tried hard to concentrate on what was happening, but failed.

'Thank you, thank you." The rector suddenly remembered what he was supposed to be saying for such a marvellous gift and he offered Lady Braithewaite a glass of raspberry punch that she accepted politely.

Montmorency could hardly move, but at the same time he wanted to rush to the side of such a vision. He looked her up and down. Almost without realising it he was taking her clothes off in the church hall. He stopped himself – that would never do.

He dutifully waltzed with Aunt Glady, polkaed with Bertha. Managed to stumble through a cotillion with Rose and a 'Dashing White Sergeant' with Gertie, when all he wanted to do was sail away with the girl from the river, but was too unsure of himself to ask her to dance.

Then the M.C. announced he wanted two circles. 'The gentlemen on the outside and the ladies on the inside – the men walk one way the ladies walk round the opposite way and when the music stops you will have a new partner.'

By an extraordinary stroke of almost magical good fortune, when the music stopped Montmorency found himself opposite the girl from the river.

'What's your name?' he almost shouted at her so she could hear him above the music.

'Leonora,' she said. 'What's yours?'

'Mont– Monty.'

'Hello, Monty!' And that was it.

The music stopped, everyone started walking around in a circle again and he had lost her. He kept craning his neck around looking for her in the room. The hall was crowded and he could not see her.

Without warning a stone lodged itself inside his chest. When he had given up hope, he suddenly noticed that Lady Braithewaite was preparing to leave.

With no thought of good manners, Montmorency pushed his way through the crush, knowing that the whole party would leave together. He followed them out into the street. Street lighting was a fairly recent thing for Stokely Bunton and Montmorency blessed it, for under the lamppost he could see her waiting for him. Her eyes shone in the silver light.

'How did you know I would follow you?'

'Of course I knew,' she teased him. 'I can't stay long they are waiting for me. Come up to the Manor tomorrow afternoon to one of the art classes.' She went up on her toes and kissed him gently on the mouth. Then she was gone, lost once again into the darkness.

Montmorency thought he was going to faint. The kiss had been so unexpected. His intimate knowledge of girls and women was limited to one experience that he would rather forget.

The rowing club had had a charabanc outing to Collins Music Hall. He had drunk far too much, trying to keep up with the men in the bar, when he found himself being shepherded by an older woman into a small room. Bust bodices, stays, whalebone corsets and voluminous bloomers took the edge off any ardour he might have summoned up. He did what was expected of him very quickly and was led back to the bar. Hoots and laughter greeted him.

'At last our Monty is deflowered and won't blush when we discuss our luscious experiences in the changing rooms.'

Montmorency put up his hands in acknowledgement and weakly lied about his prowess to keep the crew happy. In reality it had been a very depressing experience indeed.

Somehow Montmorency got through Sunday morning, even singing in the choir without being fully conscious. He ate Sunday dinner at a great rate and pulled on his jacket.

'Oh are you rowing today?' Aunt Glady expected Montmorency to spend his usual quiet Sunday in the garden or pottering in the greenhouse.

'Wont be long, Mimsy,' he replied and he was gone.

Glady found it a little mysterious, but concluded he was growing up and from now on she was not likely to know exactly where he was.

Montmorency cycled the couple of miles to the Manor and nervously walked up the stone steps to the wide open doors of the Manor. He hovered in the hallway for a while.

He studied the leaflets and brochures very carefully. He saw her name – Leonora – on the life class leaflet and the number of the room and directions to where the room could be found. He slowly made his way to where he thought she would be. He pushed the door open gently.

There were many easels arranged around the room. Some were being used but several were not. He hadn't given any thought to what he might find at the Hall and it took him by surprise to find Leonora was the teacher for the class.

Leonora came to greet him. 'You found me! I won't be long – take a seat or walk around and look at the work, they wont mind – after all they're hoping for their work to be exhibited.'

She was true to her word and soon the class was packing away their materials. The room emptied quickly and she came to him and kissed him as she had the previous night. 'I was not sure you would come.' She was wearing a loose kind of peignoir.

As she kissed him he could feel her body pressed against him. He caught hold of her and held her even more closely and kissed her more fiercely.

'Not here,' she whispered. 'Come to my room.'

Sunday afternoons became Monty's reason for living when he and Leonora made love and memories, it was an experience that took over Monty's life that golden summer.

One night, when he came home, Aunt Glady looked at him in an old-fashioned way.

Monty was unsure how to react.

Aunty Glady took his arm to reassure him. 'I am happy to see you happy Monty, it's just that I have something we must talk about. You will be twenty-five in six months and the family solicitor wants us to see him. You will soon be receiving your annuity from your father's trust and evidently you own a house in Bloomsbury. I am well provided for too. You won't be getting a

King's ransom, but with your salary from the bank – should you want to get married, you can support a family.'

'Mimsy,' Monty had to tell her something he had hoped he could avoid. 'Leonora is already married to an artist. He spends a lot of time in Scotland – paints misty Scottish mountains and stags and cattle evidently. We will never marry.'

Monty did not quite know how to explain, or how Aunty Glady would react to the unconventional life he was living, but he pressed on.

'We are close – so close – I don't think I will ever be so intimate with a woman ever again. We are completely open and honest with each other, but it's not about a cottage and roses round the door and happy ever after. We are very different people.'

'I know dear, I understand, I know more than you think. And when life beckons and it feels good and honest, don't say "No". A life of regret is the saddest thing.'

Monty was not entirely surprised by his aunt's reaction. He had long suspected that she too had loved 'not wisely but too well' and it had made her the warm compassionate person she was.

He did, however, hesitate to invite her to the New London Gallery where Leonora's huge painting of him – lying on his back, naked and half asleep with his arms and legs sprawled comfortably across the bed – was being exhibited.

Leonora believed it was high time women painted men in the nude and had their bodies on display for all to see.

Monty kept his fingers crossed that his colleagues at the bank or the rowing team and most of his friends were not art lovers.

THE STORY OF JOSEPH

The date, the time, north, south, east west, the days of the week – were all lost on him now. Joseph measured the days by the light from the window in his room – that was by turns a cell, a sick room, a church, and an asylum.

He was an ordinary man who came from an ordinary family. He lived an ordinary life he was married and had two ordinary children. Now he listened to the birds outside his window. Sometimes he managed to climb on to his rickety chair and look out at the sky and the trees, taking in the colours and the patterns of the clouds to store them in his imagination – to line the walls of his room. Sometimes he created vast panoramas of snow-capped mountains, fast-flowing rivers, deeply shadowed valleys where he roamed the hillsides on a fine black horse. At other times he was on a battlefield in the thick of a skirmish – his voice hoarse – shouting orders to young recruits hurling themselves to their death.

Joseph was not dead, but he had come close to death with some rare disease or virus unknown to doctors of his village. Joseph's family had tended him carefully but as he grew stronger they had grown weaker and when his wife died his children were taken away by the authorities to the city to be cared for and eventually adopted. Marisa, his wife, had been a strong healthy woman in her early forties and it was a great sorrow for Joseph to see her gradually slipping away from him. It had taken a while before he and Marisa could have children and now he had lost them too. For a while he was trapped inside his own despair, unaware of what had happened to him.

Joseph became surrounded by suspicion and superstition. He had become a pariah and was shunned by his friends and neighbours and his previously close community. He grew stronger and became healthier than he had ever been before. A slight limp from a childhood accident disappeared, his hair grew thicker and darker – his skin, fine and unlined, almost glowed with good health. A specialist doctor from the nearby town was asked to come and examine Joseph. In his report he pronounced that for a man nearing fifty he was as fit as a twenty year old. He had even grown several inches and from being the stocky farming man indigenous to the area he came from, he was now long limbed, lithe and walked with a manly grace. All defects and blemishes had been erased from his face and his features were now those of an imaginary perfect man. It was quite miraculous the doctor concluded.

The word 'miraculous' flew around the small rather isolated population of the peninsula. Debates took place in houses, in meeting halls and churches. Careless language like 'fear', 'alien,' 'god-like' 'the work of the devil' began to simmer and became an undercurrent in the quiet life of the region. People from other villages and even some townspeople started to visit, curious and questioning. Complete families, crammed into ramshackle old trucks, rattled into the village square asking to see Joseph – wanting to touch him, take photos of him. They wanted him to touch their sick children, to bless them – give them advice on when to plant crops and to know if it would be a good spring and a good harvest. They wanted wise words to base their lives on and comfort for their misfortunes.

The trickle of people grew to be a daily stream. The mayor and the priest became very uneasy at their unquestioned authority being gently eroded. It was of deep concern to them both, so at their various meetings they raised the issue of Joseph and his transformation. The mayor wrote serious letters to the mayor of the nearest town and the priest wrote serious letters to the bishop – saying that Joseph's presence was an intrusion in their daily lives and that of their parishioners and electors. They complained of the children making up songs and games about Joseph – clustering around his house, placing flowers and fruit on his doorstep and not paying enough attention to their lessons and their prayers.

Joseph had accepted money from some of his visitors, as he needed to make a living. This had not gone unnoticed by the village council, who, after heated conversations behind closed doors, had decided that Joseph could be an asset to the village. They could see there was money to be made from the strange man Joseph had become. They gathered together photos of him from choir outings, when he was married, in fiestas and pageants – records of his school days, his achievements and stories of adventures with his friends. They did not want him to leave and told him that his life may be in danger from the amount of attention he received – that malevolent factions wished him dead as he had been cursed by the power of nature. They told him he needed to be taken to a safe house.

At first Joseph was amenable to this suggestion, having a co-operative nature, and agreed to move to a house on the very edge of the village on a hillside that could be heavily guarded. Visitors were permitted to see him if they came in organised parties and paid a comfortable entry fee to go into the house or see the exhibition of Joseph memorabilia. He was given food and if there was anything else he needed he had only to ask the council members.

Time passed slowly for Joseph – he forgot about his children and began to slip deeper and deeper into his imagination thinking himself adrift in a desert sea looking for a lighthouse. As he became more and more lost inside himself the council decided it was better if no one actually saw Joseph, but simply to keep him as a shrine for pilgrimage. He was the miracle of their village that would become legend and a place of worship forever.

One day Joseph slipped off his rickety chair while looking up at the sky. He fell, hit his head and died instantly. The general feeling and opinion among the villagers was that it was not such a bad thing, as they would no longer be troubled by the inconvenience of watching gentle Joseph go mad. There would be a dignified funeral to which any local dignitaries would be automatically invited and perhaps the bishop and the mayor of the city closest to them, as they would bring a few photographers and journalists from the city's newspaper. They envisaged a large crowd of mourners of friends and neighbours and a procession of visitors through the village and the roads strewn with flowers and palms, which would look so picturesque in photos.

The funeral was a great success and everyone thoroughly enjoyed themselves. Children had shiny clean hair and new suits and dresses. Mum's had new hats and Dad's shoes were polished. They had photographs taken with the coffin in their best clothes. Souvenir booklets of the service with Joseph's picture on the front were passed among the crowd. The food that the villagers had provided sold well in the evening, when there was music and dancing in the main square with long trestle tables covered in shiny paper the party went on long into the early hours of the morning under a purple-velvet balmy sky.

The troublesome duty of clearing out Joseph's room fell to the ladies of the church. When all the festivities of the funeral were over, they managed to fit this little chore into their daily routine.

With an unpleasant sense of a job that has to be done, they opened up Joseph's room, they found it filled almost to bursting with large and small canvasses, huge cartoons, strange otherworldly murals. It took a long time for them to grasp that all this time he had been painting and drawing the contents of his extraordinary inner life. His years of solitude had been transformed and re-constructed into majestic works of art.

Phone lines hummed as experts were called in to assess his work. They declared him a great artist – a genius. His work attracted dealers from all over the world. Joseph, as a man, as one of them, was soon forgotten as the huge benefits they derived from him turned a small remote village into an industry – a sought after tourist destination that generated millions.

Joseph's real, inexplicable story was lost forever.

THINKING TIME

If she hadn't done this and if she hadn't done that, everything might have been different.

Sitting on the underground – the Central Line – Janice's thoughts wandered across the landscape of her life. The advertising board on the opposite side of the carriage received her entire attention. Her journey was long and she felt she had taken root in her seat.

People got on and got off the train. The carriage became crowded and then emptied again leaving Janice still sitting there.

She read the poster again. It was advertising courses in Martial Arts of various kinds. The closest Janice had ever come to Martial Arts was catching a glimpse of her son's DVDs or video games of Kung Fu fighting and other entertainments of carefully choreographed pain and brutality. She was mystified as to why anyone would find such material entertaining let alone pay large amounts of money for games for X boxes and the like.

Janice fell to pondering: if you do learn this stuff, when do you use it?

If someone annoys you at work you can hardly grab them by the waist and toss them over the photocopier in a fit of pique. She smiled slightly to herself at the vision of herself hurling her overbearing, overweight boss James Hardcastle to the floor, her foot on his chest, while he whimpered for mercy.

It was a great thought.

I'd only succeed in getting myself arrested, she told herself.

But she continued to look at the poster and ruminate on how proscribed her path in life had been. School, college, marriage, children, work – and not very challenging work at that.

Janice stopped herself. Why did I turn down that offer of promotion? she asked herself. I do the job anyway – Hardcastle's so hopeless. Why didn't I go for it like other women? Women become prisoners of an image of themselves, she decided. It's like a Merry-go-Round. All we need to do is step off – so why don't we?

She looked at the various pictures and poses on the Martial Arts poster again.

They look quite artistic really, she thought.

Janice had been quite sporty as a girl, but home and family had taken over and she had forgotten how much she'd enjoyed the sheer exhilaration of physical activity.

I'm a bit old now to go back to netball and gymnastics.

The carriage filled up again and Janice could no longer see the poster. She became aware of how many people, men, women, youngsters, wore trainers, while she was still toiling into work in high heels – not killer heels, but business office lady heels.

Janice now turned her attention to her rather dull sensible office shoes and clothes and caught the eye of the girl opposite in leggings and her friend in ripped jeans. Janice would never have been seen dead in either garments, but she was aware by the way they looked at her they were thinking the same thing of her.

She felt almost embarrassed. They looked at her in the way the family looked at her, as if she didn't quite exist. As if she was just half of something.

Janice was nearly at her stop. The train lurched a little alarmingly and she and everyone else grabbed on to anything near, to stop themselves falling into the aisle.

People collided with each other and flurries of apologies and conversation broke out.

'Didn't like that much!' said the girl in ripped jeans.

'No – hope the train's okay,' said Janice, 'I'm nearly at my station.'

'Where you off to?' asked the girl in leggings.

'My mixed Martial Arts training,' Janice said nonchalantly.

'Nooo??' the girls said admiringly.

'Gosh that must be hard – you must be tough!'

'Well, a few bruises and torn muscles comes with the territory.'

Janice looked at the poster and carefully memorised the address and phone number of the nearest Academy. She got up. 'Bye girls, this is my stop.'

As soon as she was above ground outside the station, she phoned Mr Hardcastle.

'Sorry about this James. I won't be in today – something's come up.'

Then she called the Martial Arts Academy and spoke to a very pleasant receptionist.

'Yes – I would like to enrol for beginners Karate…No, thanks very much…I think I'll leave the cage fighting until a little later.'

TIME AND PLACE

A hot wind blew in from the desert, full of sand and bad feeling, and scuffed its way around the soft yellow stone of the island. The palm trees leaned low, their fronds brushing the pavement, bowing deeply into abrasive gusts. Only faded election posters, picked at and peeling, flapped cheerfully, the urbane faces of old politicians shaking their heads reassuringly in the stiff breeze.

It was the middle of the day. The woman was alone in the bus shelter. She'd never stopped being surprised by the hot empty streets of the island noonday. The morning would unfold with the wail of traffic tuning up, staccato washing line conversations and telephones ringing in dim offices. She would turn a corner and there would be no one to be seen, as if the populace was part of some conspiracy from which she was excluded.

The bus hobbled towards her and sagged gratefully to a stop, as though never to rise again, but some indefatigable power swelled in its belly and it shuddered back to shambling life.

In the dark airless kitchen the woman took off her shoes, luxuriating in the cool of the stone floor. All the curtains were drawn, but speckles of rusty sunlight escaped round the threads of the cloth, freckling the walls and the floor.

When she had first come from plain grey skies and rain, she had resisted drawing the curtains, it had seemed ungrateful, but she had come to know the insatiable lust of the sun, eating up strength, leaving a pith sucked of its juice.

In the bedroom the woman took off her dress and lay on the bed, giving herself up to the sweet silence of the gloom. Her thoughts wandered over the cobblestones of her day-to-day life. She knew her own will had become forfeit in the extravagance of the senses that was her familiar existence.

Sometimes she would sit for hours on a rock, oblivious of its sharp jagged edge, staring out to sea, sucking in deep draughts of its blue, never satisfied – drawn to its distance, surrendering herself to some magnetism of eternity. A half-sleeping, half conscious creature at the feet of an ancient God. In this place she had come to know something, but what? She slid bonelessly into unconsciousness.

Dull disconnected sounds bounced their echoes around the warm walls of the late afternoon. She woke at once.

The old habit of anxiety flooded through her. Then she remembered, stretched her arms and yawned in a long sighing secret indulgence. She felt an eagerness for activity. She got up, peered into the mirror and pushed her fingers through her hair. The serious sounds of the day were in progress, decisions being made and money changing hands. The shops were breathing again in the shade.

Leaning over the balcony she saw her children, hot and sullen faces gleaming with sweat. Their voices came crashing like falling concrete on the stairway, as they lurched into the flat. Dropping cases, ripping shirts and buttons, walking out of school trousers. There was five minutes of symphonic explosion and they were gone. Leaving behind a ragged tidemark of their belongings, beached down the hallway.

Her husband came in, poured himself a drink and disappeared into an armchair.

The days flared and died like spent matches. There were a few places to go and a few things to do, but almost always she chose not to do them, preferring to explore the streets, greedy for moments when she could be alone, almost secretive in her desire for solitude. She had learned to be alone even when she was with people, blending into the background, yet never conspicuously silent.

It was as though she required nothing of any living person. All her needs being satisfied by the place. She chattered dutifully to others, nodding at their complaints, indignant at the gross inadequacies they perpetually encountered, but remained indifferent. Her eyes drifted towards the open window, the door, the sky.

Standing in the night, within it, encircled by it. She had written in letters they were the kind of nights that cried out in the loneliness of not being in love and yet, she was in love – she was in love with the place.

She wanted to hold the very stones close to her. Each day a promise fulfilled. The sun a more savage lover than any man. The night, murmuring, caressing, enfolding, whispering to her of old jokes in the creaking yachts on the water, telling her of dreams of the past and adventures yet to come. The net of the stars, a great ladder to be climbed taking you further into forever, but not yet.

The silken skeins of a silver sea, meshed and tangled by the lamps that wound along the edge of the creek, held her in its strands.

It was morning again. The doorbell split the silence like an axe through wood.

She was ready. At the door was a small dark-skinned woman. The heat of the island boiling up in her impatient vitality. The two women picked their way down the broken stones of the road, their feet unsure on the loose fragments.

At the end of the street a small speedboat was moored at the water's edge. The women got into the boat easily, unencumbered by weight and size. Their chatter and excited laughter warming them in the whipped breeze of the creek. The woman strapped on the great wooden skis, feeling clumsy and uncoordinated.

'Stand with your feet straight and a little apart, bend your knees and your keep your back straight and your head up.'

Her body obeyed. She was grateful for the ordinariness of the physical commands. Her hands held the towrope firmly.

The boat leapt forward into the swell and so did she. Exactly in the position she was given, she went up through the waves and skimmed along behind the boat like a trailing hand. She was thrilled, exhilarated. She had done it – without thought, without effort.

She had trusted the skill of her friend and together it had carried her along the top of the waves. She jerked inexpertly along, out into the middle of the bay. She wasn't afraid.

The land didn't look to be as far away as she had expected. It was her faith in her friend that had brought her out into the deep water. She knew without her she could never have done it.

A great wave sent her a slap on the back. She went down into the dim green sea. She had been thrown like a penny into a dark glass jar. When the momentum of her fall began to weaken she turned over and was brought back into the bright light of the morning. The pools of sunlight swayed and clung to the edge of the waves as though they too would slip into the dark depths.

She was temporarily paralysed by their brilliance, the edges of her vision curled.

A blurred face called to her. 'You okay?'

'Yes,' she coughed back.

'I'll bring the rope around,' the woman in the boat said casually.

All of her life she had been afraid of deep water, afraid that if she couldn't hold herself up on her own feet, she would be sucked down into a tight choking world that would squeeze the breath out of her and drag her down into an impenetrable darkness.

But it was not like that, she'd felt nothing but the passive weight of the sea holding her, passing her up and up, she didn't fight, she didn't struggle, she lay still and the many arms of the heavy dark waves carried her back to the surface of the water.

In this place of sticky rocks and sand that grazed the face and legs, where the sun rotted the sheets and canvas chairs and cockroaches shared the kitchen, the woman had re-discovered something she thought had been sunk without trace.

She had dipped into a moment in the past and allowed a new perspective to push back the frontiers of her small imagination. Her mind no longer beat itself ceaselessly against its own bars. She'd learned what it meant to yield.

A CELEBRATION

Laura Addison had been invited to a Ball – a Grand Valentine's Ball. A society 'bash' in London, the kind you read about in the social columns of the national papers.

'Won't I be too old?' she enquired anxiously. Laura had that ageless dancer's face, its perfect symmetry softened by years. Now she looked more approachable, more vulnerable than when she was young.

'No, you look so young and it's for the young in heart anyway.'

Laura felt warmed by the kindness of the invitation. She did want to go, for it would be such a grand occasion. Something she'd never been to before.

'Not Dad,' her son added. 'He'd have no one to talk to about mixing concrete and darts.'

'Mmm,' Laura murmured.

'The trouble with Dad is that he talks at you, not to you,' her son elaborated. 'It doesn't matter what it is he's talking about, it's as though he's addressing a meeting. He goes on and on about his snooker, or the club, but he's not really telling you anything. In a way he's telling himself, giving himself a kind of action replay, so he can enjoy the events all over again.'

'Yes, he loves those men, doesn't he?' Laura added.

Her son gave her a wry grimace.

Laura didn't even mind that much. She understood the closeness between them. Shared experiences similar background, it bound them together more firmly than any marriage. A common language of endlessly repeated anecdotes and mother tongue phrases. They remained forever boys, boys from the playground, from the play centre. The Bash Street boys, Dead End kids, never ready to grow up. Always knowing what each other would do next and yet at the same time to find each meeting fresh and young and full of surprise even enterprise. While outside the magic circle of the men everything was grey and threatening – herself most of all. She knew herself to be another country, a place her husband had no wish to go, no wish to know.

The entire pattern of her thoughts, her behaviour, her language, feelings and reactions were only important to him when she was providing a shadow, a background to his own wishes. So, she was nice to him, most of the time. Endlessly humouring him, admiring him when he did anything around the house, a dutiful wife.

Anything more spontaneous was like inviting a clap of thunder. Even a few words that held the merest whiff of challenge or the tiniest demand and his entire being shuddered and erupted as if some unstoppable emotional earthquake took charge of him. Like cheap factory glass, he would shatter into a thousand pieces at the merest pressure, however feather-light.

They lived together as amicably as possible. She was nice to him. When he arrived home late from work or had meetings or engagements at the weekend Laura was very understanding. Her name was mentioned with incredulity at his club where he stayed too long and too often.

'Doesn't Laura mind?'

'Good heavens no!'

But slowly, with that terrible slowness of the truly imperceptive kind of man he was, he began to realise how empty that niceness was and so the inevitable erosion of their relationship occurred. Year by year, any substance that might have lingered, any remnant of feeling she had for him became more and more threadbare.

Laura did not get too excited about the Ball because she knew it was to be for the young people and she was to be mostly a spectator.

'Can I wear my red dress?' she enquired.

'Oh no, it's got to be a ball dress!' Tom's friend Sophie was definite.

'A ball dress!' Laura was alarmed.

Such an imperative presented her with a serious problem. She thought about it and eventually decided on something 'ballish', but that could be worn on another occasion. She did not want to be seen competing with the young girls.

'I'll feel like the duenna.'

She made this comment several times, but no one felt moved to disagree with her. Eventually she bought a rather chic little number in white chiffon.

White did not suit her in the winter, but would be useful for the summer. She decided that if she was to be the older woman, then so be it, she would indeed be 'the older woman'. She was still attractive and as she grew older had acquired a certain style and that would have to see her through.

Her own mother enquired, a trifle waspishly, whether she thought the occasion would live up to her expectations.

Laura had replied quite firmly that it was up to her. Depending on what she put into the evening would govern what she got out of it: privately, she had planned how she would amuse herself, fairly unobtrusively.

The Albert Hall was a very large place, after all, and as there were to be various events taking place on different floors, she felt fairly sure that if she took time visiting them, returning to the box from time to time for the odd drink, she could while away the time very pleasantly indeed.

Tom had organised his troops like an army and the general meeting place for the party was his flat in Docklands. From there they travelled together to the Albert Hall.

An air of excited anticipation and blasé bonhomie bubbled and twittered among the young people.

Being introduced to her son's friends was the first hurdle to be overcome. Socially, Laura was not easy to pinpoint, her early life having been somewhat peripatetic, with little real home life: father dead, boarding school from the age of five and then passed around from Aunties to Nannies. Shuttled back and forth between East London, Surrey and Durham, her spoken language was rather mixed. They were extremely polite, even gallant. Laura hated it. She felt like a specimen in a jar.

They all looked fresh as apples, newly picked, in their hired or acquired evening suits and bow ties. Conversation was a self-consciously loud affair as they clustered on the Underground. So very obviously an evening party, relishing every ostentatious moment.

The dimly lit glass lobby, packed with excited youngsters in various styles of evening dress, was barely large enough to contain such a surge of eager partygoers. Crystal drop wall lights from inside the original foyer gave such meagre light that shadows settled soft as fluff. A dusty fusion dissolved the edges of the separate groups, drew them together into an entity that joyously heaved its way through the main door.

There was no stopping, no uncertain hovering. These were young people. They stepped confidently into the entrance way and up the stairs, light and sure of where they were going. They exuded assurance and vitality. Skipping up the carpeted stairs and along the wide landings, swishing taffeta skirts, all of them wide smiles, filled with anticipation. Laura allowed herself to be carried along by the swell of youthful exuberance.

Merely by being with them she felt herself become light and more free. The accumulated cares of years she left behind her in that dingy lobby. Swept clean, dusted and polished, brought out for this special occasion, Laura disappeared into the melee of youngsters. A new rhythm and a new pace. She captured it as easily as the girls.

The box was tiny, too small for all the party to sit in at one time. It was not to matter, nothing mattered. That was the joy, the young people were so unperturbed by anything. It was so easy.

A flurry of hats, boots and scarves were piled upon too few pegs in the anteroom that led out to the circular corridors. Drinks appeared almost from nowhere. Bottles of different kinds decorated the table that filled most of the space in the small cloakroom.

This confined space drew the party closer in a way that was not usual. Hands and shoulders touched as they moved into position and drinks were handed round. An intimacy was soon established that was to last the evening.

Sticking out on a promontory, the box felt precarious and Laura was drawn towards the edge. Most of her body seemed to be tipping forward into the centre. Veering towards the ever-increasing mass of dancers below, who moved to the music in such energetic agitation, she focused her attention on several groups. Laura watched with increasing interest, for many couples and groups danced very well.

A line of jaunty young men, some in white dinner jackets, performed a perfectly rehearsed Charleston. Complete with white gloves and a few synchronised hand movements, that gave it a certain restrained camp. All this to a rock band playing full-blooded rock and roll. Laura, a dancer herself, who fancied there was little she didn't know about dance was entranced. Fascinated by the fact that after all her years of training, practice, performance and teaching, this was a phenomenon she had never stumbled upon.

So engrossed was she in the dancing that she began to talk animatedly to her companions, pointing things out to them. She tapped her fingers on the brass rail in time to the music. Its satisfying loudness thrummed through her body. Its rhythm defying her to keep still. Laura never could keep still when there was music playing, it begged her to dance. She leaned further over.

One of her son's friends touched her arm. 'Be careful you'll loose your balance and fall over the edge,' he warned.

'Dance with me!' she demanded. 'I just can't keep still any longer.'

'Oh God, Mother's off already. Poor Kit, she'll dance his socks off!' Tom said to his mother's departing back.

I am losing my balance a bit, Laura thought to herself.

The effervescent atmosphere was fuelled by a certain sense of abandonment. This famous stately concert hall had become a playground. Laura felt unrestrained as she and Kit walked arm in arm along the circular corridor, like old friends.

'Let's go in here and have a drink first,' he suggested. All the bars were open. He led her into a small, carpeted room overlooking the park. It was almost empty.

'It's such a wonderful feeling of opulence to have a bar all to yourself.' Kit was expansive.

'Now what does my lady want to drink?'

'I'll have a glass of wine please.'

'That's not much! Have something more adventurous than that. Come on, have something exciting. Have a cocktail!' He was enjoying playing escort.

They felt it too. The young men and the girls were buoyed up by a tremendous sense of a special occasion that demanded a different kind of behaviour.

Not only were the clothes fancy, but they had brought their fancy manners to go with them.

The faded splendour of another century was working a few little tricks of its own, helped by the wine, the music and the paste jewels that imparted such respectful subdued lighting.

Once down on the dance floor they were swallowed up in the crush.

The beige lighting persisted and hung like a cloud over the dancers, enlivened a little by bevvies of balloons and giant satin hearts. Some pink, some white, some bright scarlet, a few stuck with silver darts.

Laura enjoyed dancing. Rhythms and patterns of movement entertained her. Mostly she danced for herself.

Out of his element on the dance floor, Laura became aware of Kit's waning enthusiasm.

Although she felt a twinge of disappointment, it was exactly what she'd expected. Not wishing to detain him against his will, she readily agreed to leave the floor.

They turned to make their way to the stairs.

At the same moment, a young man intervened. 'Do you waltz?'

'Do sparrows fly?' Laura replied, and without further conversation he caught her around the waist and swept her once more into the throng of dancers.

A kind of terpsichorean anarchy had broken out, a rebellion against what had been laid down by generations of dance fashions.

No questions were asked on either side as they worked their way through the Tango, Foxtrot, Paso Doble, Gay Gordons, laughing all the time as they vied with each other to find the most incongruous dances to fit music that was working its inexorable way through most of the hits of the last twenty years.

The group had stopped playing and was taking a well-earned break. A big band was taking its place, setting up stands and drum kits, giving their instruments the odd little toot in preparation for a great blast of sound.

'It's been fun, but I'd better go back now, they'll wonder what's happened to me.'

The young man walked her off the floor. 'Thanks, that was great, perhaps I'll catch you later.'

She smiled her thanks at him and began threading her way through the crowd up the stairs.

* * * * *

Once again she reached the main foyer and picked her way up the staircase. The iron balustrade finished at a wide mezzanine landing where it divided. One half went past the Casino and the other half disappeared into an anonymous looking door.

At that moment Laura realised she hadn't the slightest idea where she was. She stood and leaned over the rail looking up and down pondering how to get back.

The sheer theatricality of the place claimed her. Leaning over the wrought iron rail she allowed herself to drift along on her senses. Below she could see Guard's officers in their full dress uniform, helmets gleaming, valiantly adding a little extra sparkle to the powdery greyness. They were there to grace the occasion with a little military splendour.

Laura watched and listened. She was by nature deeply watchful and could become totally absorbed by fragments of life. There was a rhythm to the lines of the staircase. People came and went in a watery swirl of rehearsed phrases.

Scarlet jackets, swords and spurs maintained their own high-spirited tune as the band inside reared up on its hind legs, off and away at a gallop. Glass doors swung in cannon, each entrance introducing another cadence, another melody to the lilt of sound and movement.

'Are you looking for someone?' A man appeared at her elbow.

Laura realised she must have been standing there for some time. She was not used to going to public places alone and again was surprised that anyone should speak to her.

'No, I'm just lost.' She waved a hand airily, with assumed nonchalance. 'I'm in one of those boxes up there and I can't remember where it was or even which box. I know it's got "Rick something" written up outside.' She laughed at herself, while really enjoying her predicament. Laura could not remember when she had enjoyed herself so much. And it was so easy.

'Let's have a drink in the Casino, then we'll walk around until we find it.'

He showed her around, everything that was going on, bought her drinks and wouldn't hear of her refusing because she had no money with her. He tried to buy her some chips in the Casino.

This time she was definite in her refusal.

Laura was beginning to remember. Years ago, one holiday, how embarrassed she had been by the generosity of a passing Australian who had simply asked her to choose a number. It had won a ridiculous amount of money and he had casually handed her the pile of chips.

'I couldn't, really I couldn't,' she had protested. Memory was flowing now like a running tide. She was eighteen all over again. She had been slight and pretty, unsure of herself and spent most of her time saying 'no'.

It was no mystery why she had married and had children so young. Her husband was apparently strong and dominating, she felt safe with him, for a time. This night was her youth revisited.

The box was found and she thanked her rescuer.

'I'm having a wonderful time,' Laura said as she sank as gently as a fur coat across the corner of the table.

Sophie smiled, pleased with herself. 'I knew you would. Better than those ghastly club do's where the men all stand together stroking each other and the wives sit alone like oven-ready turkeys.'

Laura laughed and laughed at the thought of row upon row of shining pink breasts of turkey. She stopped suddenly. 'How do you know? You're too young to have been factory farmed.'

'My mother has told me all the grisly details.'

Laura wiped her eyes. 'Dear God, of course, there must be legions of us up and down the country, Rugby clubs, Cricket clubs, Golf clubs, Squash clubs, Working men's clubs. Dutifully trotting along on our leads. Bored out of our skulls, insulted by filthy jokes, mother-in-law jokes, 'er indoors jokes. The message is always that somehow we're holding them back!'

Tom and Sophie laughed.

'You know, all my married life all I've ever been is a Mum. I have never felt like a wife.'

'My Mum's exactly the same,' said Sophie.

'Well I'm going to get another drink.'

'Careful,' warned her son, 'You'll get pissed.'

'Frankly my dear I don't give a damn!' Laura affected her best American accent. 'Actually dahling, I'm a bit pissed already.' This time she imitated his smarter friends and she took her drink and sat on the padded velvet arm of the box with her feet up on one of the seats.

'Got you. I've been waiting for you. Now it's my turn.'

A tall thin young man squeezed himself into a non-existent space between her and the arch of the decorated plaster of the box. It was one of Sophie's friends who had come with them. Laura had been introduced, but beyond introductory pleasantries, she had taken no further notice of him. Even his strong Irish accent had not registered with her.

'Talk to me,' he ordered.

Laura was so astounded she spilled her drink down the front of her dress.

'Tis alright, it won't stain.' He dabbed at her breasts with a handkerchief he had produced from his top pocket. 'Just white wine.'

She looked down at his hands. Slim fingers with narrow palms. She could feel soft strokes across her nipples.

He was so close she was breathing him into her, his hair, the fabric of his suit, shampoo, soap, wine, the warmth of his skin. That unseen curtain that exists between people, keeping them a safe distance from each other, had been lifted, a clarity of seeing and feeling held Laura in perfect stillness, as each tiny particle of him settled on her. Like a fly in a web, his fine silkiness spun around her strand by delicate strand.

'She's not chucking the booze about now is she?' Tom passed them.

'Tis alright, I'm looking after her.'

'Be careful,' Tom warned, 'I think she's going off the rails a bit tonight.'

'Let's have some champagne then Laura.' He caught both her arms. 'Tis something to celebrate.'

'I'm sorry I can't remember your name.' Laura was forced to confess.

'Niall. Niall Degen,' he casually said his name over his shoulder as he poured the drink

He handed her a generous glass then settled back in the tiny space he had occupied before and, insisting on her entire attention, he began to talk to her. His voice poured through her like music and his eyes held hers. Lights of a fair that visits only now and then and loops and circles over the town dominating the black sky demanding that everyone stand and stare.

He fed her his words and they tasted sweet as strawberries. Popping them into her, each one tender and dawn fresh, and behind his words there sparkled a deep vein of an original experience unique to him. He knew himself to be the first to have seen and heard. Asides and observations showed him to have that capacity for penetrating the heart of something. Not merely a carefully educated intelligence, there was something beyond. Something that brought things together and recreated their meaning, as an artist will.

Laura stopped playing. It was almost as if she wasn't there. Still, quite rapt, she listened as he told her so many things of himself.

Suddenly he stopped. 'Say something then.'

'I don't know what to say. I find you totally fascinating.'

For a fraction of a second he looked a little taken aback. 'Now I know I'm with an "older woman".' His emphasis added quotes.

They talked about everything. Laura sipped her champagne, she could feel herself being drawn into him with each word, with each sentence he pulled her further and further into himself. Perched on the ledge as she was, it brought them closer in height, for he was leaning against the side. When she looked in danger of slipping down he pulled her back up to him, leaving his arm around her waist.

The box filled and emptied as the others came and went. Sometimes when the music was too loud they put their faces very close to hear each other better. His hair was shiny brown and rather long. It curled at the ends around his face and neck, she wanted to touch it.

Why you? she asked herself. What makes You different from the others who have been so nice to me this evening? What made Sean different?

They're alike, she thought, *God!*

They didn't look alike or sound alike. No accent, Sean had been no closer to Ireland than Kilburn or Tottenham.

It was a quality, this penetrating directness. Sean had been the only serious affair Laura had ever had and it had affected her more powerfully than any other. She had come out of it so changed. Split wide open. Inside that cracked shell had been a tiny kernel she felt had been swallowed by him and for the rest of her life she had looked out from inside of him. Touched things with his touch, seen things with his eyes, felt what he felt. He had given her so much, a whole landscape of love and passion, previously unknown, but he had also taken from her. Other men had been spoiled. Close friends often asked why she hadn't left her husband, or were surprised she'd never met anyone else.

Curiously, it was as though he haunted her.

Niall stood by her side and she felt the same. An imperishable magnetism.

He must be about the same age, she thought, *about twenty-five.*

Laura could feel the drink beginning to take effect. There was more general movement in the box.

'Come on tis time I danced with yer.' He pulled her to her feet and put his arm around her.

They walked along the corridor, hands on each other's waists. She could feel the delicate structure of bones and muscles through the thin cotton of his shirt.

'I can't keep up with you, you take such long steps!' She laughed at his long legs.

'I'll bet you could. I'll bet you're real good fun.'

'I was twenty years ago.' Laura regretted it the instant the words had been spoken and looked away from him not wanting to remind him of the distance between them.

Thankfully the music blared when they reached the dance floor and she danced for him.

He watched her, his eyes never leaving her body and she felt an intense pleasure in his admiration.' You've certainly got the music in you. I think you've taken a few lessons.'

Laura laughed, but couldn't be bothered to explain, wishing only to hold his attention. He showed no inclination to leave the floor, enjoying dancing with her.

Beside them was another couple who had come down with them from the box.

'Good grief, you'll dance us all off our feet, Mrs Tom!'

It was a name they had given her – and it had irritated her from the first.

Then it was the end. A last waltz was announced.

'It can't be the end, Niall!' Laura was astounded.

'It is, it's four o'clock.'

'Four o'clock!'

I have been with this boy for hours, she thought, and it has passed like minutes.

She put her arms around him and kissed him.

'I've had a wonderful time. Thank you.'

The couple beside them watched with interest. For the first time she felt him tense as their bodies touched and he held her a little away from him.

I've embarrassed him in front of his friends.

Above them the huge satin hearts were split by some unseen sword. Neatly the two halves were wrenched apart. Now broken hearts, the jagged edges painted gold, each dagger point sparkling under the lights. Smaller heart shaped balloons streamed out in all directions from the severed arteries flowing over the heads of the crowd.

And when these burst on burning cigarettes or diamante clips, showers of scarlet, heart-shaped confetti spattered hair, shoulders, jackets, skirts. Without warning these drops of blood covered everyone and even though most of it brushed away easily, it still clung in unseen crevices, stuck fast in collars, hems, turn-ups, elbows, the back of the neck. Couples swept it from each other, but not entirely. Everyone looked wounded, as though returning from battle.

In her plain white chiffon dress the confetti glared, stark and livid. Laura looked as if she had been shot. The whole of her insides had somehow exploded on to her front from a deep hole in her chest.

'My God!' he said. 'It looks like a massacre.'

'Of course,' she replied, 'The Saint Valentine's Day Massacre.'

Tom herded his party together and organised taxis to take them to the flat.

They slept where they dropped, stretched out on the floor, curled up on chairs and settees.

Thankfully Laura took off her dress, returning to sweater and jeans. She lay down in the middle of the living room. It was intensely hot and stuffy. Closing her eyes she tried to rest pretending to be asleep. No more than a few hours until daylight, but it was an eternity. Laura felt caged. She got up and carefully stepped over the sleeping figures.

Tiredness and pain were all she was conscious of. She wanted something, but she didn't know what. In the tiny kitchen she pushed open the window and tried to swallow as much cold air as she could, dabbing cold water on her face and letting the tap run on her wrists. Then she was cold. Extremes plagued her, terrible heat or shivering cold.

There was nowhere to go. The flat was too small to walk around. So many locks and bolts and inner doors made it impossible to slip outside for a walk. Only the window in the kitchen opened a little. They slept like babies.

Laura knelt beside Niall and looked at him asleep. Knees drawn up to his chest, hands together, resting as if in prayer, under his cheek. This tall young man had managed to make himself as small as a child.

Laura looked at her own son, spread-eagled, arms and legs in all directions, breathing easily at peace with the world.

Niall was older than Tom, but not in reality. Tom had a man's frame, broad-shouldered and more heavily muscled. While Niall still retained that almost delicate quality – an infant at prayer.

Is this what public school does for you? she wondered.

Wanting to touch him but not daring to, she wanted the other sleeping figures to disappear and leave them together. His shirt was undone and lay untidily around him.

Stretching out her hand to pull the ends together she brushed his bare shoulder, his eyes opened a little. Half asleep he put out his hand to her.

She moved closer, half leaning against the wall.

Sleepily he pulled himself up to her, on to her, until his head rested comfortably on her soft inner thigh.

'This is going to kill me,' she whispered.

His free arm stretched across her, inside her sweater, along her hip, his fingers reached for her warm skin. Comforted, he slipped back into sleep. He wanted to be held, she realized. He wanted to be cradled.

Laura stroked his hair. His body felt so perfect. In Laura a current tingled and rippled – she wanted him so much. She wanted to feel his naked body against her. She wanted him young and hard inside her. Why were there all these people around? If only they would go away. She would pull off the clothes that made her awkward. He would wake, touch her, kiss her, it would be so natural...

Why was she so intensely attracted to this boy? Was it a combination of lover and child? Was this an extension of that special romance between mothers and sons?

They were moving away from her now. It was a closeness she was going to miss.

Clammy sweat covered her. Hot and cold by turns she swayed dreadfully, wanting to sleep, yet wanting to keep her eyes open to stop the terrible swinging of the room.

Much later, leaning over the sink, she was sick. Convulsively sick on nothing.

Someone starved who has been fed too much, too quickly, Laura heaved up the night. Her small body contorted by retching. Above everything she wanted to be out of that flat.

Not really wanting to go home, but just go anywhere else.

Around midday, Tom took her home. Fresh air blowing in the car revived her and by the time she got inside she felt only tired.

Her husband was in his usual place in front of the television. Too absorbed by the snooker, he did not acknowledge her return.

'I'm going to bed for the rest of my life.' Laura clutched her head.

Taking off all her clothes she slid thankfully down inside the covers.

At about five o'clock her youngest son came in and stretched himself across her bed.

'Well, how's Cinderella returned from the ball?'

'Cinderella is back among the ashes and as sick as a parrot.'

'Did you have a good time? Was it worth all this agony?'

Laura lay back on her pillow and smiled at the ceiling. 'I had a fantastic time. It was worth every minute.' She paused to remember, then said. 'Be an angel, make me a cup of tea. I can't face food, but I'm so thirsty.'

A nausea persisted that she couldn't shake off. Every time food was before her a few mouthfuls were all she could manage.

Laura was distracted and forgetful. Over and over it she went, every minute of the evening. Cut off from some source, she ached to see Niall again to assuage this terrible feeling of severance.

She knew he wouldn't contact her, but she thought about him and thought about him. He'd told her a great deal about himself and she found his number in the phone book. It made him seem so near, just at the end of a telephone line.

Several times she lifted the receiver and replaced it, too frightened, not knowing what to say.

Then, one night almost without realising it she dialled, meaning to put the phone down, but it was quickly answered.

Yes, he remembered her. Yes, he was very glad she'd called. No, he didn't want to see her again.

That's okay. It was what she'd expected. It was what she wanted really. But she just thought she'd ask.

No, it didn't really matter, she just thought she'd ask.

It really didn't matter.

He was flattered.

No, she wouldn't be devastated if he said no.

It wouldn't matter...

…really…

…but of course it did.

She was grown up. She was mature. She was forty-five years old.

Goddammit, she wasn't going to be upset by it.

She wasn't going to be upset by it.

She wasn't going to be hurt, and the more she told herself, the tighter she held her arms around her own body as she sat on the floor and rocked herself, cradled herself. No tears, just this great knife that stuck in her throat and tore her insides as she moved. Chopped at her, a dry sore desiccated pain. It wrenched itself up in uneven yanks from vagina to throat.

No she wasn't going to let it upset her. She drew her body into a tighter ball and dug her nails into the soft flesh at the top of her arms.

'Why am I so fucking stupid? So fucking stupid?' She couldn't stop saying it.

Like a kind of litany it carried her along, its rhythm a current generating stronger and fiercer rocking. And at the same time, even while she chanted her curious novena, somewhere else unconnected with her pain she was glad.

Glad she had phoned him.

Glad that for once she had risked herself.

Even though she had lost, she had tried.

Behind her keening, like a counterpoint to her emotions, the time bomb of her brain ticked on.

'What would I have done if he'd said yes? I could never have handled it.'

Laura took off her clothes, looked at herself in a long mirror. Ran her hands over her pale face, over her small breasts, across her stretch-marked belly.

'You don't really look young at all. It's an illusion. You look good on stage, nicely dressed and made up under soft lights. You've had so much practice. You are professionally young, you're in a "got to keep young" kind of business. But you're not young at all – you've never been young.'

Then she cried. Unstoppable tears. She cried for herself for a loss she was born to, a lifetime of grief-ungrieved-for finally pushing its way out of her.

She grieved for the father she'd never known, killed before she could speak.

She cried for that empty, rootless childhood.

She cried for her first love who'd found her too strange and too distant to bother with.

She cried for Sean who had tried so hard with her, but left her all the same.

Laura cried for her lonely marriage. Everything that had ever happened to her conspired to drive her further into herself. Everyone had left her to the words and the music of her imagination.

Love was something she knew little of and trusted less. The tiny pieces she'd picked up had become crystallised in her imagination, for the past only exists in the imagination.

Perhaps she was finally allowed to break free.

Now. Now that she recognised what held her, she could go forward and leave all the debris of that grief behind her.

Perhaps her period of mourning was coming to an end.

Her thoughts passed to her husband, now sleeping in front of the television.

You and I are like trains racing towards each other, heading in different directions, passing at a great rate.

It seemed her husband had invested his whole life in his past.

Poor old man, she thought.

It was a past that was over even before she met him and for their entire marriage she'd watched him struggle back and back into a place that no longer existed, if it ever really did. He was now incapable of moving forward, so far had he allowed this current to drag him away from the present or the future. The only time he shone with any kind of well-being was standing by a bar in the dim lights of a pub or club, surrounded by men telling the same jokes, going over the same talk where he became a child again.

But this time he wasn't sent to sit outside on the step with his bottle of pop, but taken inside. Allowed to stand with the grown ups. Invited to join in the darts. It was so safe, they knew everything, they were always right, a wonderful warm security of soft lights; an enveloping smoky haze that would stretch on through eternity.

Heaven was a barroom, where the family sat on the step, but they had grown up and he no longer recognised them. He wanted so much to tell them what Billy and Tom had said that made him laugh so loudly and what a great time he'd had playing 'crash' and how he'd scored so many doubles with one dart and how much he liked Johnny.

We'd finished our pop and got tired of waiting on the step, Laura thought.

We liked what you're so afraid of. This new and changing world, that you can't cling to and keep ossified within four walls. What beckoned us my dear, was life.

Laura was glad. Glad she was still capable of feeling such pain, glad to have been reminded of that little miracle that occurs to human beings when another person can affect them so deeply.

That the world, for a while, slips off its axis and all your known and familiar patterns go spinning off into a dizzying conglomeration of thoughts and feelings. When even taste is slightly altered and the lightest touch is redefined. Her concentration on her regular life had deserted her.

Unusually, her husband had even noticed.

In her more relaxed moments she was aware he was irritated by her pre-occupation. But however much he attempted to remonstrate or nag her, he slowly realised he was wasting his time.

She was unreachable. Not deliberately, not by design or even conscious intention.

'You seem fed up Mum. Come with us for a drink.'

They were all around her, both her sons and their girlfriends, persuading her to go out with them.

'I think you've got fun withdrawal symptoms,' Tom teased her.

Laura put a hand on Sophie's shoulder. 'Are you sure?'

'Come on, we wouldn't ask you if we didn't want you,' Sophie chided her gently.

'Okay, thanks very much. I'll buy the drinks.'

'Of course,' her younger son said severely. 'Why do you think we asked you to come?'

'Rotter!' she said playfully and smacked his bottom. 'You can get the first one in, because I must take the dog for a quick charge about first. I'll meet you up there.'

A very thin shaft of dazzling sunlight pierced the dense clouds and for a few seconds in the chill bleakness of winter Laura was warmed by it. A dizzying brightness, that for an instant caught her off guard. A brutal pain slit her eyes like a hot knife.

Slowly they filled with water. With the back of her hand, she dabbed away the unwanted tears.

'Lovely day isn't it?' A man spoke as he passed her on the bridal path that bordered the golf course.

'Yes,' she replied and stared up again into the sky, deliberately seeking the deepest most brilliant heart of the sun.

'I think it's a reminder. A reminder of what a real hot summer is like.'

'Yes, maybe.'

The man walked on then turned and called to her. 'But we'll never see it – not this side of heaven.'

As though paradise had split its walls a sweet stream of golden stars came fluttering down before her.

Gradually these tiny slivers filled and swelled, their radiance dominating the whole sky, gilding each bud and twig, until every living thing from herself to the furthest horizon gleamed glossy and insubstantial.

A glass palace and she stood at its glittering centre, simply fixed and held. The smallest movement and it would shatter.

So many miracles, so many visions and all of them so anxious to be gone.

ABOUT WENDY WRIGHT

Born a week before World War II was declared and having spent a good portion of her life in east London, Wendy has been dancing and acting since she was a small child at boarding school.

A teacher who taught both traditional Primary School and children with Special Needs, Wendy has been writing poetry, teaching guides and even a novel over the years.

Now resident in southern France, Wendy is concentrating on her poetry and art and is regularly involved in literary festivals in France and Italy. She is also busy collaborating on a play!

www.ingramcontent.com/pod-product-compliance
Lightning Source LLC
Chambersburg PA
CBHW020241200626
46816CB00001BA/70